"What fools we've been."

Caro met her cousin's eyes, and the two women laughed softly, together. "Dupes, the pair of us," she finished.

"I was the dupe," Marian said slowly, taking hold of Caro's hand. "I most of all. I thought Francis... I hoped..." She sighed. "I should have known. He talked about you all the time." Her voice caught, and Caro pressed her hand sadly.

"He wasn't thinking of me, either. Just the house, that's all." Caro lowered her eyes and thought of the morning when he'd been so loving, and then, quite deliberately, she put the memory from her.

"So—what do we do now?" Marian asked.

"Do?" Caro's face was lit with a new, fierce determination. "We stop them! That's what we do."

VANESSA JAMES began a successful career in London as a critic and journalist and worked as an editor and writer for *Vogue*, *Harper's Bazaar* and the fashionable magazine *Queen*. She began writing books after her son was born, nonfiction as well as romance novels, which combine winning characters and a fast-paced style. She holds a master's degree in English and is a busy and most versatile writer.

Books by Vanessa James

VANESSA JAMES

chance meetings

Harlequin edition published September 1985
ISBN 0-373-10915-9

Original hardcover edition published in 1984 by Mills & Boon Limited

Harlequin Books

TORONTO • NEW YORK • LONDON
AMSTERDAM • PARIS • SYDNEY • HAMBURG
STOCKHOLM • ATHENS • TOKYO • MILAN

Harlequin Presents first edition September 1986
ISBN 0-373-10915-6

Original hardcover edition published in 1984
by Mills & Boon Limited

Printed in U.S.A

CHAPTER ONE

'I HAVE it all worked out, Marian—everything! It's perfectly simple. All I need is a man—a rich man.'

'I see.'

Lazily Marian rolled over and propped her head on her hands, so that she could look down into her cousin's face. The two women lay on a narrow tongue of land that jutted out into one of the loveliest of Cornish beaches. Beside them lay baskets, the remains of their picnic. Below them, out of sight as they lay now on the springy sea turf of the cliff, the beach curved, half a mile of white sand, deserted even in high summer, even on a day such as this one, when not one cloud marred the sharp clear blue of the sky above them. Marian yawned and smiled; stretched lazily. Until Caro had spoken, she had almost been asleep. She turned her head, looking out to sea. Below them, unseen, gulls cried, water sucked.

'Any other requirements?' she asked eventually, when Caro had added no more. 'Apart from being rich, that is.'

'Well . . .' Caro hesitated teasingly. She was chewing a long sweet grass stem, and staring up into the air with eyes which Marian found unfairly beautiful, a blue midway between sea and sky. Her hair, long, tangled, fair, spread out across the grass beneath her shoulders. 'Well . . . I suppose it would be pleasant if he were handsome, I have to admit that. Though it's extremely difficult to decide in what way. Should he be dark and brooding—you know, Byronic—"mad, bad and dangerous to know"? Or would it be better if he were blond and golden, a Greek warrior—a hero? I can't make up my mind . . .'

'I'm glad you're not being too specific,' Marian smiled drily. 'That leaves the field wide open, doesn't it? Cornwall's teeming with both kinds, of course. Hanging about on every street corner. Saw three of them in Polzeath only yesterday . . .'

5

Caro gave her a push. 'Shut up! There's lots more, and I shan't tell you if you tease . . .'

'OK, OK!' Marian assumed an expression of irritating sobriety. 'Be more specific. You've obviously given the matter considerable thought. So . . . Height?'

'Definitely over six feet. I can't bear short men, they make me feel all arms and legs.'

'That's because you are all arms and legs. All legs, anyhow. They go on for ever. It's one of the many things about you that annoys me . . .'

'Pay attention. Stop interrupting!' Caro assumed a rhapsodical expression which made her look quite absurd. 'Excellent eyes,' she went on dreamily. 'The kind that pierce you at a glance. Eyes that instantly suggest all sorts of sensual delights . . .'

'Nature?'

'Unpredictable. Possibly even a little moody. And he could have a hot temper, so we had terrible impassioned rows . . .'

'And wonderful impassioned reconciliations, I suppose?'

'Something like that.' Caro turned her head sideways and gave her cousin a wicked glance. Marian groaned aloud.

'What a pathetic specification,' she said crisply. 'It's all those lousy books you read . . . *Moody*. Have you ever lived with anyone moody? It would be extremely tiresome. You'd stand it about two and a half days.'

'That's not all.' Caro was not to be easily repressed. 'I want him to be experienced as well—to make up for my deficiencies in that respect. And masterful.' She darted a glance at Marian, who, this time, did not allow herself to be drawn. 'Not too masterful, of course, because I don't want to be bossed about. But just a bit. Determined.' She paused. 'And of course utterly, entirely and quite hopelessly devoted to me . . . Good,' she added finally, in a less dreamy voice. 'That too, naturally. Since I intend to marry him.'

Marian glanced at her suspiciously; it was difficult to be certain, sometimes, whether Caro was serious or teasing. Caro's nature was so impulsive that it was often dangerous to assume she spoke in jest; and her tendency not just to daydreaming, but to accelerated flights of fantasy, disturbed and disorientated Marian, who liked to think of herself as a rational and practical person.

'A paragon,' she said at length. 'A paragon of his sex. Splendid! I wish you luck.'

'I shall need it,' said Caro, and now her voice was not dreamy at all. 'There isn't much time, Marian.'

Marian swung round again and stared at her. Caro's eyes were now shadowed; her mouth had a determined set to it.

'Caro?' She hesitated. 'You're not serious about this? I thought we were just joking.'

'I wasn't joking. I was never more serious in my life.' Caro sat up abruptly, drawing up her knees and clasping them tightly. She looked not at Marian, but out to sea.

'When's the auction?' she said suddenly.

'Oh, come on, Caro! You know and I know.' Marian shrugged. 'In five weeks.'

'Less than that. They've moved it again. Mother saw the agent this morning. It's under a month. They don't want to wait too long in case the weather turns, because that fool thinks no one will touch the house if they see it in what he calls "adverse circumstances". Just because the roof leaks a bit, and there's that damp in the West Wing, and the potholes in the drive . . .'

Marian turned away, repressing a smile at Caro's indignant tones. When it rained, that long-neglected drive turned into a lake!

'He thinks he can get a high price, *if* we sell quickly. He thinks there's interest from developers, and of course that's all he cares about. Every time he comes he moans about something. Too many bedrooms; the wiring; not enough bathrooms. Yesterday it was the heating system. Apparently people can't survive unless they have a constant temperature of seventy-five degrees and what he calls bathrooms en suite . . .'

'Calm down, Caro!' Marian touched her arm lightly. 'Trevelyans *is* cold. Last winter there was ice on the inside of the bedroom windows.'

'So what?' Caro met her gaze angrily. 'It's beautiful. It's the most beautiful house I've ever known, and it was my father's house, and his father's, and his father's and . . .' She broke off, her voice bitter. 'And now all the agent cares about is money. He said the best chance was for someone to buy it for an hotel. An hotel! With deep-pile carpets and overheated rooms and phoney French food and bathrooms en suite . . .'

Marian sighed. She had heard most of this before, and she knew that once Caro was launched upon it, it was difficult to stop her. Caro loved Trevelyans with a passion of which Marian knew herself incapable, and occasionally this worried her, though now she listened patiently enough. After a while, as the tirade continued, her attention wandered. She thought of other things, marriage for example, and then, seeing Caro's eyes blaze, hearing her voice catch, turned back to her guiltily.

'Marian, I'm so angry with myself!' Caro was saying, and Marian sighed once more and looked away. Across the sweep of the cliff, behind the curve of the headland brilliant now in the sun, lay Trevelyans. It was invisible from where they sat. The tree that marked the entrance to the drive could just be glimpsed. It was a Wellingtonia, brought back from California by Caro's great-grandfather, one of the most distinguished botanists of the 1880s. Now Marian fixed her eyes on the summit of this tree and waited resignedly for Caro to finish.

'And so,' she said at last, when the outpouring came to an end, 'you think that's the solution? Find a rich husband? In the next four weeks?'

Caro set her lips obstinately. 'Have you a better suggestion? There's no money—only debts and more debts. The bank is pressing for a sale—you know that. There's nothing left to sell that would raise enough. No Gainsboroughs stashed away, unfortunately . . .'

'There might be something, Caro.' Marian leaned forward, trying to inject hope into her voice, although privately she had admitted to herself months before that there was none. 'You do read of such things. There might be something you'd missed. A rug worth a fortune—a painting . . .'

Caro gave a wry smile. 'It's not very likely, is it?'

'It's not very likely, even with your natural advantages, that you'll find a rich husband in under a month!'

She spoke sharply, and immediately regretted it, seeing the

pain and the panic in Caro's eyes. They looked at each other for a moment, then Caro shrugged and dropped her gaze.

'No,' she said, more calmly, her voice sad. 'Dear Marian, you're right. I'm being stupid—fantasising, dreaming . . .' She paused. 'It's just that I woke up this morning, and suddenly there the idea was, clear and sharp, as if it had come out of my dreams. A presentiment. It made everything seem very simple. I felt—I felt as if the idea came to me because it *was* possible, even likely. Do you see? Can you understand that?'

Marian looked at her closely. 'You're holding out on me,' she said suspiciously. 'Is there some candidate you have in mind? Someone you've met?'

Caro gave a light laugh. She stood, then pulled her cousin to her feet.

'No, no one, that's why it's so odd. There are no candidates. I haven't seen any of the London people for years, and here—well, they're either schoolboys or crusty old bachelors or happily married with money problems of their own. Even for the sake of Trevelyans I don't feel like marrying a schoolboy or a man old enough to be my grandfather, so that's that. My last idea, and it's quite hopeless. Come on!'

Slowly Marian began to follow her down the winding path, which curved over the headland like a ribbon, just wide enough for one person to walk. Caro strode ahead of her, shoulders braced, her arms swinging the picnic bags, her tall lithe boyish figure moving gracefully, easily, as if she had not a care in the world. But Marian was not deceived. She had seen the glint of angry tears in Caro's eyes as she set off, knew she had left so abruptly because she was too proud to let Marian know she cried.

'Caro!'

On a sudden impulse she called out to her. Caro stopped, turned, shading her eyes from the sun with her hand, then made an impatient gesture.

'Come *on*, Marian!' she called mockingly as Marian carefully began to pick her way over the loose scree where the path began its steep descent. Then she turned and bounded ahead, feet sure, careless of the sheer fall to her left. Marian watched her until she was out of sight, then turned back to the bay. It

was a perfect afternoon; late summer. The water was almost
without ripples, aquamarine and sapphire where it lay shallow
above the white sand, darker beyond. Two gulls wheeled
close; out to sea a larger bird, pure white—a gannet perhaps—
clipped the surface of the waves, arced, and then disappeared
into the thin haze that hung over the water.

Marian thought: if there were such things as wishes, if I had
one, and if I knew it would come true, I would wish . . .

She paused, smiling wryly at her own foolishness. I'd wish
Caro might keep Trevelyans, she thought. Even by means of a
rich husband. She gave herself a little shake. After all, there
were presumably worse fates for a woman than a masterful
man with an exceedingly large bank account. Were there not?

'Wait for me!' she called to the air, and then, stepping
carefully, quickened her pace after Caro.

To reach Trevelyans from the cliff where the two girls had been
sitting there was a choice of two paths. The longer, the route
Caro usually took, wound down to the bay, and then, skirting
the village of Polzeath, climbed again, over the next headland,
and back about half a mile to the road, and the entrance to the
drive. The shorter route, involving a less arduous climb, led
through the small fishing village itself, and then directly to the
crumbling walls of the estate, where—now—it was easy
enough to climb in, approaching the house through the gardens. That day, on some impulse she could not identify, Caro
paused at the point where the two paths divided.

She looked back for Marian, and saw that she was dawdling
again, staring abstractedly out to sea, watching the birds perhaps. Caro waved at her impatiently, and when she received
no response, turned down the path that led to the village.

It was small, not more than about fifty houses, set in steeply
terraced streets, each narrow and cobbled, the highest circling
the hill behind, the lowest set just above the waterfront. It was
quiet at all times, untouched by the tourism which had destroyed so many similar villages on this coast; and at this time of
day, teatime, particularly so.

A hush lay over the place; few cars could navigate these
streets anyway, they were too narrow; there was only one small

guesthouse; most of the population, all of whom Caro had known from childhood, were elderly. Their children had moved away, to the Cornish towns that offered them better jobs, cinemas, restaurants—some kind of city life. Here, since the fishing industry had failed, there was little work: the place was out of joint with time, like Trevelyans, Caro thought sadly. It had no function that suited the twentieth century.

Waiting for Marian, she walked slowly along the quayside. It was high tide; a few wooden boats, sails furled, oars stored, shifted at the edge of the water. Up the village street an old dog padded, slightly lame, panting with the heat. Caro watched him idly. She felt not even sad, but flat, as if the conversation with Marian had finally killed off something inside her, something deep and buried and so strong she had always thought it invincible: her belief in Trevelyans.

Now the optimism she herself had felt that morning seemed to Caro incomprehensible. Why on earth had she conceived this harebrained scheme, and—worse than that—allowed herself to believe in it? If she had been going to save Trevelyans she would have had to do it on her own, she saw that now. To believe some magical hero was going to materialise, like a knight on a white charger, was not just foolish, it was wrong. Angrily she kicked her heels against the wall she sat on: she was twenty-three; she had left school at seventeen. What had she done in the years between—six whole years—except drift and dream and fantasise?

And now Trevelyans would go, be sold, be altered out of existence for ever. Her fault.

She looked up, deep in thought, wondering absently where Marian was, then seeing her coming along the quay, and as she did so she heard a sound, one so unfamiliar it was a second before she realised what it was. It was the engine of a car, a powerful engine, a car going fast, accelerating down the steep hill that led into the village, a hill most cars took—very sensibly—at a cautious crawl. Marian had heard it too: both stared at each other in a second of amazement, and then whirled round.

Coming down the hill was a large grey soft-topped Bentley Continental; its bodywork gleamed in the sunlight; its roof was down. It was taking the steep gradient at what seemed to Caro a suicidal speed, and the width of the car was such that it missed the granite walls on either side of it by inches. At the bottom of the hill there was a sharp-angled corner into the quayside; even small cars negotiated it with difficulty, usually stopping and making a three-point turn; the stone walls at this point were striped with the paint of cars which had attempted it incautiously. As Caro stared, and Marian stood as if rooted to the spot, the Bentley did not even slow, but careered down the hill, its huge bonnet looming closer as it bucketed over the cobbles.

For one terrible frozen moment Caro thought its brakes must have failed, that it would crash through the low wall at her side, and career on into the water. She opened her mouth to cry out, but no sound came. Then, at the very last moment, when an accident seemed inevitable, there was a screech of brakes. The car's huge white-wall tyres spun, then held. Missing the wall beside her by five inches at most, the Bentley swung effortlessly on its axis, hugging the corner tight on the inside, and cleared the bend. There were two men in the front of the car, the driver and his passenger: Caro and Marian glimpsed them for a second as the car, gathering speed again, bowled past them both, and then, at a less breakneck pace, proceeded along to the far end of the quay, and stopped outside Polzeath's solitary guesthouse, the nearest place the village possessed to an hotel.

'Idiots!' Marian muttered, and crossed back along the road to join her cousin.

Caro was still standing at the corner, staring in the direction of the car. Marian, following her gaze, turned back to look, just as the two men got out. Two heavy doors slammed; both men turned, as if with one accord, and strolled back to the long curve of the boot, and then paused, glancing along the quay, staring in their direction as if seeing the two women for the first time. A second passed; no more than that, Marian thought afterwards.

They were too far away for her to see their faces clearly; one was dark, his eyes hidden behind black glasses. The other was fair, as fair as Caro: in the strong sunlight his hair glinted like gold. It was he who had been driving, and Marian had the impression, though she could not quite have said why, that he was the younger of the two. Anyway it was the dark man who turned away first, saying something to the golden-haired man, who laughed, and then bent to the trunk of the car.

Marian stared, unable to tear her gaze away, hardly caring that she might be thought impolite. Lifting her hand to screen her eyes from the sun, she watched as the tall dark man walked away from the Bentley, passed out of sunlight into shade, and then, bending his head, ducked into the low doorway of the guesthouse.

Beside her Caro had not moved. She stood, as if transfixed, one long slender golden arm resting easily on the low wall beside her, the breeze from the sea lifting her long hair, parting one fine strand and blowing it against her cheek. For Marian the moment had been broken when the dark man disappeared into the doorway; but not for Caro, she saw, turning back to her now. Caro was still gazing along the quay to where the younger man was lifting a large number of leather suitcases from the trunk of the car. She looked heartbreakingly lovely, as if her face were lit from within by a radiant happiness. A small smile lifted the corners of her mouth; she turned to Marian with a low laugh.

'You see, Marian? I was right this morning after all,' she said. 'He's *here*. And I'm going to save Trevelyans!'

'Wait for me, Caro!' Marian called irritably, as her cousin vaulted the crumbling garden walls and disappeared into a wilderness of rhododendrons. But Caro seemed not to have heard her; anyway she did not pause as, grumpily, out of breath, Marian hauled herself up on to the wall and then jumped clumsily down on the other side. A long bramble caught at her skirt; she scratched her hands disentangling it. Nettles stung her bare legs, a branch whipped back and caught her face as she pushed her way through the undergrowth and came out on to the grass.

Caro had not waited; Marian could see her now, striding across the lawns as if in a terrible hurry. She paused to get her breath back, a slight sense of unease beginning to well up at the back of her mind. She knew these sudden moods of her

cousin's. Caro had not spoken on the way back; now every line
of her body registered purpose and determination. She had
some mad plan, that much was obvious; Marian hoped fervently, but without great optimism, that she might not be involved
in it.

Slowly she began to walk back to the house, the sun beating
down on the back of her neck. From this distance, the decay,
the imperfections, were less apparent; the sun caught the
windows of Trevelyans and made them glint gold. The stateli-
ness, the proportions, of this, the eighteenth-century façade of
the house, were so pure, so simple, and so lovely that at such
moments even Marian could almost understand her cousin's
protective passion for the place. Time had softened and en-
riched its beauty; the roof now dipped, green and saffron with
lichen. The honey-coloured stone of its walls was patterned by
the random growth of roses and wistaria. Gloriously placed, at
the summit of a hill, with the gardens descending in a series of
deep terraces, it had, from all the windows on this side, a clear
and uninterrupted view out towards the Atlantic.

It was only as she came closer that Marian could begin to
pick out the familiar signs of neglect. The dark green stains of
damp from the broken guttering; the ill-patched gaps in the
roofing. An attic window lacked two panes of glass; subsidence
had caused even this, the more recent section of the house, to
shift. The walls bulged; there was a crazy tilt to the pediment;
to the side and the back the seventeenth-century wings of the
house were even more obviously neglected.

Marian sighed and paused, looking back across the gardens.
The hedges straggled, huge and unkempt; only a tiny area of
the great lawns was kept clipped; in the once famous her-
baceous borders, peonies and under-sized delphiniums struggled for space in a mass of nettles and thistles. Trevelyans
presided now over an encroaching wilderness. It was a lost
cause, she thought irritably, this house with its twenty-five
bedrooms, its great library in which all the books were mottled
with damp, its ballroom whose sprung floor was being eaten
away by dry rot. Anyone else would have given up years ago,
Marian said to herself crossly. Why couldn't Caro?

But then Caro did not see the house like that. Marian was

not sure how she did see it. Bathed in the flow of childhood memories, perhaps. Linked inextricably to her memories of her father, whom she had loved so fiercely, that too. Yet she was not blind to its defects. She must know the hopelessness of the task, yet she went on trying. Caro was a fighter, Marian thought, and for an instant, as she stepped into the shadowy hall, had a memory of her at school—Caro, her defender, her protector, Caro who could fight like a boy, and did so, fists at the ready, long hair flying, whenever her shy, plain cousin was cornered or teased.

Affection caught at her heart, and because such emotion embarrassed her and made her awkward, she greeted Caro surlily, her words at odds with her heart, when she caught up with her at last, and found her, alone, looking out at the sea, in the drawing room.

She flopped into a chair; its springs sagged under her. Caro did not answer her, and for a moment they were both silent, an odd unspoken tension palpable between them. Marian looked around her. In the late afternoon sun, the long room looked less shabby than it did in the clear light of noon, but still the signs of faded splendour were apparent enough. The rugs worn smooth by the passage of feet; the threadbare chair covers, the faded needlepoint. One of the curtains was a little torn; the windows, twelve feet tall, needed cleaning.

Marian sighed and relaxed, feeling her irritability subside. She looked at her cousin, leaning now with her odd coltish grace against the window frame. The sun caught her hair; she was, even to Marian, startlingly beautiful. She might have married anyone, Marian thought, thinking of Caro's years in London, of the suitors so indifferently dismissed, her haste to return here to Trevelyans. She was without vanity; for someone so beautiful, that was odd. She felt the old protective compassion stir in her heart, and when she spoke at last, it was more gently.

'You're being silly, Caro,' she said. 'They're probably just passing through. They'll be gone in the morning.'

Caro swung round, her brows creasing with a momentary anxiety. 'I don't believe it,' she said firmly. 'They can't be. Not now they're here. Now *he's* here.'

'Now who's here? As if I hadn't noticed. You stared quite shamelessly. I was embarrassed.'

'The fair one was driving.' Caro paused, her eyes dreamy. 'And it was a beautiful car, didn't you think, Marian?'

'A rich man's car, you mean.'

Caro blushed. 'I wonder where Mother is?'

'Don't change the subject.'

'All right, I won't.' Caro rose, moving easily in one fluid movement, so her tall slender frame in its shabby blue cotton frock was outlined against the light. 'Listen, Marian. I woke up this morning with an idea from nowhere. To get married. I never even thought of getting married before—never wanted to, truly. And to a wonderful man, who just happened to be rich enough to save Trevelyans. I didn't mean all those things we talked about. You know—Byron, and Greek gods and everything. That was just embroidering, having fun. But I'd thought of a way out, don't you see? The only one possible— and I told you, and you, as usual, poured cold water on the whole thing, and I thought I was being stupid—and then . . .' she spread her hands wide, 'there he was! Obviously as rich as Croesus—*and* with taste, because you have to admit it's a splendid car, not vulgar and flashy in the least. Someone with a car like that would see the point of Trevelyans straight away, I know he would. And . . .' she paused wickedly, and looked sideways at her cousin, 'you also have to admit that he was *extremely* good-looking. I thought . . .' She paused. 'I thought his hair was *amazing*. Like a golden helmet. He looked like a warrior: a hero, and . . .'

'Oh, really?' Marian grinned. 'And what about his friend?'

'I didn't notice his friend.' Caro paused. 'You did.'

Marian looked away. 'I was looking at the car.'

Caro was not to be deceived. 'No, you weren't,' she said crisply. 'You weren't at all. I could tell. And so . . .' she paused, 'you'll be glad to know that we're going down to Polzeath this evening, you and I. We'll have dinner with Mother as usual. Then we're going down to the Luggers' Arms. We'll buy ourselves a drink and sit there and wait. They're sure to come in—there's absolutely nothing else to do in Polzeath, and they're bound to get a bit desperate and want a whisky or something. And when they do—*voilà*, there we are, the women of their dreams, waiting for them, across a crowded Cornish bar!'

'Oh, my God,' Marian groaned. 'You can't be serious! You can't do this.' She paused, desperately trying to think of a way out, though she knew there would be none when Caro was in this mood. 'They're probably married.'

'They're not.'

'They're homosexual.'

'Rubbish!'

'They'll ignore us.'

'Oh no, they won't.' Caro smiled grimly. 'I shall make quite sure of that.'

Marian stood up, cross with herself because in spite of everything she felt a rising excitement, the old sense of anticipation she had always when Caro was launched on one of her madder schemes.

'I thought you said you believed in Fate,' she said drily. 'If so, why not wait for them to come to us? It'll happen anyway, according to you.'

'Marian,' Caro took her hands, 'I believe in Fate! I also believe in giving Fate a hefty push when necessary. You're twenty-seven, and in danger of ending up on the shelf. I'm twenty-three, with less than a month's grace, and I'm desperate. Fate has handed us a straight flush, and I intend to play it. Now go and change, and put on the red dress with the immodest neckline—don't *argue*. We'll be at the Luggers' Arms at nine, and then . . .'

'And then what?'

'I haven't the least idea,' said Caro, eyes gleaming. 'But one way or another, something's going to happen—and that can't be bad, can it, Marian?'

'It might be,' said Marian, laughing, but allowing herself to be drawn from the room.

'I don't care,' said Caro, bounding up the stairs two at a time. 'It's worth the risk, isn't it, Marian?'

'I wish . . . I *sincerely* wish,' said Marian, as they teetered down the hill into Polzeath, 'that you hadn't worn that dress.'

'Why not?' Caro caught the spiky heel of her shoe in a cobble and cursed.

'Because it's so damn conspicuous, that's why. And ridiculous. Everyone will stare.'

'Just so long as *they* stare,' Caro said firmly. 'That's all that matters.'

Marian had brought a woollen stole, and she now wrapped it more tightly about her own shoulders so that it totally obscured the neckline of her dress. Beside her, Caro shimmered. She had put on her one best dress: it would have been conspicuous in a London disco, Marian thought dourly, let alone a Cornish fishing village. It was a mesh of silver sequins, and it ended halfway up Caro's breathtakingly tanned legs. Caro had also put on some earrings, which surprised Marian, for normally her cousin hated to wear jewellery, claiming it bothered and fussed her. The earrings, like the dress, were conspicuous. Long, and of bright silver, they now gleamed and jingled, as Caro—who always wore tennis shoes or sandals—now navigated unsurely in four-inch sling-backs.

'Oh, God!' Marian groaned. 'In the first place they won't be there, and in the second, if they are, they'll think we're maniacs.'

'No, they won't.' Caro sounded supremely confident. 'In the first place they will be there, and in the second they'll think we're wonderful. And they'll be quite right—we are.'

'Well, I don't feel wonderful. I feel an idiot.'

When they finally entered the small pub, it was even worse than Marian had imagined. It was quite full, and entirely occupied by men. Desperately she glanced along the bar, into the tobaccoey gloom beyond, and her heart sank. Not a woman in the place. Just a lot of elderly men in caps and fishermen's sweaters – many of whom she knew. Villagers. Caro had swung back the door, hot upon entrance, and narrowly missed being decapitated by the low beams of the ceiling. As they entered, the impressiveness of the entrance somewhat marred, Marian felt, by Caro's last-minute duck, an appalling silence fell. The men at the bar seemed to turn in one solid rank, and they met, full force, the unblinking stare of at least fifteen pairs of eyes. The barman, John, whom Caro had known since childhood, froze in mid-gesture, in the act of drying a glass. Even Caro was disconcerted, Marian could see that, and hurried with conspicuous haste to the shelter of a tall wooden bench near the empty fireplace.

'You get the drinks,' she hissed.

'Thanks a bunch. You get them – I'm not running that gauntlet.'

And Caro, recovering her nerve as always, did.

'Two—er—gin and tonics, please, John,' she said firmly, sequins a-glitter at the bar, and that—mercifully—seemed to break the moment. With one accord, and a few embarrassed greetings, the men at the bar turned back to the serious business of their bitter ale, and studiously ignored them.

Caro returned, balancing the drinks inexpertly, her cheeks flame red.

'Done it,' she said in a dramatic whisper. 'Now all we have to do is wait. And for God's sake don't drink this too fast, I've only just enough money for two more.'

Marian sighed. Caro rarely drank, claiming she disliked the taste of alcohol, and the thought of what might happen to her after a large gin and tonic made Marian feel ill. To make matters worse, Caro was now fumbling in her beaded evening bag, and produced a packet of her mother's cigarettes and a kitchen-sized box of matches. Marian sat, fascinated, while Caro alternated her attempts to look like an experienced smoker with speculations as to what the two strangers could be doing in a place like Polzeath.

The pub clock showed nine-fifteen when Marian's patience suddenly gave way.

'Oh, come on, Caro—this is daft. They're not going to turn up anyway, so I can't think why we're . . .'

Marian's voice died in her throat. Even as she spoke, the door to the pub opened. From where she sat she had a clear view of the new arrivals: Caro, with her back to the door, had not, but the change in Marian's expression was enough. She leant forward eagerly, almost knocking over her glass.

'Is it them? Oh, my God—I told you! Now, behave totally naturally, for goodness' sake. Where are those cigarettes?'

CHAPTER TWO

As usual in Cornish village pubs, and particularly in Polzeath where such an event was a rarity, the arrival of strangers caused a sudden hush in the buzz of conversation at the bar. Marian noted that the two men were greeted, as she and Caro had been, by the unblinking gaze, the curious appraisal, of many pairs of eyes, and she felt a grudging admiration that neither appeared in the least intimidated by it. The younger man led the way, looking neither to right or left, crossing to the bar as if he came to this place every night of his life. The older man followed him more slowly, glancing around him: he registered their presence, Marian felt sure of it, though he gave no sign.

'Whisky?'

'Brandy, I think.'

The younger man turned to the barman; the other, leaning lazily against the bar as around him the conversation started up again, looked directly at Marian. Furious with herself, Marian felt herself blush. Caro was twisting about in her seat, and obviously resisting the temptation to turn round with extreme difficulty.

'Well?'

Marian lowered her eyes and directed her words to the beer mat in front of them. 'They're here. You were right.'

'And?'

'They've ordered a whisky and brandy.'

Caro groaned softly. 'I've got ears, I heard that. Do something! We've got to get them over here. Smile at them, for heaven's sake. I don't know—nod. Anything!'

At precisely that moment Marian's eyes met those of the dark-haired man lolling against the bar. Before she could stop herself, Caro's words acting as a kind of automatic trigger, she realised to her horror that she had, indeed, given him a glassy smile, and had even—oh, the shame of it—inclined her head in a gesture that would not have disgraced the Queen Mother. Caro saw the smile, registered the gesture, and obviously decided she had better take the matter into her own hands, because with a swift movement she tossed off the rest of the gin and tonic, and rose to her feet.

'Let me get you another, Marian,' she said sweetly, glaring at the inch of gin left in Marian's glass, and Marian dutifully drained it. Before she had time to swallow the glass was out of her hand, and Caro was halfway across the room to the bar.

At least she had the subtlety not to stand next to them, Marian thought, as Caro asked John for two more gin and tonics, but still she had the impression that the obviousness of her move had not escaped the older of the two strangers at the bar. As Caro collected the drinks, he moved forward swiftly.

'Perhaps I could help you with that?' he said smoothly, and took the two glasses from Caro's hands before she could even reply.

It was as easy as that. Within a minute he and his companion were standing opposite them across the small scarred pub table.

'Would you mind if we joined you?' the younger man said, inclining his head politely to both of them, while Marian sat silent and Caro smiled dazzlingly.

'Oh no . . . please . . .'

Two chairs scraped back. It was done. Caro gave Marian a sideways look of triumph. Her cheeks were flushed; her eyes glowed. She had quickly put out one cigarette, and was now fumbling with another.

'Allow me.' The elder of the two men produced a slender gold lighter, and Caro bent towards it with shaking hands. She promptly put its flame out, and the man gravely re-lit it. Beside him, his companion stretched lazily and decoratively in his chair.

Marian, tightening her stole around her shoulder, leaned back out of the light, able at last to see both men clearly. She had expected, told herself she must expect, disappointment. To her alarm there was none. Both men were, if possible, even more attractive at close quarters than they had seemed at a distance. Wishing she had not drunk the gin so quickly, Marian stared at them, trying to force herself to be objective.

The older man was perhaps thirty-five, the other a little younger, but not as much as she had thought—perhaps he was thirty. The elder wore immaculately tailored tweeds, slightly worn, as if he sought deliberately to disguise himself as a certain type and class of Englishman. The younger wore international denim: a faded jacket, jeans, a Levi shirt, an expensive belt, and a silk scarf that exactly matched the deep brown of his eyes. The manner of the younger man was immediately pleasant; he gave an impression of openness, even innocence. Marian raked his face for any sign of mockery, and could find none. He was staring at Caro with an expression she found only too familiar on men's faces when they encountered her cousin for the first time: one of stupefied admiration. Yet he was not a callow boy: his mouth was determined, his eyes observant.

His companion was altogether more dour. His darkly handsome face wore a closed and abstracted expression, as if he regretted this meeting already. When he entered the pub he had been carrying a book; now he held it before him, flicked it open, closed it again, and put it down on the chair beside him reluctantly, as if he would much rather read than talk. He was not at his ease; his high cheekbones had flushed darkly when his companion suggested they should sit down; now he looked irritable. His hair was cut short, his skin was very tanned; he looked like a man who spent much of his time out of doors, and who found the company of women tedious. A sportsman? A farmer? No—neither pigeonhole seemed to fit him. There was an arrogance in the way he glanced at Caro, who was talking rubbish, and then looked at his watch without any attempt to disguise the gesture. Mesmerised, Marian found herself staring at his hands: they were long-fingered, beautifully formed and strong; their fingers now drummed restlessly on the table.

'We've just been for a walk,' the younger man said, directing his remark to Caro. 'Along the cliff. It's beautiful here.'

'Isn't it?' said Caro at once. She paused, took a huge swallow of gin and tonic, then fixed both men with a wide-eyed gaze. 'You're staying in the village?'

'Yes, at the guesthouse on the quay. Mrs Trelawney's.'

'Oh, how lovely,' Caro said idiotically. 'Are you staying long?'

There was a second's hesitation, then the younger man smiled.

'We're not quite sure. We're playing it by ear at the moment. And you? Are you on holiday here?'

'Oh no, we live here. That is . . .' Caro paused in momentary confusion, waving her cigarette a little wildly in the air, 'I live here all the time, and Marian—this is Marian, my cousin—she lives here sometimes. When she's not—er—away.'

'I see.' The young man regarded them both gravely. 'How lucky for you both. It must be marvellous for you, Marian and . . .' He duly hesitated, and Caro promptly cut in.

'Caro—Caroline. But everyone calls me Caro . . .'

Her voice trailed away, and Marian stared fixedly in front of her, not daring to look up. This was even worse than she could possibly have imagined. It was as if they were all engaged in a ridiculous formal dance, going through the steps of what was, in effect, a pick-up—a politely decorous affair, but a pick-up nonetheless.

The younger of the two men duly made the next appointed move.

He smiled widely, charmingly, as if he knew they must find all this as absurd as he did, but was willing to go through with the charade.

'My name is William—Will. And oddly enough, this is *my* cousin, Francis. We . . .'

'I think that if we're going to do this at all, we should do it properly, Will.' The older man spoke for the first time since they had been seated, leaning forward with a suddenness that startled Marian, and an expression on his face that she could see clearly was one of mockery.

'Albany,' he said firmly, before his companion could speak again; 'Our name is Albany.' To Marian's dismay he held out his hand across the table.

'Oh . . .' Caro stared at him. 'I'm Trevelyan—Caro Trevelyan, and . . .'

'And I'm Marian Fox,' Marian interjected firmly, because

Caro appeared to have forgotten her name, she was in such a state of confusion.

'How do you do?'

Before Marian could move, she found her hand clasped for a second in his; then it was being extended to Caro, and Caro, eyes bright, cheeks flushed, made an awkward hesitatory grab for it, missed, and knocked her gin and tonic right down the front of her dress.

'Oh hell!' Instantly she was on her feet, Will was on his, and a large, immaculately laundered handkerchief had been produced, with which Caro dabbed ineffectively at her sequins.

'What a shame! It's such a beautiful dress . . .'

'No, please, it doesn't matter—look, it just sort of shakes off . . .'

'Please, let me get you another drink . . .'

Francis Albany, who had not moved during this little diversion, smiled coldly at Marian.

'But we've seen each other before, I think,' he said. 'Haven't we, Miss Fox?'

Marian stared at him stupidly. 'Er—no,' she managed, 'I don't think . . .'

'Oh, but surely,' he interrupted smoothly. 'Weren't you on the quay this afternoon, you and your cousin? I feel sure I saw you both then—when Will and I arrived.'

His eyes had moved lazily over her dress, up to her face. At Caro's insistence she had put on more make-up than usual, and she felt sure he was taking it all in—the over-bright blusher, the ghastly blue eye-shadow, which had surely been a mistake. He *knows*, she thought miserably. He knows we saw him, and that that's why we're here, wearing these ridiculous clothes . . .

'But of course!' To her eternal relief, Caro had recovered herself, and now interjected. 'Of course we saw you! How silly. That must have been you in that wonderful car.' She gave Francis Albany her most ravishing smile, which failed remarkably to elicit any response. 'You were driving very dangerously. I thought you'd never make the bend . . .'

'Will was driving,' he said shortly, and turned away with an expression of ill-disguised boredom.

'Yes, I was.' Will had returned with the drinks. 'I couldn't resist letting her go a bit—on the hill, you know. Then suddenly I saw the bend, and . . .' He spread his hands with a smile. 'Still, we got round. Just.'

'Perhaps you're not very used to our roads?' Caro looked at him speculatively. 'You're not from Cornwall?'

'No, no—London.' There was a pause. 'Francis and I are just down here on a holiday—a motoring holiday. The weather's been so fine, and it was years since either of us had been to Cornwall, and so . . .'

Caro's face had fallen. 'Then you'll be moving on soon?'

Oddly, the question seemed to make the two men hesitate. A glance passed between them that Marian did not much like, and before Will could answer, Francis Albany cut in.

'No, I don't think so,' he said. 'We like it here very much.' He paused, and when his cousin said nothing, went on, 'The area seems mercifully free of tourists, which is more than you can say for much of this coast, alas. Neither of us has been to this part of Cornwall before, and our time is our own and so . . .'

Caro's face had lit up. 'I'm so *glad*,' she said warmly. 'There are wonderful beaches, you know—places you can only reach on foot, so no one goes to them, even in high summer.' She paused significantly. 'Of course, if you don't know the area, they might be a little difficult to find . . .'

She looked at Will pleadingly as she said this, and Marian gave her a sharp poke on the ankle.

'Nonsense, Caro,' she said robustly, finding her voice in desperation. 'All you need is an Ordnance Survey map and . . .'

'But we don't have any maps, do we, Will?' Francis Albany spoke lazily, and his eyes met Marian's for a second in a kind of mocking challenge.

'They sell them at the village store,' she answered coldly.

Caro made a noise that could have been a squeak of indignation at such treachery, or could possibly have been a hiccup. 'You are not,' she said grandly, 'to take any notice at all of my bearish cousin. If you need any suggestions—any suggestions at all—about where to go, we'd be happy to help. The coastline further east is very wild, and it's terribly easy to get lost, and . . .'

'I'm sure it is,' Will Albany put in soothingly. He hesitated, and again Marian saw a glance pass between the two men. 'Of course, I suppose you're both much too busy? But if you had the time, it would be delightful if you could be our guides one day—I mean, obviously you know the area terribly well . . .'

Marian knew her mouth had set in a straight line: it was too bad, she thought angrily. It was perfectly clear to her that they were both being sent up. She stared at the two handsome men across the table with dislike: she could just imagine what they were thinking—two girls, dressed up to the nines, practically throwing themselves at them. No doubt they'd go back to the guesthouse and laugh about it together.

'You see . . .' Will had leaned forward, 'I'm very interested in architecture.'

'In church architecture,' Francis put in.

'Yes—church architecture. And I believe there are some rather interesting examples of—er—early monastic buildings on this part of the coast.'

'Oh, really?' Marian fixed Will with what she profoundly hoped was a supercilious smile. 'What period?'

'Norman,' said his cousin.

There was a brief silence. Marian had the curious sensation that she had played what she thought to be a winning card only to have it trumped.

'I tell you what.' It was Will who broke the silence, leaning forward and directing his words to Caro. 'If it's fine, we had thought of driving out somewhere later this week—taking a picnic, you know. I suppose we couldn't persuade you both to come with us? Thursday? Friday?' He gave both girls such an easy bewitching smile that even Marian felt some of her doubts disperse.

'I know you don't really know us or anything, but we'd come to your house to collect you, of course.' He paused fractionally. 'Do you live in the village?'

'No,' said Caro, before Marian could stop her. 'We live at Trevelyans. It's about half a mile the other side of Polzeath—on the Bodinnick road.'

'No!' Will smiled at them widely. 'But this is extraordinary. Then we must have some friends in common. Lady Amhurst?' He looked from one to the other. 'I'm sure she mentioned your house to me once. I was at school with her son, Mark. You must know Mark . . .'

'But of course I do!' Caro's face had cleared rapturously. 'He taught me to swim. And Lucy Amhurst's my sort of unofficial godmother . . .'

'Oh well, that's settled, then. You must come for a picnic with us—will you? Do please both say you will?'

'But of course we will—it would be lovely, wouldn't it, Marian?' Caro beamed, and to Marian's immense relief, the barman called, 'Time'. Marian stood up quickly.

'Caro, we must go,' she said firmly, gripping her cousin's arm in a vice-like grip.

There was a flurry of slightly embarrassed goodbyes; the offer of a lift back to Trevelyans which Marian sternly refused, and which—she saw—Francis prevented Will from pressing, with a light touch on his arm.

'Until Thursday, then,' said Will, as they all paused awkwardly outside the pub. 'If we called for you about eleven?'

'Wonderful,' said Caro.

'Goodnight,' said Marian.

Will Albany raised his hand in a gesture of farewell; Francis nodded curtly. Marian managed to propel Caro firmly around the corner, and up the dark warren of streets that led towards the hill.

There, looking out across the bay at the moon high in the sky, the water quite black, lit only with a pale surface radiance, and dotted with the tiny lights of ships' masts, she paused. Caro swayed against her.

'What are we doing?' she hissed. 'That's the way home!'

'I know the way home—probably better than you do, the state you're in,' Marian said grimly. 'Just wait a minute. I've had an idea.'

'All right.' Caro sagged on to a low stone wall. 'I don't mind sitting for a bit, actually. My legs feel sort of funny. I must have cramp.'

Quietly, trying to make no sound on the cobbles, Marian edged her way back towards the quayside. Here, in the oldest part of the village, the alleyways between the houses were extremely narrow and dark. It was quite possible to slip from doorway to doorway down to the quay, and to be almost invisible in the shadows. Just above the quayside she paused, listening, until she heard a door shut, the sound of voices abruptly cut off. Then she edged forward.

Just in front of her the water glinted; a cat yowled, startling her. She waited, peering up at one of the houses until she saw lights in the upstairs windows. Then, making sure their curtains were closed, she inched forward. In front of her, ghostly in the moonlight, was the great Bentley car. Making no sound, she tiptoed towards it, and pressed her face against the glass of its windows. Then—after a little while—she made her way silently back to Caro, feeling proud of herself.

'Where have you been?' Caro moaned peevishly. 'I feel ghastly. What on earth are you doing, skulking around at this time of night?'

'Doing a little detective work,' Marian put her arm through her cousin's and levered her to her feet.

'Detective work?'

'Just taking a look at that Bentley, that's all.'

'At the Bentley? Whatever for? Oh, come *on*, Marian, this is stupid, let's go home . . .'

'OK, if you say so. *This* way, Caro . . .'

Caro tripped, then giggled.

'Well,' she said, as they reached the hill, 'don't hold out on me! What did you find? Is it stolen? False number plates? A body in the boot?'

'Don't be ridiculous. Nothing so dramatic . . .' Marian hesitated.

Caro yawned. 'Then if you've had enough Sherlock Holmes for one evening, can we please hurry? These shoes are killing me!'

'Sure.' Marian quickened her pace, pulling Caro after her. By the time they had reached the top of the hill Caro had recovered her spirits; she began to talk animatedly, and Marian listened with half a mind. She wouldn't tell Caro,

she thought. It might sound stupid, and yet . . . An unease
nagged at the back of her mind. The Bentley had been
locked, and empty. Except that on the back seat, strewn in
profusion, had been maps, many of them. A road atlas;
ordinary touring maps, and Ordnance Survey maps, the really
detailed ones drawn up for walkers, an inch to the mile.

Marian wrinkled her brow. It was not just the lie, she
decided, it was something more. There was an oddness about
the two men, something she could not quite pin down. The
glances exchanged between them; the hesitation—almost as if
they had been giving each other cues . . .

At the great iron gates that led into the drive of Trevelyans,
Caro paused. She leaned dreamily against them, and the gates
whined on their rusty hinges.

'Think of it, Marian,' she said. 'The gates could be properly
repaired at last. We could restore the Lodge, and someone
could live there. There would be smoke coming out of the
chimney; you'd see it as you drove up the road, the way we
used to when we were children, do you remember? The tennis
courts could be re-surfaced; we could get a gardener; the
kitchen garden could be rescued from the weeds. There'd be
asparagus for dinner, and raspberries in the summer, just the
way there used to be. The house would be beautiful again. Oh,
Marian!' She gave an absurd skip and a jump and began
dancing up the moonlit driveway. 'Caroline Albany. I think it
sounds wonderful, don't you?'

Marian did not answer. She would telephone Lucy
Amhurst, she resolved, before Thursday.

The morning of the picnic Marian was up first, which was
unusual, but she had slept badly. She washed, quickly ran a
comb through her short, dark hair, then paused, looking at
herself in the glass. She looked better without all the make-up
Caro had persuaded her to wear the night at the pub. Now her
own face was, at least, familiar. Delicately she traced the lines
that already marked her forehead, then rubbed ineffectively at
the shadows under her eyes. Her age was beginning to show,
and she had never been pretty. She had good eyes, she
thought; not large, but of a clear hazel: 'Your lovely *candid*

eyes,' Caro called them. Yes, perhaps her eyes were her one good feature; for the rest, she was unremarkable. Neither tall nor short, fat nor thin: a forgettable face.

Normally she did not mind it, could pass almost an entire term teaching without giving her appearance a second thought. In the holidays she would content herself with an observer's role: sitting back, and watching the predictable progress of Caro's fascination. Although the other night . . . She paused, and a tiny frown deepened the lines between her brows. That night it had been a little different. Of Will Albany she could not speak for certain; she still had not weighed him up in her mind. But Francis Albany had quite definitely not responded in the usual manner. Without the ease of manner of his cousin, he had seemed to her a little remote, surprisingly uncharmed by Caro—almost disapproving.

Marian felt her heart give an odd unexpected little skip. She had pulled on a shapeless old sweater, for it was cold at Trevelyans even on summer mornings; now she resolved to change later. After breakfast.

In the kitchen it was warmer; the old-fashioned range was lit; there was a delicious smell of bacon cooking. Caro's mother was sitting at the long deal kitchen table, a pile of papers and documents in front of her, her spectacles, as always, slipping down on her nose.

'Aunt Meg.' Briefly and affectionately Marian bent to kiss her lowered head, receiving a brief, vague acknowledgement. She looked tired, Marian thought, and worn; much older than her years.

'There's some bacon for you, Marian—do you want an egg?'

'I'll see to it—don't you bother.'

With a sigh Meg Trevelyan bent over her papers once more.

'It's so dreadful, Marian,' she said tiredly. 'All this business about the sale. Why do these things have to be so complicated? Mr Bell from the bank must have explained it a hundred times, and I still can't make head or tail of it.' With a weary gesture she pushed the papers away and removed her spectacles. Her blue eyes, perhaps as lovely as Caro's once, but now faded, watched Marian as she bent over the stove.

'I'll go through them later with you, Aunt Meg, if you'd like. It can't be that difficult. I'm sure I could explain.'

'I'm sure you could—you're so quick and clever, Marian.' There was a pause. 'Tell me—' her aunt's voice was now less vague, 'is Caro taking this very hard? She seemed so angry after the agent left, but she won't discuss it with me.' She paused. 'I suppose she stopped confiding in me long ago, and it's only now I'm aware of it. It's sad, when that happens.'

Marian turned quickly. 'Oh, Aunt Meg, I'm sure she'd like to talk to you, to confide in you. And she is taking it hard—I knew she would. But you know what she's like—awfully stubborn and proud, somehow. She thinks she would worry you, I expect, that's all.'

'Her father was just the same.' Meg's voice was resigned, yet affectionate. 'He left things in a terrible mess, you know, Marian. I think sometimes that if it hadn't been like that, if all his affairs had been in proper order—well, then I might have made a go of things. Of this house. But there were so many debts, even then . . .'

There was a little silence as Marian lifted the bacon on to her plate, and gave the ancient electric toaster the sharp tap which was necessary to make it work.

'What are your plans today?' Meg Trevelyan was gathering up her papers.

Marian kept her voice neutral. 'We might go for a drive. We met some friends of Lady Amhurst's the other evening. They're staying in the village.'

'Of Lucy's—and staying in the village? How odd.'

'Yes. They seemed very nice. They wanted to see some of the beaches. They mentioned something about a picnic . . .'

'A picnic?' Meg paused in the doorway, animation returning to her face. 'How lovely! We used to have such wonderful picnics here in the old days. When Philip was alive, you know. Champagne, and old Mrs Penhallow used to make up the most wonderful hampers—pies and home made bread, and peaches from the hothouse. We had caviar once, I remember, and Philip tipped it over on to the sand, and we tried to scrape the sand off the caviar because it was too good to waste . . .' She laughed, and Marian felt a wave of pity for her. 'Well, you have a lovely time, both of you—and perhaps, Marian, you might have a look at these papers with me later on. Will you do that?' Her aunt turned, peering at her short sightedly. 'It's this planning permission, you see. The man from the estate agents says we'd get so much better a price for the house if there was permission to turn it into an hotel.' She shrugged. 'I hate the idea, naturally, but you can see the sense of it, and really, the money would be a great help. So . . .'

'Of course, Aunt Meg. I'll go over it with you later on.'

'Bless you, my dear. And enjoy your picnic. I think it's going to be another lovely day . . .'

She drifted away down the passage to the small room she used as an office for all the estate work, and Marian sat, sipping her coffee and thinking.

After a little while she roused herself, washed up the breakfast things, then walked purposefully back through the hall and into the morning room, shutting the door firmly. She listened for a moment, then, hearing no one on the stairs, no sounds of movement from Caro's room above, she picked up the telephone and dialled a number. It rang for what seemed an age, then, just as she was about to give up, she heard Lucy Amhurst's stentorian tones, with—in the background—a cacophany of dogs barking.

Marian had her excuse for telephoning worked out: some question to do with the Women's Institute, on which organisation Lucy Amhurst was the moving force, and Meg Trevelyan an unenthusiastic recruit.

'Yes. What? Good lord, no—I told Meg that last week. What? Down, Chisholm, *down*, Grainger!' The noise of barking redoubled in the background. 'Look, Marian, is this urgent? Because I'm all saddled up, and it is Friday, you know.'

Marian looked at her watch and silently cursed. Friday was the day of the local hunt, on which Lucy Amhurst was as energetic a force as she was on practically every other local organisation.

'No, no,' she said hastily, 'that's fine. Oh, and Lady Amhurst—I thought you might like to know. We met some friends of Mark the other night, Caro and I. They're staying in Polzeath, and I just thought that you . . .'

'Friends of Mark? Who?'

'Albany. William and Francis Albany.'

'What? Can't make you out, my dear. William and Francis? Oh yes, I think I recall them. Tall, aren't they? Rode? Or did we shoot at their place once? Yes. Well, tell them to tell Mark to write. Never does write. Most inconsiderate. What? No. Is that all, Marian?'

'Yes, Lady Amhurst.'

'Good. I'll be off, then. Fine day. Think we might have a kill. You'll be in charge of the cakes stall at the bazaar as usual, won't you, Marian? The twenty-first. Put it in your diary. Useful things, diaries. I put everything in them myself, then I never forget arrangements and have to waste time checking up on them. Give Meg my love. And Caro.'

The receiver was replaced with a bang.

Marian stood for a moment, listening to the dial tone, then, on a sudden impulse, she dialled Directory Enquiries. No Albany with the right initials was listed in the London area. She was turning away from the receiver, guiltily, when Caro burst into the room.

'Marian! Isn't it the most wonderful day?' She hugged her cousin. 'I thought it would never come. Aren't you excited? I am! *And* I'm starving. You look a bit grim. Didn't you sleep well? I did—like a log all night. I dreamed of Will—it was wonderful! Then Francis came in, just when it was getting interesting. And then I woke up.' She paused for breath. 'Who did you dream of?'

'I don't remember,' said Marian, untruthfully.

CHAPTER THREE

'Your cousin's being remarkably tactful.' Will Albany held out his hand to Caro as they descended the steep cliff to the bay. She half turned, looking up at him, and he gave her a wicked grin. 'So is Francis, of course, but then he's under strict instructions . . .'

'Strict instructions?' said Caro faintly, knowing her breath was coming a little quickly, and hoping Will would attribute this—should he notice it—to the stiffness of their climb.

'But of course.' He gestured up to the headland above them where, in the distance, the tiny figures of Marian and Francis could just be glimpsed, walking purposefully towards the point. 'Francis suggested looking at the view before coming down here: Marian said she'd go with him. I wanted to be alone with you, so I think it's worked out remarkably well, don't you?'

He gave her a sideways glance beneath the thick, dark eyelashes, and Caro laughed.

'I should think so. I'm not sure yet—I haven't decided. Race you to the bottom . . .'

'Race?' He stared at her departing back in mock horror. 'Down this path? I'm not a mountain goat!'

'Coward!' Caro called back, laughing over her shoulder, and started to run. She outstripped him easily, for she knew each bend, dip and turn of the treacherous path from childhood. So, when she paused, perhaps a hundred feet above the beach, at the point where the path turned and the bay became fully visible for the first time, she had a moment before he caught up with her, a moment to collect herself.

'There,' she turned to him, gesturing ahead, as he reached her side, 'Isn't that beautiful? Worth the haul?'

Will Albany stopped short, and was silent for a minute, looking down at the great arc of pale sand, the steep, dark cliffs, the patterning of grass and lichens and stone crops, green

34

and gold and rose in the sunlight.

'Yes,' he said at last, 'it's very beautiful. Extraordinary. And quite deserted.'

'It usually is,' Caro smiled. 'People can't face the trek across the fields, and if they do, they give up when they see the climb. I love it here. It's my favourite beach.'

'Then it shall be mine too.' Briefly, as if by accident, she felt his hand brush hers. 'Shall we go down? At a less precipitate pace? If I'm going to reach the sea I think I'd rather do it in one piece!'

Even so, going more slowly, Caro reached the sand ahead of him. She turned back with a laughing gesture of encouragement as he clambered over the last steep rocks, then set off towards the water. Gulls dipped over its surface; a light breeze blew off the ocean; apart from the cry of the birds it was absolutely silent. She felt her heart lift as it always did when she came to this place; experienced briefly a sudden extraordinary sense of well-being and happiness in which the influence of the place, and of the man with her, mixed intoxicatingly.

She *liked* him, she thought—had liked him from the moment he had arrived at the house that morning. Liked his unassuming open friendliness, the kindness and politeness he had shown her mother. Had liked, above all, his reaction to Trevelyans, the interest he had at once shown in the house and its history. He was easy to talk to; he had a light, teasing way with him, a flirtatiousness tempered by amusement that she responded to at once. Yet there was something more, something in his eyes: an astuteness, an intentness.

She turned then, watching him walk towards her across the expanse of sand, his head thrown back, the thick hair glinting against the light, as he looked up to the birds wheeling in the sky. He seemed to her, in that moment, the most handsome man she had ever seen. Tall, strong, moving with an easy grace. He reminded her, just a little, of her father.

'It's a magical place,' he said, as he reached her side. 'A little enchanted, perhaps.' He looked at her speculatively. 'I can't quite believe that I'm here, that it's real. Or you.' He turned back to look at the cliff. 'And I certainly can't believe we just came down that. No, you've materialised, out of the waves. You're not a woman, you're a nereid.'

'In shorts?' Caro looked at him mockingly. His eyes met hers lazily, ran down from her face to the thin tee-shirt which the wind blew tight against her slender body, down to her long legs, her feet gold against the pale crushed shells. She turned away quickly, and he gave a low laugh, breaking the moment.

'Here.' He took off his jacket and laid it down on the sand. 'Is it safe there? Is the tide going in or out?'

'Out. It's just turned.'

'Then let's sit down.' He reached out a hand to draw her down beside him. 'Here. We can sit and watch the sea—and the others when they start to negotiate that cliff.'

'All right.' Caro lowered herself down beside him with a smile. 'Marian has no head for heights,' she said, 'she loathes that path. It's a nightmare for her.'

'Oh, Francis will take care of her,' Will said negligently, as if the subject of Marian should not concern them. 'He climbs. She'll be all right with him. Now,' he turned back to her with that easy, bewitching smile, 'I have you to myself for a little while, and I want to hear all about you.' He paused. 'A woman of mystery. What are you doing here, in the depths of Cornwall? How is it we've never met before? Do you never come to London?'

'Sometimes.' Caro hesitated. 'I spent a couple of seasons there, a year or two ago. I didn't come out, Mother didn't have the money. But Lucy Amhurst took me under her wing. Mark's sister, Jennifer—you must know Jennifer? Dalton she's called now— she's remarried. I used to stay with her. I went to quite a lot of parties and so on.' She shrugged. 'But I didn't meet you. I would have remembered.'

His eyebrows lifted just a fraction, and Caro wondered if she should have been so frank, but he merely laughed.

'A little too late for me, I'm afraid. I went through the deb circus myself once, but that was ten years ago at least . . .' He hesitated. 'You don't like London, then?'

'Not very much. I'd rather be here.'

'Really?' She saw his gaze travel the length of the beach. 'It's a shame, though, that so few people should come here, don't you think?' He lay back lazily in the sand, shielding his eyes from the sun so that he could regard her quizzically. 'Don't you ever feel guilty, keeping all this . . . beauty . . . to yourself?'

Caro flushed. It was clear from the tone of his voice that he did not refer to the beauty of the scenery, but she chose to disregard that.

'No,' she said firmly, 'I don't. Anyone can come here, after all. It's not a private beach. It just requires determination. And not minding when you get here that there's nothing but the sea and the sand. No horrible cafés, no boats for hire . . .'

'I'm not sure about the boats. Or the cafés. It would be an amazing place to wind-surf—have you ever done that? And Francis is going to have to lug the picnic things all down that cliff. Now, don't you think it would be rather marvellous if— just over there—there were a very discreet and very expensive restaurant, not the sort of place to attract trippers at all, where we could wander across now, and sip cold champagne under an awning? Eat a little fresh lobster, perhaps? Some grilled fish caught that morning? Wouldn't that tempt you?'

'No, it wouldn't.' He was teasing her, Caro thought, and she smiled. 'I'd rather have ham sandwiches, and good cheese, and apples, and warm beer.'

'Warm beer?' Will wrinkled his nose in distaste. 'You'll be having no such thing. I brought some champagne. All we'll need to do is leave it in the sea for half an hour, and then—hey presto, civilisation!'

Slowly he took out a cigarette and lit it, his eyes travelling absently along the line of the cliff behind them.

'Your house, Trevelyans . . .' he gestured across the sands to the far side of the bay, 'it must be over there, just behind that headland?'

'That's right,' Caro said proudly. 'You can't see the house from here. But that's our land, at the top of the cliff. The far side of the beach marks the edge of the estate.'

'Really?' He gestured back to where they lay on the sand. 'But not this side of the bay?'

'No, not now. The whole bay was ours, but we leased parts of it off. It was very large, you see, too much for my mother to cope with . . .' Caro hesitated.

'So who has it now?'

'This part? Oh, the man who farms the fields we came through up there. John Trelawney; he's Mrs Trelawney's son—you know, the woman who runs your guesthouse.'

'You ought to get it back.' He smiled at her. 'It would be romantic, wouldn't it, to own a beach like this one. For it to be your very own.'

Caro drew a deep breath. 'That's impossible,' she said flatly. 'There's no money. In fact . . .' she hesitated, 'Trevelyans is to be sold.'

'Sold?' He sat up abruptly. 'You can't mean that?'

'I'm afraid so.' Caro had to force her voice out, her tongue seemed reluctant to form the words. She had meant to tell him all this, of course, but perhaps not so soon, not so quickly. After all, she didn't know him at all well, and he might not understand. But he was looking at her with such an expression of interest—of concern, she thought—that she gained courage.

'My father died, you see. Years ago now. And the place is so huge. It was never very efficient, and my mother isn't a natural business woman—neither am I. So—it was inevitable, sooner or later. The debts mounted up. And now it just isn't possible to carry on any longer. There's going to be an auction, next month.'

'So soon?' Will spoke sharply, and seeing anger momentarily veil his eyes, Caro felt her heart lift. He understood, she thought; he did, just as she had known he would.

'The bank is more or less forcing the sale,' she explained. 'We can't borrow any more, you see. And they say that if the house is left any longer without major repairs, it will deteriorate, and it's our only asset . . .' Her voice tailed away; he was regarding her intently.

'Oh, *banks*,' he said at last, carelessly, tossing the end of his cigarette into the sea. There was a pause. 'Which are you dealing with?'

'Which bank, you mean?' Caro felt confused. 'Why, our own bank, in St Austell. They've handled all our affairs since my father died.'

'Oh, I see—a local bank. And your solicitors, are they local too—or do you use a London firm?'

'No, a local one. In St Austell . . .' As she said the words, he echoed them, and they both smiled.

'You think that's a mistake?' Caro looked at him anxiously, and he shrugged.

'No, no, probably not. Some of these local people can be very good. It's just that they can be—well, a bit over-cautious, a bit stick-in-the-mud, you know.' Will hesitated. 'You must feel very upset?'

Suddenly, when the moment had come, Caro found she could hardly speak. She wasn't, in any case, quite sure how she had pictured this moment: herself expressing dignified but clearly deepfelt grief perhaps, after which he took her into his arms, and murmured words to the effect that she need worry no longer, he would take care of everything. But clearly, the moment had come too soon for that; she wished, in fact, that it hadn't come at all. So, suddenly embarrassed, she looked away.

'Yes,' she said dully, 'I am. Sad.'

To her relief he reached across and touched her arm; with a marvellous gentleness, she thought. 'Tell me . . .' His voice now sounded a little vague, as if he realised she might find it distasteful to be questioned too much. 'Are the repairs needed very extensive? Structural? Decorative?'

Caro swallowed. 'Fairly extensive,' she said cautiously, hoping she could be forgiven a white lie, and trying not to think about dry rot.

'Then maybe it will be all right after all,' he said. 'You'll find a way out, perhaps. These old houses are always a terrible headache. Cheer up, Caro.' And, using her name for the first time properly, he turned to her, touching her face gently, just a brush of the fingers against her skin, but Caro felt the touch soar through her blood, exactly the way she had read of in books. It works! she thought confusedly. It's true! It really is like that! Will leaned towards her, and suddenly the air was immensely still, humming with silence. Their eyes met, focused on each other, as if they saw one another for the first time, Caro thought, gripped suddenly with an immense excitement and equally fierce panic. She had just begun to hope fervently that he knew what to do next, because she hadn't the least idea, when there was a loud shout from the cliff path.

'Will! Come and give me a hand with all this stuff, goddammit!'

Instantly they drew apart, and Will pulled a face.

'Francis,' he said. 'So much for his tact. We'll have to continue this conversation another time.'

He rose to his feet and set off at a run, while Caro leaned back luxuriating in the warmth of the sand against her back. Damn Francis, she thought lazily; how typical of him to turn up at just that moment. There was something of the spoilsport about him; she had sensed it the night they met, again at Trevelyans that morning, when he had behaved with notable lack of charm, had merely given the house a cursory glance, had ignored her and crossed straight to Marian . . .

Marian! Suddenly she sat up, all her senses alert, and looked back to the cliff path. Will had scrambled up the rocks to his cousin, and was in the act of taking the picnic bags from him. The reason Francis needed this assistance was now clear. He needed both hands free to help Marian, who was venturing down the path an inch at a time, and clasping his hand tightly.

Caro smiled to herself. While it was perfectly true that Marian had no head for heights, and disliked the path she was now negotiating so cautiously, she was perfectly capable of getting down it on her own, unaided—had done so often enough, with Caro. Caro's smile changed to a wide delighted grin: so even Marian, who allegedly scorned such subterfuge, was capable of exaggerating her fears just so that Francis Albany would be forced to take her hand!

Caro stared: she ought to have noticed, of course, the night they met, when Marian had gazed so at the silent dark man opposite her. Or if not then, this morning, when Marian had disappeared upstairs and had spent a considerable time changing for a picnic to which she feigned indifference. But Francis Albany had seemed so unapproachable, so cold, rather like a disapproving uncle, the spectre at the feast, Caro thought, giggling to herself, that it simply hadn't occurred to her that Marian might find him attractive. And yet why not? He was handsome, and apparently rather serious, which should suit

Marian, and perhaps that coldness was really shyness, or awkwardness, with strangers.

By the time she saw her cousin clambering over the rocks, still clasping Francis Albany's hand, she saw them deeply in love. By the time Marian said something, unheard, and Francis laughed, they were engaged. By the time, with an odd mocking gesture, he lifted Marian bodily the last few feet to the sand, they were married, with children. The rightness of it was so splendid Caro wanted to get up and execute a mad dance—they would both be *Mrs Albany*!

'Hello!' She leapt to her feet as the three crossed the sand to her, fixing Francis with a look of rapturous welcome which appeared to disconcert him considerably. 'Hello!' she said again, idiotically, she knew, but she couldn't stop herself because—although he might not know it—this tall, charmless, dour man had suddenly become an ally, the means to her cousin and friend's lasting happiness. She clasped his hands, just managing to prevent herself from flinging her arms around him and giving him a hug. 'You were *splendid* on the cliff. Marian would never have made it without you!'

'Really?' He spoke drily, gently disengaging his hand. 'Have you not ventured down here before, then, Marian?'

Marian had gone a dull brick red. Caro gave them both what she profoundly hoped was a smile of sweetly knowing understanding.

'Sometimes,' she said. 'But I'm sure you *helped*. After all . . .' she felt Francis Albany's eyes upon her and floundered a little, 'well, you *climb*, don't you? I mean, you probably go up the Matterhorn before breakfast. This is nothing to someone like you . . .' Her voice tailed away. Francis Albany was looking at her rather in the manner of a biologist looking at a particularly dull specimen he was about, reluctantly, to dissect.

He shrugged. There was a little silence. Then to Caro's delight he moved off, with Marian, to the water's edge. She went quickly to help Will with the food. What a strange man Francis was, she thought. So dry, so humourless. But still, obviously kind, and obviously concerned with Marian. Caro felt her heart glow. She *must* not rush things: she always did—Marian said it was her worst fault. But still—it did seem so miraculous, so perfect—as if it had been willed by particularly beneficient gods.

'Has your cousin been drinking?' Francis Albany was standing, hands in pockets, staring out to sea, with Marian beside him, shoulder to shoulder. He made the remark out of the blue, in a perfectly matter-of-fact tone, rather as another man might have said, been swimming? or walking?

'No, of course not. Caro doesn't drink.' The words came out sharply before she could stop them, and she saw his eyebrows lift fractionally. Not surprisingly: the night they met Caro had knocked back the gins in the manner of one dying of thirst in the desert. 'She's—very high-spirited,' she said quickly. 'Impulsive, that's all. Is there something wrong with that?'

He shrugged. 'It might be—perhaps—a little wearing.'

'I don't find it so. Caro is my dearest friend.' Marian spoke snubbingly, angry with him for being so outspoken, so rude—and also disappointed. The conversation when they were on the clifftop had been sporadic, a little forced, but it had gone well enough, she had felt.

When Francis didn't answer her, but merely continued to stare imperturbably out to sea, she paused, drew in a breath to steady herself.

'And besides,' she said, 'she's been under a lot of stress recently.'

This seemed to attract his attention.

'Stress?' He turned on her that rather cold, distant regard, and it took all Marian's strength not to quail before it.

'Well, Trevelyans . . .' she hesitated.

'The house is in a bad way,' he interrupted. 'That much was obvious.'

'It's to be sold,' Marian blurted, noting even in her confusion that this piece of information appeared not to surprise him. 'And she loves the house very much, you see. She's taking the loss of it very hard.'

'That's understandable. It's a particularly beautiful house.' He paused, kicking the sands beneath his feet idly with the toe of one immaculate shoe. He was hardly dressed for a beach expedition, Marian thought, wondering for the first time if she had been right to like him. She swallowed. 'You're interested in houses?' she said waspishly. 'As well as churches?'

That got a response; the corners of his lips curved very slightly.

'Yes. But then I'm an architect, so it would be odd if I were not.'

'Oh . . .'

'So, of course, I'm interested in Trevelyans.' He hesitated, as if aware at last that he might have sounded rude, then turned to her, his tone more conciliatory. 'When I realised who your cousin was, it was a little awkward. You see, it is buildings that interest me, not their owners. I'd like to look at Trevelyans, naturally, but I should prefer to do so on my own. When the house was empty. I find people in houses a distraction. One becomes caught up in their problems, their existence—their identity.'

'You must explain that to Caro,' said Marian. 'I'm sure if you do, she'll be delighted to help. You can look at Trevelyans in total isolation if that's what you require. But you'd better do it quickly, while you're here. The auction is next month.'

She turned away as she spoke, nervously anxious that her snub should be final, that he should have no opportunity to reply. To her irritation, she saw he intended no answer; he simply turned back to the sea.

Marian walked slowly back across the beach to where Will Albany and Caro were laughing together, spreading a huge white linen cloth on the sand. She wished they had not come on this expedition. The conversation with Francis had left her on edge: all her customary equilibrium was gone. What a cold fish the man was; a scholar—dead from the neck down, probably. Quite insufferably rude, and arrogant to boot. Yet earlier—when they came down the cliff path—he had seemed kind, gentle. It had been all right then, she thought, as she fought, and failed, to marry the two impressions. It had been all right until Caro had greeted them in that lunatic fashion. Then it had gone wrong. She shook herself impatiently, resolutely resisting the impulse to turn back and see what Francis Albany was doing. It was ridiculous; today her normal calmness had fled; her mind felt like a whirligig.

'Champagne . . . bravo!' Caro was executing a mad kind of Indian dance. Will Albany was holding a bottle aloft, attempting to ease out the cork. 'Shake it—oh, go on, Will! I know one shouldn't, but I love it when the cork makes an explosion. It's more exciting, festive, somehow. Go on!'

'Then you just waste half of it, Caro,' Marian said.

'Who cares? There's another bottle . . .' Will had been infected by Caro's mood. He held the bottle aloft and shook it wildly, like some warrior with a victory prize. Quite suddenly the cork shot out, with a terrific noise, like a gunshot. Champagne foamed over Will's wrists; Caro cried out; the gulls wheeled and yelped in alarm. Caro rushed forward, attempting to catch the foaming wine in a paper cup, and spilling much of it. They were laughing, both of them, Will and Caro, their two golden heads thrown back against the sunlight. They seemed to Marian like twins—two of a kind, both so young and so beautiful—radiant with health and vitality and an eternal, golden youthfulness.

'A toast, a toast. We have to have a toast!' Will was hastily filling the other paper cups.

'I have a toast, the perfect toast. I know exactly what it should be!' Caro sang out, her voice ringing clear across the beach.

Suddenly there was a silence; everyone looked expectantly towards her, and in that moment Francis Albany joined the group. His shadow fell across Marian's body; he approached quite silently. Caro lifted the white cup to the sun.

'To . . . chance meetings,' she said, almost defiantly, holding each of them for a second in a challenging, compelling regard as blue as the sky, as if daring any of them, then, to mock her.

Will Albany laughed. 'But of course. Chance meetings,' he said, and he and Caro drained their cups in a single tilt.

Marian sipped hers more slowly. Francis Albany, she saw, had not moved, and her cousin became aware of it, stiffening a little as the empty cup was lowered. He stared at Caro coldly; and he did not drink.

*

It was an odd sort of picnic, Marian found, although, thanks to the champagne, which seemed to melt even Francis Albany's frosty manner a little, it gradually became more relaxed, Will proving to be an entertaining host. He was wearing old clothes that day; faded jeans, a pale denim shirt, scuffed running shoes. He sprawled on the sand next to Caro; it was he who did most of the talking. Beside him, Caro also sprawled. She had kicked off her sandals, her long golden legs were stretched out before her; when she leaned across to reach the fruit piled in the centre of the white cloth, the loose neck of her much-washed tee-shirt sagged open, revealing, Marian thought, far too much of her high, rounded and unclad breasts: it was a point of contention between the two of them that Caro refused resolutely to wear a bra.

Francis Albany at least had the discretion to look away when Caro leaned forward, she noted; ridiculously, it was Marian herself who blushed. She sat, she was aware of it, a little stiffly, her full skirt drawn tightly down over her legs; she didn't eat very much. She had decided it really was time she lost some weight; she was getting too plump—suddenly she'd noticed in the glass that morning. So, now, although the long walk and the sea air had made her extraordinarily hungry, she ate only a little salad and fruit, and refused the wonderful pies which Will had bought that morning in the village. Next to her, a little apart from them all, sat Francis Albany. In spite of the heat, he was wearing a shirt and tie, an exquisitely made linen suit. He had a book with him, and periodically he would pick it up and read, then briefly enter the conversation, then return to his book. Marian tried delicately, while reaching for an apple, to see its title; but the book was old, leather-bound, and its lettering was tiny; she could not make it out.

'Oh, for God's sake, Francis!' Will said impatiently, when he had returned to its pages for perhaps the fifth time. He turned to the two women with a smile. 'Francis never goes anywhere without a book. It's pure affectation. I swear half the time he has it upside-down.'

Francis did not answer, but merely turned the book lazily in their direction, so there was just time to see the injustice of

Will's allegation but no more, and returned to its pages with a smile.

'This is a *picnic*, not a seminar,' Will groaned. 'I apologise—' he smiled at Caro and Marian. 'We must be boring you both very much.'

'Of course you're not.' Caro had the beneficent expression on her face that indicated, Marian knew, that she had drunk too much champagne too quickly. 'It's *us*. We're boring Francis. Or I am. I talk too much.'

Francis shut the book with a bang.

'On the contrary, it has all been quite delightful,' he said, failing utterly to inject any sincerity into the compliment. 'And you've proved to be the most excellent guides. You could hardly have brought us anywhere more beautiful.' He paused, looking along the beach. 'A wonderful place. I shall have to come here again. On my own.'

A little silence greeted this remark, then Will burst out laughing.

'Francis is so tactful,' he said. 'But you mustn't mind. He's a loner. And he works too much. So when he actually meets people he hasn't the least idea how to behave. Also he's a mysogynist—no, don't deny it, Francis, you are. He simply can't talk to women. Never could.'

'How terribly unfair of you, Will.' Francis leaned back lazily on the sand, quite unperturbed by his cousin's remarks. 'When I try so hard. When I have all the required social graces. I open doors; I carry packages; I give up my seat on the tube; I'm the most considerate of escorts, the most conscientious of guests. I dance—well, more or less dance. And I can carry on a conversation with a woman for at least five minutes—ten when I'm on form. Even with the most unsettling of women—you know, the kind who are never still . . .'

His voice trailed away languidly; Caro, who had been in the act of rearranging her long legs more comfortably, suddenly froze.

Marian looked at him coldly, though she was amused in spite of herself. 'Is it really such an ordeal, a conversation with a woman?'

'Well, yes, you know, I find that generally speaking, it *is*.'

Francis regarded her with intent seriousness. 'You see, I'm full of admiration for women—full of it. They're so very different from us. They see significance in what I had thought to be trivia; they can converse so charmingly and at such length on where they spent the previous evening, and with whom, and who they met there. They have such a fascinating grasp of the complexities of relationships; they keep pace with them; they know always who's with whom and since when and with whom they were previously. I adore to hear them discourse on dress, for example; or interior decoration; or the charms of Tunisia versus those of Morocco. I find them endlessly fascinating. So fascinating they seem to strike me quite dumb. I can't think of a thing to say that's worthy of their presence. An English education, I expect . . .'

Caro had leaned forward, and was listening to this speech—by far the longest he had made since they met, his conversation consisting largely of monosyllables—with an air of attention.

'But that's *terrible*!' she exclaimed at last when he had finished. 'It's so *sad*. I mean, I don't think women are like that *at all*. Marian and I aren't interested in dresses and stuff. Well, not very.' She paused. 'I've always thought,' she finished, with great seriousness, 'that I was exactly the same as a boy—a man. I like doing all the same things men do—climbing and walking and riding and tinkering with cars. I can't do any of the feminine things at all—I can't sew or cook, and I'm hopeless with babies. They bawl as soon as they set eyes on me.' She hesitated, and glanced at Will. 'I *like* babies, of course,' she added hastily, 'it's just that I've not had much practice with them.'

Will laughed easily. 'Caro,' he said, 'I believe every word you say, naturally, and I can't wait to see you fix a carburettor, but I'm here to tell you—I'm afraid there's simply no chance of your being regarded as a man.'

He glanced at Caro as he said this, his manner much as it had been since they met, slightly flirtatious, slightly teasing. But there was something more in his expression: Marian, watching him, sensed it instantly. Instantly she felt her cheeks burn; something tight seemed to constrict her heart and her throat. No one had ever looked at her like that, and suddenly, passionately, she was filled with a sense of injustice. She wanted to do something mad, something incomprehensible: I'm a woman too, she wanted to say. She smoothed down her skirts. Francis Albany, in the little silence that followed, stretched lazily and rose to his feet.

'It's going to cloud over, I think,' he said as he turned back to them. 'We might think of leaving now, perhaps?'

'Oh, must we?' Caro turned to Will. He hesitated.

'Well,' he said, 'you and I could walk back if you liked. There's that path you pointed out to me, the one that runs along the cliff back to Trevelyans. We could go that way, and Francis and Marian could take the car and meet us back at the house . . .'

'What a lovely idea!' Caro was already on her feet. 'It's a beautiful walk, I'd like to show it to you, Will.' She paused. 'Would you mind, Marian? Francis?'

Marian was too embarrassed to answer; Francis appeared not to care either way. He didn't reply at once, and when he did so, it was almost absentmindedly.

'But of course,' he said politely. 'You go on. We'll see you back there.'

Caro and Will helped, briefly, to pack up the picnic things. There was much horseplay between them, and gigglings and whisperings, as if suddenly something had sprung up in Will which could be satisfied only with touching of some kind, and this almost adolescent pushing and teasing were the only acceptable way—others being present—that this feeling could be expressed. Marian averted her eyes from them miserably.

'Do go on, you two,' Francis said at last, impatiently. 'Marian and I can manage the rest.'

Will needed no more urging. Without a backward glance he and Caro ran off across the beach. Caro's laughter drifted back on the wind; as they rounded an outcrop of rock they both slowed, and fell into pace side by side. Will put an arm around her shoulders; they passed out of sight.

Francis stood watching them depart, his face closed.

'Well,' he said at last, 'shall we go back?'

'I'm sorry.' Marian turned to him impulsively, feeling somehow, obscurely, that she should apologise for her cousin. Francis Albany's mouth lifted briefly in a grim smile; he made no pretence of not understanding her.

'Don't be,' he said, more gently than she had expected. He shrugged. 'It just makes me feel rather old.'

'Me too.'

'Don't be ridiculous.' Her words seemed to arrest him, and he gave her a brief, searching glance. He paused. 'Why don't we stop for a drink on the way back? I don't think they'll miss us, do you?'

'So—let me see if I've got this straight.' Francis returned from the bar, and placed another whisky in front of Marian. 'Your mother was Caro's mother's sister, and you've lived with her family since—when?'

'Oh, since I was very young—eight. My parents were killed in an air crash. So I went to Trevelyans. Caro and I were brought up together.'

'Her father was alive then?'

'Yes, he was. He died at sea—in a yachting accident when I was about fourteen and Caro was nine.' Marian paused. The whisky she had drunk warmed her; she felt relaxed. Francis sat opposite her; the tiny pub was almost empty; just one old man, at the far end of the room, talked to the barman about the price of sheep. She felt, suddenly, an overwhelming desire to confide in this man—as if, for no proper reason at all, she wanted to pour out the story of her life.

'I see.' He regarded her intently. 'So, you were almost brought up as sisters. I see now what you meant.'

'Yes, we were. We went to school together—then later, when I had my degree and I started teaching, I always came back to Trevelyans in the holidays.' She paused. 'It's my home too. Almost the only one I remember.'

There was a little silence. 'It's very sad,' he said finally, 'that it should go. I can see it means a lot—to you both.'

'Yes, it does. But it's quite hopeless.' Marian met his eyes frankly. 'You can't say that to Caro. She won't face it. No, that's not true, she has faced it now, now the auction is fixed and everything, but . . .'

'She has some plan? Is it possible the house could be saved—even now?'

Marian blushed. 'I don't think so,' she said quickly. 'No—Caro hopes, of course. She's an optimist . . .' Her voice trailed away.

'Really? Or a dreamer?' He was watching her closely.

'I'm not sure.' She paused. 'Caro's a fighter,' she said at last. 'She doesn't give up easily, even when the odds are stacked against her. And of course they are stacked against her now—she realises that.' Marian shrugged. 'It's something a lot of women have to face at one time or another, don't you think? Coming up against financial realities. And generally we're so ill equipped. I'm not much good with figures—Caro's hopeless—she can't add up. She used to be very scornful about people who did understand money; I think she thought it was vulgar. Now it's different. We'd both give quite a lot to have had a good commercial education. Not all that French and dancing classes and lacrosse . . .' She smiled ruefully.

'She doesn't work, then, your cousin?'

'No—not at the moment. She's been helping her mother these last few months, since the crisis over Trevelyans really blew up. And before that—well, Caro's wild. She doesn't find it easy to settle to things, routine, office hours. So . . .'

Marian sipped her whisky; Francis Albany lit a cigarette.

'It's stupid, really,' Marian went on. 'Caro's very clever, actually, and with her looks there are so many things she could do. When she was in London, for instance, there was this agency—they were desperate for Caro to model for them. It was one of the top places: she could have made a lot of money, they said. But she wouldn't.'

'She wouldn't?' He looked a little surprised.

'Absolutely not.' Marian smiled. 'You see, in a way, Caro's a rarity. I don't think she realises quite how beautiful she is, and if she does, she's not interested. She said she thought modelling was stupid, and that most of the people involved in it were horrible. And it would have meant leaving Trevelyans. So . . .' she shrugged, 'what she said at lunch was quite true, you see. She is like that. She was always a tomboy; her father brought her up like a boy—I think he wanted a son.'

She hesitated. 'There was another child after Caro, a little boy, stillborn. After that her mother couldn't have any more children.'

'I see.' He paused. 'Did Caro realise her father was so anxious for a son?'

Marian's brow wrinkled. 'It's difficult to say. Caro was six when it happened. I was eleven, so I suppose I remember it more clearly. There was great excitement—plans; her father was wildly excited, her mother was overjoyed. Of course, afterwards it was terrible. Maybe Caro sensed it; she worshipped her father, you see. But even though I know Caro so well, I couldn't be sure. She never talks about that time. It's odd, isn't it, that one can spend the best part of one's life with someone and yet know them so little.' She paused. 'Do you have brothers or sisters?'

'No, none. An only child.'

'And were you and Will very close—as children?'

'Not terribly.'

'You went to school together?'

'Yes. But I was quite senior to Will—there's five years between us.'

Marian sighed. It was like getting blood out of a stone: even now he looked at his watch. She felt her heart sink.

'Perhaps we should go back now?'

'Yes, perhaps we should.'

Together they went out of the pub into the evening air; a breeze had blown up from the sea, and it felt suddenly chilly. Gratefully Marian ducked into the warmth of the car, sinking back on the old leather seats as Francis started the engine.

'It's the most beautiful car, this,' Marian said.

'And a hopelessly impractical one.' He smiled drily. 'Twelve miles to the gallon, and the devil to park in London. I keep it for sentimental reasons. It was my father's. He had something of a collection—but this was always his favourite. He proposed to my mother in it.'

He glanced sideways at Marian as he said this, as if it amused him to give her now, unasked, the kind of information she had sought and failed to obtain earlier. Marian felt her heart miss a beat; the switch from frosty formality to warmth, or approximate warmth, was so sudden it caught her unawares. Did he realise, she wondered, that his charm was the more potent for being usually withheld?

'How romantic,' she muttered, staring fixedly at the rose-wood dashboard. Her mind spun, then set. *It was his car, not Will's.*

They drove on a little way, in silence, while Marian fought down her own cowardice, and wondered whether she had the gall to ask any more direct questions.

As they reached the hill above Trevelyans, she cleared her throat.

'Is Will an architect too?' she asked, as casually as she could.

'Will? No.' Francis paused. 'Will works in the City.'

'Oh—I just wondered. You said you were both interested in architecture . . .'

'Will is primarily interested in money,' he said shortly. 'Any interest he has in architecture is . . .' He broke off. 'Well, perhaps some of my interest has rubbed off on him.'

Marian stared at him in surprise, for his tone had suddenly changed.

'You mean he's a banker? A merchant banker? My father worked in the City.'

'Of sorts.' He shrugged, glanced in the driving mirror. 'You'd have to ask him. I've never really been interested in the complexities of high finance.' He gestured to the road ahead. 'Is that the turning there?'

'Yes, it's rather sharp . . . and the gates mayn't be open.' Marian craned her neck. 'Oh, they are, it's all right.'

'Good.' He swung the powerful car round and switched on the headlamps, for the light was beginning to fade. In silence they drove slowly up the long winding drive, the wheels hissing on the uneven pockmarked gravel, the lights revealing to left and right the wilderness of overgrown rhododendrons.

As Francis pulled up in front of the house, Marian leaned forward.

'Oh, look!' She pointed to a large battered old Rover, half its back bumper tied on with string, which was parked in front of the doors. Two black labradors, tongues lolling, were looking out of its rear windows. 'Lady Amhurst's,' she said. 'She must be here to nag Aunt Meg about the WI. Poor Meg, she hates all that, we'd better go and help her out.' She turned to Francis. 'You'll come in for a drink? If Will isn't back yet you can wait for him here.'

'Thank you, but no.' He paused. 'I have some work to do—and I'm sure Will is capable of making his own way back. So, if you don't mind . . .'

He made as if to get out of the car, and Marian quickly forestalled him.

'Well,' she said awkwardly, 'thank you. It was a lovely day—and thank you for the drinks, for driving me back . . .'

'Not at all.'

'Goodbye, then.' Still she lingered. Surely he would say something more, perhaps suggest another meeting. But he said nothing, seemed impatient to get away; his hand was already on the gear lever.

'Goodbye, Marian. And thank *you*—most interesting . . .' His voice tailed away, his eyes were on the door, he spoke almost absentmindedly. Sadly Marian got out; he accelerated away the moment she reached the steps.

Marian watched the car disappear down the drive; she felt hurt. Not surprised; she had experienced that kind of brush-off too often before for that, its patterns were all too familiar to her.

Then, hearing Lucy Amhurst's loud voice from the hall, and Meg's more muted one, she paused. Had Francis been so anxious to get away because of her—or because of Lucy Amhurst? Which of them was he avoiding?

CHAPTER FOUR

THE dress was too expensive.

Caro, her nose pressed to the windows of the shop, did some more mental arithmetic, and swore softly under her breath. Not that it was the most wonderful dress she'd ever seen, but it was the best she was likely to find in a place like St Austell, which had few pretensions and fewer fashionable shops.

She sighed irritably; what was the point? She had just taken out her entire savings from the bank, and they weren't even enough to buy a new dress in St Austell. There was no time to go anywhere else, because the dinner was tonight.

'Damn!' she said loudly to her own reflection in the glass, and behind her a woman laughed.

'Caro? I thought it was you. Why the temper?'

She swung round.

Jennifer Dalton was standing just behind her, balancing a box of groceries under one arm, and tugging ineffectually at a large black labrador dog on a long leash with the other.

The two stared at each other for a moment and then they both laughed. Caro gave her a quick hug, then held her at arm's length.

'I didn't know you were down here,' she said. 'Lucy didn't mention it. What have you been doing to yourself—you look terrific!'

There was a little silence. Last time they had met Jennifer had just been through the divorce, she'd looked overweight, exhausted, washed out. Now she glowed.

'New man, new marriage—Ma told you about that?'

Caro nodded.

'She doesn't approve, of course. A journalist. She thinks all journalists are little men in dirty macs who write nasty stories about her friends for the gossip columns. However . . .'
Jennifer shrugged, 'strict diet, new hairdresser, a shopping

spree in London before I came down, and general joie de vivre. Oh, you know, Caro, I feel happy.'

Caro smiled. 'I'm glad.'

'And Peter is in Brussels, so I thought I'd make a flying visit. Try and talk Ma round a bit.' Jennifer paused. 'And you?' She looked at Caro searchingly. 'Ma told me about the house. I'm sorry, Caro.'

'Yes, well—I haven't given up. Not yet.' Caro looked away. 'Don't let's talk about that, or I'll start being boring.' She gestured to the shop window. 'I came to buy a dress, and they're all too expensive. Hence the temper.'

'I see. For a special occasion? A special man?' Jennifer grinned. 'I know the symptoms—don't pretend!'

Caro blushed.

'All right, all right, I shan't ask questions.' Jennifer paused. 'How soon do you need it? Tonight? Nothing simpler!' She linked her arm through Caro's. 'Look, you hold this bloody dog before he pulls my arm out of its sockets, and come home with me. I've got the car, and you must have come on the bus—right?'

Caro nodded, grabbed the lead, and was instantly nearly pulled over as the labrador sensed freedom for a second.

'Come on . . .' Jennifer tugged at her other arm. 'Are you still size eight?'

'Yes.'

'Then you're in luck. Thank my diet. How does a little black chiffon number sound to you? Silk chiffon at that, lined, cut so it clings, just a bit, and with the most divine lace top which suggests everything and reveals nothing and cost me a bomb last week in Harvey Nichols?'

Caro stopped dead in her tracks.

'You mean it?'

'Of course I mean it, idiot. I can't think why I brought it with me, because it's utterly wasted until Peter gets back. I don't need it and you can borrow it. Just don't spill soup down the front, OK?'

'You're an angel!' Caro turned to her rapturously. 'I'll take great care, I swear. No soup, and I won't crease it and—oh, Jennifer.' She stopped, a seraphic expression on her face. 'It's

Fate again. It must be, meeting you like this, just when I'd given up and . . .' She paused sobering. 'I've never worn black. Will I look all right? I won't look idiotic?'

'Lamb dressed as mutton, you mean?' Jennifer shot her a dry glance. 'I shouldn't worry if I were you, Caro. Come on—you can try it on back at the house.'

In Jennifer's room, which Caro remembered from her schooldays, from the long summers when she and Jennifer and Mark had all gone swimming and riding together, Jennifer flung herself down in an armchair.

'God, this room!' She grinned at Caro. 'Doesn't it bring it all back? Do you remember that time you stayed with us, and we spent half the night talking about Life, and Love, and what would become of us all? Mark, and you and I and Marian.' She paused. 'How is Marian?'

'OK.' Caro was looking around her with curiosity. It did bring it all back. The room had hardly changed. She pulled herself back to the present with difficulty. 'I mean, she's fine,' she said. 'Still at the same school. She likes it, I think.'

'Not married?'

'No. She hasn't married.'

Jennifer sighed. 'Well, that doesn't surprise me altogether. We never thought she would, do you remember? We had it all so worked out, didn't we? I was going to be deb of the year and make a brilliant marriage, and give wonderful parties. Mark was going to be the youngest ambassador to America in diplomatic history. And you—' She paused. 'You were the odd one out, I suppose. We could never decide what you would do. An architect, you thought once. Do you remember, Caro?'

Caro hesitated. 'No,' she said at last, 'we never could decide. But then I don't think I knew myself what I wanted.'

'Maybe you were right. After all, look at us.' Jennifer pulled a face. 'Mark's thirty, and a minor official in Berlin—quite successful. Nothing startling. Marian—well, who knows with Marian whether she's happy or not? And me . . .'

'You're happy now?'

'Yes. Yes, I am.' Jennifer sat up. 'Second time lucky. Touch wood!'

Caro stared at her; she could feel something beginning to

work on her. Perhaps it was the room, the past it brought back so suddenly—whispered confidentialities, hopes. 'Jennifer . . .' she began.

'Yes?'

'How do you know . . . I mean, when you met Peter, this time. Did it feel different—from before, from the first time?'

'How do you mean?'

'Well, you were in love then—when you got married, the first time.' Caro turned to her impulsively. 'We talked about it, in your flat in London. You must remember? So how did you know—this time—that it was different?'

There was a little silence.

'If I'm going to be honest I'd have to say I don't know.' Jennifer's voice was flat. 'It felt the same, I suppose—in some ways. You know—all the madnesses. Worrying whether he was going to phone, worrying where he was when he wasn't with me. Thinking he must find me terribly dull and boring and stupid. Being over the moon one minute and down in the depths the next—all that. The disease, that's what we used to call it—do you remember? You were terribly scornful.' She smiled. 'The symptoms were just the same. I was different, perhaps, and I knew that.' She shrugged. 'This time perhaps I looked for different things in a man: someone I could talk to. Someone I liked, and respected. Someone who was truthful, because I'd had enough cheap lies to last me a lifetime.' She sighed. 'The first time it was all very obvious—good looks, fast cars, winning ways, charm—well, you remember what Jack was like. Peter's very different.' She paused. 'Why the inquisition?' she went on. 'What are you asking me, Caro? How do you know when you're in love?'

'I suppose so. Something like that.'

'I *see*.' Jennifer gave her a long look.

'Well, I'd just like to *know*,' Caro said defensively. 'Who else can I ask, for heaven's sake? I can't ask Marian . . .'

'No, I don't think that would help. Not much anyway. Marian's too afraid of risks . . .' Jennifer paused, and then abruptly she laughed. 'Oh, Caro, don't you see? I can't tell you either. You'll know. And if you're wrong, you'll find out, sooner or later.' She caught Caro by the arm. 'Stop treating me like a grandmother! I hate advice—giving it or taking it. Now, why don't we look at that dress?'

As if determined to end the conversation she moved away to the wardrobe, reached inside, and brought out a dress that made Caro catch her breath. Jennifer laid it reverently on the bed, and Caro stared at it.

'It's beautiful,' she said at last. 'Even I can see that. But Jennifer, I can't . . .'

'You can and you will. Now try it on.'

Hands trembling, Caro pulled off her old clothes, and slipped the dress over her head. The silk slithered cool against her skin.

'Without the tennis shoes, I think. Try these.'

Caro kicked off her worn sneakers and pulled on the pair of high heeled shoes. Jennifer drew her in front of the glass, and Caro stared at her own reflection in silence. Jennifer stared too, and at last she sighed.

'It doesn't look like that on me,' she said. 'Even with the diet. Life's unfair. You must wear it, Caro.'

'Do you think . . .'

'I think it'll knock him sideways. Provided you're prepared for that.'

Caro didn't answer; she couldn't believe the girl in the glass was herself. Jennifer watched her, and then smiled.

'You're not going to tell me his name, I suppose?'

'Not yet.' Caro hesitated. 'Not just yet. Do you mind?'

'No,' Jennifer grinned. 'I'm consumed with curiosity, but I'll hold it in check—for a bit. I shall want a full report, though. Here . . .' she reached in a drawer, 'these go with the dress. Awfully sinful, but it deserves it.' She held up some wisps of lace: a black suspender belt, a pair of silk stockings.

'I can't wear *those!*'

'Of course you can. You must dress the part. Now come on—I'll drive you home.'

In Jennifer's Volvo, speeding back along the lanes to Trevelyans, Caro clutched the dress tight in her lap. She felt blinded by excitement. Sightlessly, noting nothing, she stared out of the windows of the car at the blur of trees and grass. Tonight, her mind said, over and over again, in the most maddening way. Tonight—something would happen, it must. Yesterday, when they had walked back from the beach, Will had held her hand, put his arm around her. She had been expecting him to kiss her, and had been preparing herself for the moment when he did more rationally than she had anticipated. She was hoping she wouldn't make a fool of herself, that she'd know how to hold him, what to do with her mouth. In the movies the heroines always ran their hands up to the hero's hair, and sort of *meshed* their fingers in it and stroked it at the same time, and it looked perfectly easy and natural, but suddenly, walking back along the cliff-top in the gathering dusk, Caro had had her doubts. Maybe it wasn't that simple. Maybe she would do it all wrongly, maybe she would be a total turn-off . . .

Once they had reached the cliff-top his manner had changed a little; he had seemed to Caro distracted, as if he answered her remarks with only half a mind. So, when they finally reached Trevelyans, and he had kissed her, thoroughly, and without preliminaries, it had almost been a relief. Why, she had almost decided he was more interested in their surroundings than in her. It was for that reason—she had been feeling so muddled and tense—that the kiss hadn't gone terribly well. So she told herself. Not that Will seemed to notice, but Caro had felt like a marionette, as he held her and touched her, and pressed his lips hard against hers. If he had been more *gradual*, maybe it would have been easier, as it was he needed a shave and his skin rubbed painfully against hers, and she had been so flustered she hadn't known whether to open her lips—as he seemed to expect—or not, and in the end hadn't. Of course, she thought now, such confusion and shyness was probably a good sign. If she hadn't been worrying so idiotically about the etiquette of kissing and whether she ought to respond fervently, and if so, to what degree, it would all have gone much better. As it was, she had probably just been a little overcome. Probably she was falling in love with him, she thought, listening anxiously to the pulsing of her own mind, and feeling—yes, she did—its rhythms skip as his name sprang into her mind. Oh, Will, she thought, and was pleased to hear herself sigh.

'Goodness, what a car!'

Caro started; Jennifer was gesturing to the side of the road.

They were just passing Jack Trelawney's fields, and there, pulled off the road, tucked away down the track that led to his farm, was the sleek grey Bentley. Caro stared. How odd, she thought, as Jennifer accelerated past. What could Will want at Trelawneys' farm? Then she realised; probably Francis had taken the car, left it, and walked on to the beach—it was the quickest route, and he had said he wanted to return there.

What an odd man he was, she thought dreamily, recovering her composure. So dour. Marian said he had fine eyes. She hadn't noticed that; they had seemed unremarkable to her. Still, she must remember to notice them another time, if only for Marian's sake. Marian was clearly interested in him. Caro sighed. She hoped Marian knew what she was doing. She hoped she wouldn't get hurt.

'Why don't you tell Marian to come over and have supper with us tonight?' Jennifer was turning into the drive. 'I'd love to see her again. She could bring your mother too—they might as well, don't you think, while you're out on the town. It's the cook's day off, and Ma's cooking, so it's bound to be fish pie, but they won't mind that, will they? I'll raid the cellar. Tell them to come . . . okay?'

'All right. I'm sure they'd love that.' Caro felt a momentary wave of guilt; Francis had not asked Marian out, that much had been clear from her demeanour at breakfast.

'And thank you, Jennifer,' she said, as she clambered out of the car with her parcels.

Jennifer laughed and let in the clutch.

'I'll be thinking of you,' she said. 'Good luck!'

There was a long looking glass in the hall, and Caro looked in it anxiously. It was old, its mercury backing bubbled and scarred; the light in the hall was not strong. So, as Caro peered at her own reflection, the image the glass gave back was curious, blurred, shadowy, as if she viewed herself through water.

Marian and her mother had already left for the Amhursts'; the great house was now silent around her. Except for the tiny periodic shiftings and creakings which it always made, the summer evening's air was hushed. The little sounds did not make Caro nervous; she was used to them and she loved them.

They were a product of the building's age, the sounds of its old timbers contracting, moving, in the cooling air. The noises calmed her; they were part of the house's life; at such times Trevelyans seemed to her to breathe, to be alive.

Will was a little late. She looked at the watch on her wrist, which said seven-thirty-five, and then, mindful of Marian's instructions not to spoil the effect of the dress, took the watch off, and laid it down on a table. Seven-thirty-six. Perhaps she should occupy herself.

Brakes; a car door banged; footsteps. I must count, she thought, not rush to the door like an idiot. So, as the old bell clanged somewhere at the back of the house, she stood still in a corner of the hall; forty-seven, forty-eight, forty-nine. She could bear it no longer.

She hurried across the hall, Jennifer's shoes tapping and clicking her progress across the stone slab paving, and a terrible gripping nervousness clutching her chest, making it suddenly hard to breathe. She flung back the door and stared out into the twilight.

'Oh!'

'Good evening. May I come in?' Francis Albany stepped past her into the hall.

The disappointment was so acute it hurt; she could not even speak. Francis had moved beyond her, turned, and now stood regarding her solemnly. He was wearing the kind of clothes she had come to associate with him: conservative clothes; a plain black suit, perfectly cut, a dark tie, a white shirt. In this light he looked to her suddenly even taller, immovable, a little grim.

'But . . .'

'I know. I'm so sorry, I have brought a note.'

He did not smile, but merely handed her a large cream envelope, with *Caro* written on the outside of it in a large sprawling hand.

Caro ripped the envelope open jaggedly, pulled out the single piece of paper inside; the words swam before her eyes, leaping and jumping, and it was a while before they made any sense to her, although the message was short. *Darling Caro*, he had written. *Some boring business problem has just come up and I've had to dash to London at a moment's notice. Will you*

*forgive me? Francis has promised to look after you—not too
well, I hope, and I should be back tomorrow or the day after at
the latest. Will you let me take you for dinner then? Please say
yes. I shall be thinking of you, and of Cornwall.* He had signed
the letter simply with a 'W'.

Caro looked up at Francis, who was standing regarding the
paintings without any apparent embarrassment. She said
crossly:

'He might have telephoned!'

'I know. But it was very sudden. The City, you know.'
He shrugged. 'I think he did try to get you, but the line
was engaged.' He paused. 'So I hope I shall be allowed to
deputise?'

'Deputise?'

'Take you out to dinner. It's the least I can do.' He spoke
without any degree of enthusiasm, formally, as if this were a
task his duty bade him do, and so he would go through with it.
Caro felt piqued. She moved forward a step, and the silk dress
rustled, moved against her hips and thighs; on the air she
caught suddenly the scent of the perfume she wore, borrowed
from her mother, rich, heady, strange; it did not belong to her.
The movement, perhaps the scent—l'Heure Bleue—caught
his attention.

He appeared embarrassed now, a little, and that gave Caro
confidence. She smiled at him.

'Don't be silly,' she said. 'These things happen. It doesn't
matter. I'm sure you have other more important things to do
and . . .'

'No.' He looked at her seriously. 'And I've booked a table.'

Caro sighed, and glanced down at the note in her hands.
Darling Caro. It was—encouraging. Definitely encouraging.
Tomorrow he would be back, and meanwhile he was thinking
of her. She gave Francis a rapturous smile, hardly seeing
him.

'All right,' she said, more happily. 'That would be lovely.
Thank you.'

They would talk about Will, she promised herself; and she
could tell him about Marian. Of course. It was the perfect
opportunity. She wouldn't rush it this time, and be idiotic, but

would plan it carefully, convey to him something of what
Marian was—her strength, her goodness, her shyness . . .

'I like your dress.'

'I'm sorry?' She stared at him, returning with difficulty from
her thoughts.

'I said that I liked your dress.' Francis gave her the most
extraordinary half bow, and an inclination of the head, so
formal, so old-fashioned she almost laughed aloud; clearly he
was not used to paying women compliments.

'So do I,' she said lightly. 'I'm afraid it's not mine. I
borrowed it specially.'

'For Will's benefit?' he smiled.

Caro felt herself warming to him. 'Yes,' she said. 'It was,
actually.'

'Then I shall make a point of describing it to him. In detail.'
She caught the expression in his eyes then, for he had turned
his face slightly, so the light caught the planes of his cheeks,
and she suspected him for a moment of mocking her, their
expression surprising her. It was warmer, more alive, quicker
than she had expected. Marian was right, she thought absently.
He had fine eyes; intelligent, perceptive eyes. She felt a
moment's indecision, a confusion.

'Would you like a drink?'

He looked at his watch. 'I think not. I booked the table for
eight. Shall we have one there?'

Caro did not demur, glad that she didn't have to sit across
the great drawing room at Trevelyans and make conversation
with this odd staid man. He made her feel tongue-tied and
stupid; she would feel safer in some anonymous place— a
restaurant, a bar.

'Is this your coat? You may need it—it's not that warm.'

Before Caro could protest he had picked up her old worn
black coat, which was draped over a chair, and had put it, very
gently, around her shoulders. She was thinking of Will as he
did it, thinking of where they might go, and of what might
happen when he returned from London. As Francis lifted the
coat around her his hand brushed the skin at the back of her
neck; the skin was at once suffused with sensation: erotic,
warm, it pulsed for a second through her whole body, shocking

her. Just the thought of Will and an accidental touch could do that to her, she thought, wonderingly, as she followed Francis out to the car. Maybe it was true, maybe she was, already, a little in love with him. After all, such things could happen very quickly—everyone said so. *Will*, she said to herself silently, holding the name in her mind like a talisman, hardly noticing that Francis was now beside her and had started the car.

It was a restaurant Caro had heard of, but never visited. Small, discreet, and—she thought worriedly—probably terribly expensive, it took up the ground floor of a Georgian country house some miles inland on the edge of Bodmin Moor. In the dining room beyond were set beautiful tables, with white linen cloths, flowers, silver, candles. From where she sat came the discreet buzz of conversation; in this room, painted dark green, a fire had been lit; there were deep velvet sofas; it reminded her a little of Trevelyans. Francis was at the bar now; he had his back to her, was ordering some drinks. She watched him curiously. Normally she might not have noticed, but her senses were sharpened by the strangeness of the occasion, by a residual nervousness at the evening to be navigated, and so she saw the glances of the other women in the room as Francis came in, stood now with his hands resting on the mahogany counter in front of him. The glances were more than curious, they were slightly envious, almost predatory; Caro smiled to herself, following their gaze. He was, she supposed, very good-looking. His body was tall, lean and athletic, his shoulders wide; he moved with an easy grace. His face was powerful, dark, the planes strongly marked, and the eyes watchful. It was not easy to know what he was thinking; there was continually the possibility that he was bored, or that he mocked. His face lacked the animation that lit Will's, lacked his gaiety. And his eyebrows were too straight, Caro judged. They made his face look stern, even hard, without humour.

He was coming back. In his hand he held what looked like a whisky, and a large cocktail with a foamy surface and a cherry on a stick. Caro looked at it doubtfully; she had never drunk a cocktail. Seeing her gaze, Francis, too looked momentarily uncertain, as if he were not in the habit of buying women drinks.

'Well, you said anything.' He paused. 'And I thought it went with the dress.'

'What is it?'

'A dry Manhattan.'

'Oh.' Caro sipped it. It was delicious, not like alcohol at all, she thought cheerfully, her courage rising. She took a larger swallow, aware that Francis was staring at her.

'It's terrific—all lemony.'

'Yes. I should be careful, though. I think they're quite strong.'

'Oh, it's all right.' Caro gave him a dazzling smile. 'I don't drink, much. Not usually.'

She mustn't let him see she was nervous, she decided. There were too many things she needed to ask, needed to say. She stretched, then, remembering the dress, hastily crossed her legs in the way they had shown them in movement classes at school. The silk of her stockings, the silk of the dress, felt good. Francis had followed the movement as if mesmerised, and Caro instantly sat still. He did not like restless women, she remembered.

'You're an architect,' she said, in her best opening conversation manner. 'Marian told me.'

'Yes, I am. An architect.' His eyes were still riveted on her stockinged legs, and Caro wondered irritably if they had a hole or ladder.

'How fascinating. What kind of buildings do you design?'

'Er—houses. I design houses. Sometimes.' He turned his attention back to her face with apparent difficulty. 'But I also write. About architecture. And I act as a consultant, occasionally.'

Caro's heart sank. Marian had said he wasn't frightfully easy to draw out, and that had been the understatement of the year, she thought rebelliously. You could have a better conversation with a computer!

'Marian's very interested in architecture,' she said firmly. This was not strictly true—she herself was, had inherited a passionate interest in buildings from her father—but she thought she could be forgiven the untruth. 'And you're a consultant? To whom?'

He sighed. 'Oh, to various bodies—the National Trust, the Mayflower Foundation. My speciality is sixteenth and seventeenth-century English architecture. I'm called in sometimes when the Trust acquires a property that needs extensive restoration . . .'

Caro's face lit up with more genuine enthusiasm. 'Trevelyans is seventeenth-century,' she said eagerly. 'That is, the side wing of the house as it is now. The front wing is Queen Anne, of course, and Lutyens . . .'

'Yes, I know. I noticed.'

'But you must look at the house.' His tone had been cold, but she would not let it discourage her, she determined. 'It would interest you—I know it would. Will you let me show you round some time?'

'That would be delightful.'

'Or perhaps Marian.' Caro blushed. He had sounded distinctly unenthralled at the invitation. 'Marian could show you. She knows the house almost as well as I do . . .'

'I'm sure not quite as well,' he interrupted smoothly.

'Well no, but . . .' She broke off. This was awful, she thought suddenly, utterly ghastly, and she was no good at it whatsoever. It was hateful trying to have a conversation, and being on your guard all the time, and being watched every moment by those cold, dark eyes which radiated disapproval. She took a large swallow of the Manhattan and drew in her breath.

'Look,' she said, leaning across the table, 'this is hopeless. I know you don't like me, and I can see I get on your nerves, and you think I'm an empty-headed idiot, chattering on and on. And it's very polite and nice of you to do this, but really you needn't. Why don't we call it quits now, and just go home?'

There was a silence; she had surprised him, she thought, but then she had surprised herself. She hadn't exactly meant to say all that, but now she had she felt a great deal better.

Francis' straight brows drew together momentarily in a frown; then to her astonishment he began to laugh. It was the first time she had heard him laugh—she hadn't even seen him give more than a tight, frosty smile that never reached the eyes—and the laughter transformed his face.

'Oh dear,' he said at last. 'Is it that bad? I'm so sorry. I warned you I was no good at talking to women. But I can assure you I was thinking no such thing.' He paused. 'I don't think you're an idiot, or in the least empty-headed. Impulsive, of course, but . . .'

'There's no need to be polite.' Caro looked at him crossly. 'I mean, we both know you're only deputising for Will, and . . .'

'But this dinner was my idea. Will didn't suggest that. I wanted to come.'

Caro stared at him. 'Really? Is that the truth?'

'Word of honour.' He looked at her solemnly. 'Cut the throat and all that.'

'Oh.' She gave a sigh of relief. 'Well, that's all right, then. I just thought . . .' She broke off. 'I suppose—you couldn't just sort of try and forget I was a woman, could you? The way we talked about on the beach yesterday? You know, just treat me as if I were a man you'd met and were dining with. Then you mightn't feel so—awkward.'

'I could try.' His eyes met hers, and Caro felt oddly held by them. 'In fact,' he smiled, 'I'm sure you're right. It's the obvious solution. There's only one difficulty.'

'What's that?' Caro looked at him suspiciously.

'Well, how do you regard me?'

'Oh, that's not a problem,' Caro laughed with relief. 'You see, I don't really think of you as a *man*—not in that sense, you know.'

He quirked an eyebrow, and Caro blushed.

'No, you know what I mean. Obviously, I think of you— well, as a friend. And if I know I'm not driving you mad, and irritating you, I expect I'll settle down and just talk normally, the way I would to anyone else.'

'Splendid.' Francis gave a slightly cold smile. 'Then that's settled. No more selfconsciousness. We shall have a marvellous evening and a most interesting talk. Man to man. Agreed?'

'Agreed.' He had held out his hand, as if to shake on a deal, and Caro grasped it firmly. He had beautiful hands, she had noticed them before, and his grasp was dry and firm against her skin. She liked him, she thought, holding his hand a little too long because it felt cool and pleasant. I like him after all; and he is *perfect* for Marian.

CHAPTER FIVE

'WILL you have a pudding, Caro?'

'Oh yes, *please*!' Caro looked at the trolley with delight. The meal they had eaten had been light and delicious; now, spread before her was the most exquisite array of dishes; tiny oranges in a golden glaze; almond tartlets filled with fresh raspberries; a glorious wine red mousse, ivory cabinet puddings vivid with glacé fruit, a confection of meringues and whipped cream.

'Aren't they beautiful?' She hesitated. 'I can't make up my mind.'

'Have two. Have as many as you like.' Francis was watching her with amusement.

'No, I'd better not do that. I'll have one of those—the little ones that look like castles.'

Solemnly the waiter placed two cabinet puddings on a gold and white plate, and handed her a sauce boat.

'An egg custard, madame. Made with cream. Sir?'

'Just a little Stilton, I think.'

Caro prodded one of the little puddings.

'Aren't they lovely? I haven't had these since I was a child. Mrs Penhallow, our cook, used to make them at Christmas. And trifles, proper ones, and tipsy cake.' She sighed. 'I used to think they looked like jewels—all those beautiful colours, and the shiny glass dishes. Much better than rubies and diamonds.' She paused and gave Francis a wry grin. 'Also they taste quite wonderful. Would you like a taste?'

Francis looked at her solemnly; he was crumbling a Bath Oliver biscuit. 'I wondered if you were ever going to ask.'

'Here you are, then.' Caro held her spoon out to him, and Francis gravely tasted the cabinet pudding.

'Heavenly?'

'Definitely. No other word would be adequate.'

Caro warmed to him. Really, she thought, as the waiter

brought them coffee, she had enjoyed herself. Francis was easy to talk to once you relaxed, and the claret he'd ordered had been sumptuous, like velvet, and provided you asked no personal questions whatsoever, he became less reserved, and talked most interestingly. She had learned a lot from him; his work with the preservation groups was fascinating. The quickness of his mind, the sharpness of his judgment, and the depth of his knowledge impressed her.

She paused, sipping her coffee, and looked at him carefully. She felt now that he was a friend; perhaps even an ally.

'Francis,' she said, determining suddenly to take the plunge, 'if you were in my situation, I mean about Trevelyans—what would you do? What would you advise me to do?'

He was in the act of lighting a cigarette, and he paused.

'It's difficult to say. The auction's very close. You haven't much time. And I don't know all the circumstances, so I'm hardly in a position to . . .'

'The circumstances are simple,' Caro interrupted quickly. 'We're broke—or nearly. The roof timbers have dry rot. There's bad subsidence in the East Wing. The wall on the front façade is starting to lean. The drains need fixing; the place hasn't been re-wired since about 1930. The gardens—well, you've seen the gardens. And that's just for starters. The full list from the last survey is about ten pages long.'

'A fairly typical case.' He smiled. 'I've dealt with worse than that.'

'But the money . . .' Caro leaned forward. 'You see, I realise the National Trust can't help—we tried them. They would love the house, but they won't take it on without a sizeable endowment, so that's out. We tried for a grant from the Department of the Environment, and the paperwork nearly drove Mother insane, and so now . . .' Her voice trailed away and she looked at him pleadingly. 'The auction is next month. Please, Francis, you're an expert. What would you do?'

'In your place, with under a month's grace?' He looked at her narrowly. 'I'd marry a rich man.'

Caro went scarlet; her coffee cup clattered as she set it down in its saucer. She stared at him, her eyes round, and Francis stared back impeturbably.

'Marian told you!'

'Marian?'

'She told you! Oh, it's too bad!' Her mind began to accelerate. Suddenly the whole sequence of events fell into place with a horrid accuracy. 'She told you, and you told Will, and that's why he's gone to London, and why he sent that note. Only he doesn't mean what he wrote there at all. Not at all. And now I shall probably never see him again!' Her voice had risen to a wail, and across the dining room, heads turned. Francis gestured to the waiter.

'We'll have this conversation elsewhere, I think.' He stood up, before Caro could protest, his mouth tight, his cheeks slightly flushed—though whether with embarrassment or anger, Caro could not tell, and at that moment didn't care. To Caro's fury and surprise he gripped her arm in a vice-like and painful grip, and propelled her—fast—from the dining room. At the desk, when he paused to pay the bill, Caro opened her mouth to protest.

'Outside,' he said grimly, silencing her with a look of such direct, dark anger that even she quailed.

'Get in the car.'

'Where are we going?'

'I'm taking you home.'

Francis pushed her into the Bentley without more ceremony, and then got in himself. The door slammed, and Caro rounded on him furiously.

'How *dare* you! What do you think you're doing? Why, you practically frogmarched me out of there! You are the most arrogant, rude . . . what makes you think you have the right to . . .'

'Stop being so damn childish.' Francis cut across her words, his own voice tight with anger. 'You have less self-control than any woman I've ever encountered, do you know that? What the hell do you think you're doing, starting a scene like that, about nothing, in the middle of a restaurant?'

'It's not about nothing, and I'll start a scene anywhere I damn well like. I don't need your permission!' Caro glared at him furiously. 'I'm not a pompous stuffed shirt like you! I couldn't care less what those boring people in there think. Why should I care?'

'Because it's damn bad manners, that's why.'

'And I suppose it's good manners to suggest I'm trying to hook your cousin, that I'm . . . I'm some kind of gold-digger or something! And to go talking and gossiping behind my back, laughing at me, leading me on, and all the time thinking . . . Damn you, I wish I'd never come out with you tonight!'

'No more than I do, I assure you.' He leaned across the car quite suddenly, took hold of her shoulders, and shook her. 'And now, if you'll calm down a little, and stop shouting like a fishwife, you can just listen to me for a moment.'

'I'll do no such thing! Just let me out of this damn car—I'll walk home!'

There was a sudden dangerous silence; Caro heard her own words echo in it, and felt ridiculous. Francis let go of her.

'The door's not locked.'

'*What?*' Caro stared at him. He had turned away from her; his hands now rested on the steering wheel, and he was staring straight ahead of him.

'I said, the door's not locked.'

'OK. Fine. The hell with it!'

She was not going to back down now, she thought. Damn him and his superior, sarcastic manner. He was calling her bluff, he thought she wouldn't do it. Well, he was wrong!

With a toss of her head, Caro heaved on the door handle, pushed back the door, clambered out, then slammed it with as much violence as she could muster. The wind hit her like a knife.

'You've forgotten your coat.' Francis had wound down his window, and held it out to her. Caro ignored him, and so, after a pause, he simply dropped it on to the ground.

'Trevelyans is that way.' He gestured down the road with icy politeness. 'The other way leads to the moor, and I wouldn't advise taking it. Goodnight.'

With which he rolled up the window, started the engine, and accelerated away.

Caro stared after him, shaking with impotent rage.

'Louse! Creep!' she shouted after the departing Bentley, and the wind took her words and blew them back in her face. She stared down the road. He was already out of sight. Quickly, shivering, she bent down and pulled on the coat. Then she hesitated, glancing back to the lights of the restaurant. She could always go back there, and telephone home—but no, that was too galling. Everyone would stare and whisper, and besides, Marian and her mother might not even be back yet. She set her face to the wind. No, she would walk back. He thought she wouldn't, of course, which was all the more reason to do it.

Insufferable, arrogant beast. Well, he would not get the better of her! It wasn't that far: actually, she wasn't sure how far it was, but it couldn't be more than eight miles, and she'd walked that distance hundreds of times. Someone she knew from the village might pass and offer her a lift. She wasn't absolutely certain where she was, of course, but she thought she remembered having followed this road when they came, so if she just pressed on, sooner or later she'd come to a signpost.

Right! Pulling the coat tight around her, she turned her back to the comforting lights of the restaurant, and set off into the dark.

By the time she'd gone half a mile her feet were in agony. Jennifer's high-heeled shoes tilted and slipped on the uneven road, and they pinched her toes badly. Caro cursed. There was nothing for it: she'd have to take them off, and the ridiculous silk stockings. Limping to the side of the road, she bent down and pulled off the shoes. Immediately she felt better; her spirits began to revive. She tucked the shoes, one into each pocket of her coat, and then, checking quickly each way for approaching headlights, fumbled under her skirt at the black suspenders that held up the stockings. There! They were off! She pushed the wispy stockings into her now bulging pockets, and curled her toes luxuriously in the cool grass of the verge. That was better. Now she'd do it easily. In summer she often went barefoot, the soles of her feet were like concrete, Marian said. Just as well now. She peered ahead down the road. It stretched into the distance, narrow, unlit, bordered with steep banks, almost roofed with trees. It was terribly dark; the sky was clouded, there was scarcely even a moon. Still, she was not afraid of the dark, and never had been, and it was cold. She'd better set off.

Bending her head against the wind, she walked determinedly at a fast pace down the road, imagining as she went, and with increasing pleasure, all the horrible things she would say and do to Francis Albany if she ever had the chance. Obviously, somehow, Marian must have let something slip. She couldn't believe her cousin would have told him straight out—no, she would never do that. But she must have said something, and that horrible, conceited, devious man had put two and two together. Obviously he'd realised some time ago; he must have been waiting all through dinner for the chance to come out with it. In fact—now she saw it clearly—that was obviously why he'd taken her to dinner in the first place. How horrible! How cold-blooded! All that rubbish about man-to-man conversations. Why, the man obviously hated her, and had done from the first, and no doubt he'd been absolutely delighted to pass on his discovery to Will. She could just imagine the conversation: 'I wouldn't go too fast if I were you, Will. You realise she's just after your money.' She paused momentarily, her stride faltering.

Of course, in one way, depending on how you looked at it, that was true. But the gloss was all wrong; it was a distortion. Once she had seen Will, met him, talked to him—all those ideas had evaporated like the dew. She had liked him for himself; more than liked him. She didn't even know if he *were* rich, dammit. After all, Marian had said the car belonged to Francis, so Will might indeed be poor.

And if he were, she didn't care. It didn't alter her feelings for him one shred. Not a shred, her mind repeated firmly. It was Francis who was obviously rich, with his beastly swanky car, and his pompous Savile Row suits, and his horrible expensive restaurants. So if she were what he had suggested, she'd have turned her attentions to him, and she wasn't going to do *that*, God forbid, and that *proved* it.

She thought of Will, then, as she had seen him on the beach, tall and golden and strong and—somehow—invincible, and her heart caught. Whatever happened, she would see Will again, Francis should not stop her, and then she would tell him exactly how it had all come about, and how muddled she had been, but how, really, almost immediately she had realised— yes—that she loved him.

She stopped. There, it was out! She had let her mind speak the words without qualification, and as soon as she did so, she felt tremendously elated. It was true: she was in love. And next to the strength of that feeling, nothing else mattered. I would live with Will in a cottage, she thought to herself, pleased by the image, and for the next mile let her mind ramble contentedly over the picture she conjured up. The two of them, in a remote place; a little garden, with roses growing over the door, and a warm fire in the winter, and they would sit there together in the evenings, and talk, and be happy, and—make love—she thought, feeling rather breathless. And horrible cousin Francis would most definitely not be welcome: no idyllic weekends in the country for *him!* She stopped again, annoyed with herself. Why had she had to think of him again? Now the whole picture was spoiled, the image had fled. And it was really damned cold.

Just ahead, she could see, the road divided, and she hastened forward, looking for a signpost. To her relief it rose up, white and ghostly in the dark. She hesitated, rubbing her foot. The roads were harder than she had imagined, and she could feel a blister forming. Also, it was beginning to rain. Damn, she could feel it. Soft Cornish rain, that came in off the sea like mist, and felt silky against the skin, and left you more saturated than a torrent.

Damn Francis! Now she began to regret, a little, her impulsiveness and temper. Maybe she should have maintained an icy dignified silence, and demanded to be driven home, and not said a word until she'd had a chance to talk to Marian. Still, she had not. Now there was nothing else for it but to press on. She had, she admitted now, rather expected him to have come back for her when his own temper had cooled, or at least to find him waiting for her, further along the road. But obviously now that was out of the question. Why, he was probably in bed and fast asleep by now. She hoped he had nightmares!

Abruptly she turned. The road began to climb steeply almost at once, and Caro groaned. Her coat was soaked already, her feet were sore, only residual anger kept her warm, for her bare legs were already frozen, and the stupid suspender things, with no stockings to keep them taut, rubbed and banged against her thighs. Forcing herself to go on, feeling tiredness begin to pull her muscles, she stumbled, and half fell. The fall shook her; no great harm was done, but the suddenness of the hurt alarmed her. To her fury she realised she was near to tears. What if she were really lost? She could be out here all night at this rate, anything could happen. She might die of exposure . . . You're being ridiculous, she said to herself crossly. People don't die of exposure in Cornwall in September. She would be all right. Once she saw the sea, she would know where she was.

She crested the rise. It was there: black, glittering, shifting. The sea. She stared around her in the darkness. The area was desolate. Not a farm, not a light, nothing, just windswept grass, a few bent trees. With a sigh that came out like a choking sob she realised that, even now, she had no idea where she was. Was Trevelyans to the east or the west, and which way was she facing? The coastline here was so beaten, so indented, you could never be certain, and Caro was used to orientating herself by the sun.

Suddenly she realised she felt utterly exhausted. All the fight and the anger had gone out of her; she felt drained of everything except misery. Trevelyans would be sold; she would probably never see Will again: her life was a pointless, directionless mess, and perhaps worst of all, Francis had been a little right. She was rude and impulsive and thoughtless, and maybe she had not behaved entirely honourably. After all, she had sought Will out, quite deliberately, that first night, and had pretended it was accidental, a chance meeting. Now her cheeks burned with shame at the memory. How could she have been so *stupid*?

She sank down by the roadside and cried. Then, revived by this unusual indulgence, and also feeling cramped and cold, she stood up again. Whatever else, it was no good giving up. She had to get home somehow. But first, she thought, hitching up her skirt, and feeling a momentary guilt because Jennifer's beautiful dress was wet with rain, *first* she was going to get rid of those damn suspenders.

It was extraordinarily awkward. Her coat hampered her; her clothes were now so wet they stuck to her skin, and the beastly thing had a whole series of little hooks and eyes at the back of the waist that were stiff. Damn, damn, damn, she muttered, pulling the dress higher, bending forward in concentration, and trying to force her numb fingers to undo the hooks. Rain beat against her bare thighs; one hook came out. Just one more and then . . .

The wind was so loud in her ears that she never heard it; the car crested the hill at such a speed she would hardly have had time to do anything anyway. Her head was bent against her chest, and she did not see its lights, until, as the car levelled off, its headlamps caught her, full beam, standing by the edge of the road, skirt awry, legs bared, pale in the light, and the rest of her body quite naked to the waist except for a pair of tiny black lace panties and the suspender belt, which, Caro thought furiously, had taken on the dimensions of an octopus. She was beyond caring. The hook gave as the car skidded to a halt, and with a gesture of triumph, she wrenched the offending garment off. She could see nothing, the headlamps, still on, blinded her totally.

A car door had opened; she blinked, and with as much decorum as she could muster straightened her skirts, adjusted her coat, wound the suspender belt into a ball and stuffed it into her bulging pockets.

She glared into the lights. Into the pool they cast on the road appeared a pair of feet, clad in impeccable black shoes. Above them she could see black trousers, but no more, for the rest of the man's body was in shadow, and her eyes dazzled. The feet came to a halt. There was a little silence.

Then she recognised the shoes and her heart sank. It was, of course, Francis Albany. Caro glared.

'Don't you think you'd better get back in the car?' he said.

For a moment, even then, she was tempted to refuse. She hesitated; Francis stepped forward.

· 'Well?' he said pleasantly, his face grim. 'Are you coming, or do I have to use brute force? It's up to you.'

Caro glowered. He was quite capable of it, and he looked fearfully strong. She tilted her chin.

'Very well. Since you leave me no alternative . . .'

She brushed past him without a second glance and climbed into the Bentley. After a brief pause Francis got in beside her and slammed his door. Then he reached to the dashboard and switched on a light. Then he turned and gave her a long, cool look. Then he laughed:

'You look like a drowned rat, do you know that?'

She shivered suddenly as he spoke, and then to her horror sneezed, and at once Francis's manner changed. He reached across and felt her hand. Caro snatched it away and he sighed.

'You're freezing,' he said more gently. 'You'll get pneumonia, if you're not careful. Here, you'd better take that coat off, it's soaked. There's a rug in the back of the car.'

'I'm fine.'

'I said, take it off.'

Caro didn't dare disobey him, and the coat did feel horrible, so reluctantly she allowed him to help her off with it, and then to drape a large soft cashmere travelling rug around her. Instantly she felt better, and snuggled deeply under its folds. Francis leaned across to tuck it around her legs and then suddenly stopped.

'You've cut yourself.'

'Yes. I fell over.'

Before Caro could stop him, he had pulled the rug aside and was looking at her legs. He lifted them gently so the light shone on them, holding her firmly and yet soothingly, as a doctor might.

'And your feet are bleeding. Your legs feel like ice. Honestly, Caro . . .' He reached across to the glove compartment and pulled out a silver flask. 'You're colder than I realised. You'd better have some of this—it's brandy. Sip it slowly—it'll help to warm you.'

Suddenly he was in charge, and Caro realised she was glad of it. She felt much weaker than she had realised, almost lightheaded, as if she might faint, and events were beginning to slow, to move at a dreamlike pace. She took a gulp of the brandy and choked.

'I said sip it, not drain the flask. Now . . .' Francis reached for her wrist and she realised he was taking her pulse.

'I'm all right,' she said dreamily, her own voice seeming to come to her from the distance. 'Really I am.'

'I'll be the judge of that. Now, listen . . .' he hesitated. 'Can you rub your legs, rhythmically, upwards—like that?' She felt a hard hand grip her calf and move up to the knee, flexing and massaging her skin. She sighed and leaned back. It felt wonderful.

'Try.' His voice was impatient. Caro bent forward and reached for her legs. Her hands seemed surprisingly weak. Francis gave an irritable exclamation.

'That's no good. Here, let me.'

She let her hand fall back to her lap. Francis lifted her right leg and began to move his hand back and forth, exerting pressure and then releasing it, down, in a firm sweep to the ankle, then up, compressing and relaxing, to the knee. Caro felt the blood start to return to her feet; her skin tingled.

'That's amazing,' she said. 'Amazing. How did you learn to do that?'

Francis paused and looked up at her for a second. 'I climb. I often go out with the mountain rescue teams in Scotland—on Skye. There we have special bags to zip you into, thermal bags. But then a climber out in the Cuillins is considerably worse off. You're all right. We just need to get the circulation going, that's all.'

He lowered her right leg, and lifted the other. His hands, firm and cool, moved smoothly over her skin. Caro sighed, and looked down at him, his dark head bent in concentration, his strong tanned hands moving back and forth, back and forth. Again she was reminded of a doctor; he had the same impersonal confident touch, and for some reason it slightly piqued her. They did not interest her particularly, but everyone always said she had beautiful legs. As far as Francis Albany was concerned, she thought crossly, they weren't a woman's legs at all. They were just—legs. She sighed, and as his hands moved she just allowed herself to flex slightly. Nothing much, just a slight arching back, a lifting of the leg, so for a second her skin brushed against his face, his lips.

'Mmmm,' she said dreamily. 'That feels wonderful. There, just there.' Instantly he released her, and set her foot back on the floor with a bump.

'You're all right now,' he said, a little grimly. He tucked the rug back around her.

'You're very cold too,' she turned her head to him slowly. 'Would you like me to do the same for you? Get the circulation going?'

'No, thank you.' He met her eyes directly. 'You wouldn't know which muscles to go for, and your rhythms would be all wrong.'

There was a little silence. Caro expected him, then, to reach forward to start the car, but he didn't, and for some reason she felt glad. The windows had misted up, and the two of them sat now, side by side, the only sound their own breathing and the distant suck and crash of the sea. Caro found, to her surprise, that she felt amazingly tranquil and at peace. Francis was not looking at her, and he seemed to hesitate before he finally spoke.

'I should just like to get one thing clear,' he said at last, 'before I drive you home. You jumped to a lot of conclusions in the restaurant this evening. It wasn't too easy to follow your reasoning, but you should understand. What I said to you—it had nothing to do with Marian at all. I wouldn't dream of discussing you in that way with your cousin, and as I'm sure you know, she wouldn't . . .'

'Stop!' Caro leaned forward impulsively. Suddenly, she realised, she had no anger or irritation left; she felt contrite. 'You're right. You see, I reacted like that because I felt guilty. If I explain, now, do you promise not to tell Will, ever?'

He made no answer, and his face, shadowed in the soft light from the dash board was impossible to read. Caro hesitated and then went on.

'You see, I'd become almost desperate about Trevelyans. I can't bear to see it go. Some days ago I woke up in the morning, and I found that somehow—during the night—a solution had come to me. I would . . .' She hesitated. 'Well, as you said. I would marry a rich man. Someone who would understand and love the house as I do—who would see the point of saving it. There were things I might have done, earlier, if I hadn't been stupid and irresponsible, but it was too late for that. So I thought, when I woke up, I know, I will marry a rich man.' She paused. 'Just the way you said.'

'Did you have a candidate in mind?'

'No—that was what was so odd.' Caro turned to him pleadingly. 'I had this feeling—you must think this very stupid, but I did. As if it wasn't just an idea, but something that was really going to happen . . .' Francis turned to her abruptly, enquiringly, and seeing she had his attention, she continued. 'Then, later that day, just when I decided that of course I was being ridiculous, I was walking home with Marian. We went through the village, which we rarely do, and—I saw your car.' She paused, her face glowing. 'I saw Will.'

'Chance meetings,' Francis murmured, and Caro blushed.

'I know. I *did* go to the pub in the hope of seeing Will—I admit it. But you see, by then I was in such a *muddle*. I never meant to be cold and calculating, I'd like you to believe that.' She paused. 'And, once I met Will, it was different anyway.'

'Different?' He looked at her unsmilingly. 'Why?'

'Because as soon as I met him everything changed. Then, it wasn't because of Trevelyans that I wanted to see him again. It was because of him.' She paused and took a deep breath. 'I love him,' she said, firmly, partly because she wanted to hear how the words sounded spoken aloud, partly because, although she could not have explained why, she wanted to see Francis' reaction.

It was swift. He gave a gesture of disgust. 'On the basis of two encounters? Really!'

'I don't see why not.' Caro turned to him fiercely, stung by his tone. 'I believe in love at first sight. My mother always says that the very first time she met my father, she *knew*. I think that can happen. Oh, I know you're not the kind of man to believe that—you'll dismiss it as rubbish and romanticism.'

'So.' He turned away from her, his face suddenly hard. 'Why have you decided to tell me all this? This . . .' he paused fastidiously, 'this woman's magazine story?'

His words cut her, but Caro forced down her temper.

'Because . . .' she hesitated, unsure. 'I don't know why,' she said finally. 'I suppose you'd made it pretty clear what you thought of me, and I wanted you to know you were wrong. That it wasn't like that. *I* wasn't like that.' She paused. 'I'm not a gold digger, Francis.'

'I never said you were. You asked my advice and I gave it. It's as simple as that.'

Caro stared at him. 'Is that true?' she said. 'Really? You just meant to give me advice?'

Francis shrugged; the whole conversation was beginning to bore him, she could sense it; his coldness was increasing by the second.

'Certainly. I wouldn't pretend it was particularly moral, just pragmatic. You need to save Trevelyans. There's very little time. You're . . .' he paused, 'you're an attractive girl, you're unmarried. It seemed a solution. I wasn't being altogether serious, you must forgive me.'

'You hadn't realised, then, what I felt for Will?'

'I hadn't given it a moment's thought, if it's any consolation to you. And if you want my opinion, your feelings for Will, as you call them, are half wish-fulfilment and half imagination.' He paused, then spoke more gently. 'I think, Caro, that perhaps you would be wise to be a little cautious. You are impulsive, even you will admit that, and . . .'

'Oh, for God's sake!' Caro interrupted. 'I'm twenty-three. I'm not a child. I . . .' she paused, then sighed. He was looking at her with a slightly odd expression, almost sadly. 'Oh, dear!' She gave a groan. 'I see what you're doing. You're trying to let me down gently. You think Will won't, that he doesn't . . . He's engaged! He's in love with someone else—that's it, isn't it!'

Francis repressed a smile. 'Caro,' he said patiently, 'as far as I know Will isn't engaged. And I don't think he's in love with anyone else. But you must ask him that, mustn't you?'

'He isn't engaged?' Caro's hopes rose, and then were immediately dashed as another idea came to her. 'Oh,' she said glumly, 'I see. You mean he won't fall in love with me. I'm not his type.'

'I didn't . . .'

'I suppose you're right. After all, why should he? I'm broke, scatterbrained, impractical. I had a stupid, rotten girl's education. I talk too much.' She sighed. 'And what's more, I'm hopelessly inexperienced. I mean—why should he? He probably knows lots and lots of absolutely wonderful women, who are terribly clever, and know how to dress, and who can talk about all the right things and . . .'

'And?'

'Well . . .' Caro hesitated, but the brandy was giving her confidence, she was warming to her theme, and really Francis did seem quite approachable now.

'Well,' she said again, 'Francis, tell me honestly, a man does prefer a woman to be—a bit experienced, don't you think?'

'I'd say it depends on the man. And the woman.'

Caro peered at him closely; she suspected him of mockery again, but his face was quite serious. She took another swallow of brandy.

'You see, the trouble is I'm not.' She paused. 'There was a time, ages ago, when I lived in London, when I thought, this is no good. I've got to get on with it. My virginity, I mean.' She looked at Francis confidentially. 'It was beginning to be—almost a burden, a sort of albatross around the neck. So, I'd almost decided to get rid of it, you know in one fell swoop, so I didn't have to bother about it any more. You see—' she paused, 'it always seemed to me fundamentally immoral only to sleep with someone if they were going to marry you. It's a bit like being bought, isn't it? With a ring. But on the other hand, if you were still a virgin, it was always an issue. So I decided to stop being one. I was very organised and practical about the whole thing and . . .'

'Did you succeed?'

'No, that's the awful part. I didn't. I'd selected the man and everything. He was perfect in a way because I knew he'd take the whole thing very casually, and I didn't even like him very much, so there was no danger of its becoming emotional. It was all going to be very cool and scientific. Then, when I was out with him, we were having dinner in some restaurant, I suddenly thought—No, this won't do, it's a waste. If I'm going to give it away, I should give it away to someone I really love. So it would be special, a kind of present to them.' She paused. 'Do you think that was stupid?'

'I think it was remarkably sensible. So what did you do?'

'Oh, nothing,' Caro said airily. 'I just explained and told him I'd changed my mind, and then I called a cab and I left him there, still having his soup. He was cross.'

'This was at the soup stage?'

'Oh yes. It didn't take long. Once I'd been reminded how utterly awful he was, there wasn't much point in staying. However . . .'

'Yes?'

'Well, the point of all this is that as a result I'm awfully ignorant. I thought, you see, that it would be better to avoid men rather, until I met the one—the special one. So—now I have and I don't know what to do.'

'You don't know what to do?'

'Absolutely not. I don't know what to do with my hands, or my mouth, or . . .'

Francis began to laugh. Caro stared at him indignantly.

'It's not funny,' she said. 'It's all very well for you to laugh!'

'I apologise.' He paused. 'You don't think you could just trust to your instincts, when the moment came?'

'No, I don't,' Caro said firmly. 'I shall only make a mess of it. What I need is some practice. I see that now.'

There was a little silence. She looked at Francis sideways; an idea was coming to her—a splendid idea . . .

'Francis . . .' she said.

'Yes?'

'You don't find me attractive, do you? I mean, I'm not your type?'

Francis regarded her solemnly. 'That's rather difficult to say,' he answered. 'I've never met anyone quite like you.'

'Oh, I'm sure I'm not.' Caro turned to him pleadingly. 'I suppose you wouldn't consider—well, teaching me a little?'

'Teaching you?' Francis looked alarmed.

'Oh, not very much,' Caro said hastily. 'Just what to do with my arms and things. Don't you see? Between us there would be no danger of complications of any kind. It could just be *scientific*, like learning Latin grammar or something . . .'

'Thank you very much. You think my kisses would be like Latin grammar?'

Caro blushed, since that was precisely what she did think. 'No, no,' she said quickly. 'But you're so much older than I am and you're a man of the world, and so obviously you'd know the technicalities at least . . .'

'I might manage the technicalities, yes.'

'There you are, then! That's all I need. Oh, *please*, Francis! I'd listen to you, honestly I would, because you're so sensible. You were sensible this evening, when I was stupid. And when you touched me earlier on—when you were—er—massaging my legs and everything, it was so wonderfully impersonal, just like a doctor, and . . .'

'What had you in mind?' Francis's tone was dry. 'An introductory course, or full graduation?'

'Oh, just introductory,' Caro said nervously. 'Just to get me over the initial hurdles. Please, Francis. You can't imagine what a help it would be. I'd be so much more *confident*, and then . . .'

'All right. When would you like to start? Now?'

CHAPTER SIX

HE turned towards her as he spoke, and Caro met his eyes. His face was softened by the light, amusement curved his lips. Suddenly, for the first time since she had met him, she was aware of both his strength and his masculinity. It frightened her a little, and she almost changed her mind, but the opportunity seemed too good to miss, and Will might be returning the next day, she told herself quickly, so, lowering her eyes, she nodded silently.

'Very well.' He moved a little closer to her, and Caro caught the scent of his skin and his hair, a tangy sharp male scent; it was definitely attractive, and at once she drew back.

'I think, perhaps, the rug . . .' Very gently and firmly he eased the rug from her shoulders. Caro stiffened.

'Do you really?'

'Yes, definitely. A man can't kiss a woman properly when she's wrapped in a rug. Lesson number one, Caro. Now . . .'

He lifted his hands and gripped her shoulders firmly.

'If you could just turn a little towards me . . . that's right.'

He held her close to him with an easy negligent strength; Caro blinked; it felt extraordinarily pleasant.

'Very good. Now, if you could just . . . look at me . . .' Very gently his hand moved caressingly up her arm, across her shoulder to her neck, cradling her face up to him. As his hand slipped under her hair and touched her skin, Caro felt a pulse shoot through her whole body. Her eyes widened.

Francis was looking down into her face, his features intent. He was an awfully good actor, she thought with surprise. Really awfully good. He was apparently completely serious.

'Darling,' he said, and she froze.

'Darling?'

'But of course.' He smiled at her, a slightly lazy, dangerous smile. 'Verisimilitude. Don't worry. Now, where was I? Ah yes, darling . . .'

He bent his head and very gently brushed his lips across her forehead. Caro sighed. She closed her eyes.

'My dear.' He kissed her lips. It was the gentlest of touches; his mouth was firm, warm against hers, the pressure of his lips very slight. It felt very warm, very gentle, quite wonderful, Caro thought, and almost before she had realised what she was doing, she had lifted her arms and encircled him in them. He drew back a little, and looked down into her face.

She swallowed. 'I . . . is that right?' she said, hearing her own voice falter a little.

'But of course.' He took one of her hands and drew it to his lips, placing a kiss against her palm. Caro stared at him. Really, he was almost *too* good at this, she decided. His movements were so fluid, so determined, so practised. He must be a much more experienced man than she had thought.

'Now, if you could just lift your face a little. That's right. Relax . . .' He was stroking her back and her neck, and, hesitantly, Caro allowed her own hand to move, just a little, so she touched his neck, his face. His skin felt slightly rough under her fingers, and to her surprise her touch seemed to affect him. He moved suddenly, catching her hand and holding it against his face; his breath seemed to come more quickly. A needle of suspicion began to probe at the back of Caro's mind; she was not altogether sure that he was treating all this in the right scientific spirit . . .

'Francis . . .' she said.

As her lips parted he bent his head and kissed her again full on the mouth. As his lips touched hers, parted them further, gently, then more fiercely, and his arms suddenly tightened around her, a dart of extraordinary pleasure shot through her whole body. She gasped, feeling herself weaken against him, feeling herself tremble. The kiss went on for a long time; how long Caro could not have said, for she was finding it increasingly difficult to be objective; but at last Francis drew back a little and looked down into her face. Caro stared, hypnotised by his eyes. Why, they were extraordinary eyes. Quite extraordinary. Tawny, with flecks of gold in their depths . . .

'Well?' Francis smiled at her. 'How did that feel?'

'Oh . . .' With some difficulty Caro found her voice, though it refused to function normally, and to her consternation sounded husky, little more than a whisper. 'I thought it was very good . . .'

He frowned. '*Good*,' he said firmly. 'Not very good. Not yet.'

'Really?' Caro's eyes widened in consternation. 'What was I doing wrong?'

'You should be a little nearer, I think. Like *that* . . .' With one easy movement he pulled her tight against him, so her breasts under the thin lace dress were pressed against the hard muscles of his chest.

'Oh!' She caught her breath. Something extraordinary was beginning to happen to her; suddenly it seemed difficult to keep still. She wanted to move, she realised, to press her body against his.

'I think . . .' There were tiny buttons at the throat of her dress. Gently but insistently he began to undo them, and she stiffened.

'Do you really think . . . ?'

'But of course . . .'

He had undone the dress with amazing ease as far as the division of her breasts. Before Caro could move or protest, she felt his lips against her neck, kissing her skin with soft lingering kisses, then moving a little lower, a little lower. His head was bent. Impulsively, not pausing to think, Caro cradled him against her with a sigh, touching his hair, moving her fingers through it.

'Caro . . .' he said, his own voice sounding a little less cool now, slightly thick, and he moved one hand just a fraction so he cupped her right breast in his palm. She felt her nipples harden under his hand as, very gently, he moved his thumb over the lace that covered the tips of her breasts, then, as she felt her whole body pliant against him, he kissed her again on the mouth, hard this time, his own breath coming fast.

Caro heard herself give a soft moan, and his kiss deepened. She wriggled closer to him, her thighs pressing against his, possessed suddenly with a desire to touch him as he touched her. Francis drew back. Gently but swiftly he released her. Then, as if nothing whatsoever had happened, he roughly straightened his hair and adjusted his tie. Then he looked at his watch.

Caro stared at him.

'Well?' she said finally.

'Quite good,' he said pleasantly. 'For a first attempt, promising, definitely.'

'Only promising?' Caro's eyes widened. 'I thought I was doing quite well.'

'But you were.' He smiled at her. 'You could relax a little more. Some of the movements are a little jerky still. And you were leaning against my arm too heavily. I was getting cramp.'

'Cramp?' Caro's voice came out in a squeak. 'Is that what you were thinking?'

'I have to be objective about it, Caro. That's the whole point, surely? And I was getting cramp, definitely.'

'What were you thinking about?' She looked at him sulkily.

'Thinking about? Then? Oh, some plans I've been drawing up for a house. And also how you were moving and so on—I was trying to note that.'

'But didn't you . . .' She hesitated. 'Didn't you feel anything?' She paused. Francis was staring at her blankly as if he couldn't comprehend her meaning. Caro gave a groan. 'There you are,' she said gloomily. 'I'm no good, I knew that would happen. I mean, if I were any good, you'd have felt something, wouldn't you?' She paused. 'I did.'

'Good,' he said briskly. 'That's a very good sign. We're getting somewhere. When did you feel something?'

She hesitated. 'Well, straight away, really,' she said. 'And then when you—er—that is . . .'

'When I touched your breasts? You responded very well then, I thought. No coy protestations. Excellent. And you have lovely breasts.'

She looked at him suspiciously.

'It seems to me,' she said darkly. 'It seems to *me* that you're a good deal more experienced at all this than I expected.' She gave a sudden giggle. 'I think you're a bit of a rake, Francis.'

'A rake? Me?' He looked at her innocently. 'Well, perhaps in my younger days. Even now, occasionally . . .'

'I thought you were an intellectual.'

'So I am. An intellectual rake. Now one comes to think of it, the perfect tutor in matters of this kind.'

'Are you sure you were thinking about your designs for that house, Francis?' Caro gave him a sharp look. 'Your breathing changed, I noticed.'

'Of course my breathing changed.' He returned her look with an air of injured innocence. 'It has to, when you're kissing someone. Otherwise you'd suffocate.'

'Do you think, Francis . . .' she hesitated. 'Do you think I could try just once more? Just to make sure I was getting the hang of it?'

'No, Caro, I really think . . .'

'Oh, just once, please!' Caro's eyes shone. This time I'll show him, wretched man, she thought. Thinking about his designs for a house indeed!

Before Francis could draw back she lifted her arms very deliberately and twined them around his neck, drawing his face down to hers. Then, before he could protest, she reached her mouth up and kissed him. This time she made sure she did not lose control; she concentrated on what she was doing. His mouth was beautiful, she thought, as she touched his lips delicately with the tip of her tongue, then felt them part under hers. She kissed him for a long while, making sure she did not lean on his arm and give him cramp, and willing him to respond. When he gave a low ragged groan, and moved closer to her, she took his hand, and—greatly daring—pressed it against the soft swell of her breast. Then, with a sweet smile, she drew back.

'Well?'

Francis cleared his throat. 'Improving,' he said grudgingly. 'certainly improving. I don't think you need any more tuition from me, Caro.'

She stiffened. For some reason, this was not the reaction she had wanted.

'In fact,' he looked at his watch in a businesslike manner, 'I think I should really take you home. It's getting very late. This was supposed to be just the introductory course, if you remember.'

'All right.' Caro felt sad.

He started the car, swore, and then had to wipe all the steamed-up windows. They drove back almost all the way in silence, Francis never taking his eyes from the road, his manner thoughtful.

'What an exceedingly odd evening,' he said at last, when they reached Trevelyans. Caro smiled.

'Yes,' she said, 'it was, wasn't it? But I liked it.' She hesitated, feeling there was something she wanted to say, and yet not sure what it was.

'Francis,' she said finally, as he pulled up outside the darkened house.

'Yes?'

'Do you feel we're friends now—after all that? I do.' She turned to him frankly. 'I've discovered I like you. I didn't think I would at first. I thought you were a bit—well, stuffy. But you're not at all. And you were very kind this evening. Thank you.' She paused. 'Do you think Will will be back tomorrow?'

'Impossible to say.' He spoke a little stiffly. 'If he is I'm sure he'll contact you at once.' He gave her an odd sideways glance. 'And then you'll be able to put all your new found knowledge to good use, won't you?'

'Maybe.' Caro sighed. 'Am I forgiven for being so—rude—and impetuous, earlier?'

'Already forgotten.' His voice was light and dismissive. 'Though I think you might do well to guard against your tendency to impetuosity.'

'Why?'

'Oh, because you might get hurt, that's all. Now, run along in, like a good girl. It's terribly late.'

In spite of his dismissiveness, Caro still paused. She looked at him curiously.

'Why do you say that?'

Francis gave an exasperated sigh. 'Has no one ever told you, Caro? You ask too many questions. It's extremely provocative.'

Caro smiled widely. 'Good,' she said. 'I like being provocative.'

'So I noticed. Now go in and get warm and get some sleep.'

'May I ask one more question?'

Francis sighed. 'What?'

'Will you let me show you the house? One day, before you leave? Please, Francis.' She smiled at him impishly. 'It's to say thank you, for my tuition.'

'Go *in*,' he said. 'Before I spank you.'

Caro grinned and jumped out of the car. She had left her coat behind, and to her delight, Francis appeared not to notice. His face was abstracted.

'Goodnight, Francis,' she called meekly through the glass.

'Goodnight,' he said curtly. He started to move off, then stopped again and wound down the window.

'I'll telephone you tomorrow,' he said gruffly. 'Just to make sure you're all right, that there's no ill effects . . .'

'Thank you, Francis,' said Caro, and went indoors feeling oddly triumphant.

It was cold in the library. All the rooms at Trevelyans were cold in the mornings, but the library was freezing. Marian shifted awkwardly on her perch at the top of the library steps and flexed her feet. She glanced out of the window; the weather had cleared overnight. With a sigh she lifted the heavy book from her knee and flicked one last time through its pages; she was wasting her time. Caro's father had a fine collection of books on architecture, and Caro herself had added to them. The one she had been consulting—*New Directions in British Architecture: The Post-Modernists*—was pretty dull.

Gloomily she stared at a photograph of the new lecture hall, Cambridge, by someone called Jim Stirling. She'd never heard of him, and the brutalism of the building's design repelled her. Anyway, the book was pretty useless; it didn't seem to go much beyond 1960; there was no reference to anyone called Albany in the index.

It might have been interesting, just to see what kind of work he did, she thought, though really how Caro could get interested in all this stuff was beyond her. She didn't really like elaborate houses anyway, even Trevelyans, for all its beauty. Such houses created too many problems, they took over people's lives. Something was always going wrong with them; they made a simple orderly life impossible, and Marian preferred her life to be as uncomplicated, as orderly, as possible. She pushed the heavy book back on the shelves; Caro always said that if Marian had her way, she would live utterly anonymously in a small tidy flat, with everything painted white, and electric heating, and a porter on the premises in case anything went wrong.

It was true, she thought, and for a moment an image of such a place swam into her mind; somewhere central in London, and she knew just how she would furnish it, very simply, in pale clean colours. There'd be a small, efficient kitchen, with lots of cupboards so there would be no clutter. She saw herself, for a moment, in such a kitchen, preparing a casserole in one of those splendid electric pots that cooked by themselves and used hardly any electricity. She was wearing a pretty, clean, flowered apron, and Francis Albany had just walked in the door, in one of those wonderful suits he wore, with a bottle of Bordeaux in his briefcase. 'Marian,' he said, in that beautiful voice of his, with its slight drawl, its odd hesitations that seemed to give weight to his simplest utterances: 'Marian'.

Irritably she got up and climbed down from the steps. She was getting as bad as Caro; what was the matter with her? She was not usually given to daydreaming.

She went out into the hall. She would go for a walk, she decided; the house was getting on her nerves that morning. On the stairs was Caro. She looked terrible; she was swathed from head to foot in her father's old woollen dressing-gown, and her hair looked like a bird's nest; her nose was red.

'You're late up.'

'I'm not up. It's an illusion. I'm going back to bed, I feel ghastly.'

'Probably a hangover.'

Caro turned. 'Is it a hangover when your head aches, and your eyes feel all sort of itchy, and your nose is stuffed up?'

'Very possibly. Take some aspirin.' Marian paused. 'Did you have a good time last night?'

'Sort of. An odd time. I'll tell you later, when this drum in my head stops banging. If it ever does.'

Caro disappeared, and Marian smiled to herself. Caro had been very late back. Lying awake, unable to sleep, she had heard the car at about two a.m. She pulled on a thick tweed jacket, and wrapped a headscarf over her hair. She would walk along the cliff, she decided. Fresh air might make her feel better, and for some reason she felt drawn to the bay where they had all picnicked together. She needn't go down to the beach; just along the cliff path at the top. That should blow the cobwebs away.

The wind was gusting and Marian felt cold. For a moment, passing Trelawneys' farm, she hesitated and almost decided to go back. She did not share Caro's enthusiasm for walking. Jack Trelawney was there, opening the gate into his lane for his tractor, and Marian waved to him hopefully; sometimes Jack gave her a lift up to his farm, and she had tea in the kitchen with him and his wife. But today he seemed in a hurry; he gave her the briefest, most cursory of acknowledgements and then hurriedly climbed back into the tractor and drove off. Why, he hadn't even shut the gate behind him, Marian saw as she reached it, went through and latched it. How odd, it was almost as if he was avoiding her.

Resignedly she took the track that led to the cliff. On all sides the banks, crested with gorse, were thick with flowers. Marian paused, trying to remember their names. She pressed flowers sometimes, and their botanical names interested her; they were a challenge, resisting easy classification, and Marian liked to classify things, So, now, she bent to the flowers, looking closely at their leaf formations, at the number and alignment of their petals, for that was the surest method of identification.

'Cinquefoil,' said a voice, startling her. 'And that's crows-foot, and that one—by your hand—that's rue.'

Marian blushed; she knew she did not blush prettily, as Caro did, so she took her time straightening up, turning.

'Hello,' she said. 'What are you doing here?'

Francis Albany smiled, and Marian cursed herself for sounding so peremptory.

'Walking.' He shrugged. 'Thinking. I felt drawn to the beach. Wonderful day, isn't it?'

'It's very fresh, yes.'

'Were you going on to the cliff?'

'No,' she said quickly. 'No, I'm not a great walker. I was just looking at the flowers, then I was going back.'

'I'll walk with you.' To her surprise he offered her his arm, and awkwardly Marian rested one gloved hand in the crook of it.

'Where's Will today?' she asked, when they had walked a little way in silence.

'Will? Oh, he's still in London.'

'In London?' She turned to him in surprise. 'Did he go up today, then?'

'Today? No, yesterday.'

'But I thought . . .' She stared at him. 'Surely—last night? Caro and he . . .'

Francis paused in his stride. 'No, he was called away yesterday afternoon. I deputised for him—Caro had dinner with me last night.' He walked on again a few paces. 'She didn't mention it to you?'

'No. No, she said nothing this morning.'

'Oh.' He sounded slightly irritable at this, and Marian glanced at him curiously; perhaps he was a little vain, she thought suddenly; he sounded oddly affronted.

Marian sighed, hoping Caro had not been indiscreet. She cleared her throat. 'Will your cousin be away long?'

'I don't know. He thought just a couple of days at most. But he rang this morning and said he might have to stay a bit longer. Business, you know.'

'What a pity.' Marian hesitated. 'Caro will be disappointed.'

He gave a frosty smile. 'So I gathered; we talked of it last night.'

Marian bit her lip. Caro *had* been indiscreet. She might have known it.

'She's very *sudden*, your cousin,' he said, in a disapproving voice. 'Very headstrong.' He paused, glancing down at her. 'Very different from you.'

'Well, yes.' Marian felt a glow of pleasure; it fought with her natural loyalty to Caro. 'But Caro's not—light,' she added. 'She's a person of very strong affections. Devotions . . .' Her voice tailed away.

'Would you say so?' He sounded bored. They were within

sight of the Bentley which he had parked across the fields. 'I suppose . . .' he turned to her, touching her gloved hand with the lightest of pressures, 'I suppose you wouldn't like to have lunch with me, would you, Marian?'

'Lunch?' Her voice came out in a sort of croak and he smiled.

'There's a fish place in Fowey, just over the river. It's ten minutes from here in the car. And it is lunchtime.'

'Well, yes.' Marian kept her voice perfectly casual; her heartbeat seemed to her to have doubled in a second, and a ridiculous wild joy and hopefulness lifted her whole body. 'Yes. That would be very nice.'

'Good.' Francis removed his hand, and quickened his pace. Marian stumbled to keep up with him.

The beastly iron didn't work properly.

Caro slammed it back down on the ironing board, and looked at Jennifer's dress doubtfully. She found it difficult to iron a handkerchief without making the edges go wavy, and the skirt on this dress seemed to have yards of material in it, it was driving her mad. She had already burnt her arm on the iron, and she was so terrified of scorching the silk that it was now too cool to be any good. Its thermostat didn't work properly. She looked at her watch; past one. Her mother was seeing the solicitors, she knew that. But where was Marian? She'd been looking forward to telling her about last night; not all of it, because there were parts she felt she'd rather keep to herself, but a carefully edited account. And now, nothing. What was more, Will must be still in London, when he could surely have taken the early train if he were that keen to see her, and Francis Albany hadn't even had the courtesy to telephone to see how she was. Nor had he returned the coat, shoes, stockings and suspender belt.

She had a moment's image of his lifting the coat from the car, and discovering the wispy underclothes, and she giggled. The idea of Francis Albany with a suspender belt in his hands was so incongruous . . . And yet was it? Caro paused and then blushed. What had she been thinking of last night? It must have been the brandy, and the after-effects of that ghastly walk. She must have been mad. Why, she'd told him things she'd never discussed with anyone before, not even Marian, and then . . .

She frowned, as the memory of Francis with his arms around her, Francis kissing her, came back with a startlingly pleasant physical clarity. The sensation increased her irritability. Who would have thought that such a cold haughty man, a man who was apparently totally impervious to women, who hadn't even bothered to pursue Marian and ask her out, should be so, so . . . Her mind reached for the word. Skilful, she decided finally. Definitely skilful. With reserves of quite unexpected passion, presumably if the right woman awoke it, so he forgot about house designs and getting cramp in his arms and . . .

Quite suddenly she felt dreadfully guilty. Marian! Why, last night, she'd forgotten about Marian altogether. She'd tried to talk about her at dinner, but Francis kept changing the subject. And then, in the car—why, she'd forgotten her altogether. She, Caro, had suggested to Francis that he should kiss her, and how would that appear to Marian? She would be jealous, hurt—of course she would. Because Marian would never understand that of course there had been nothing in it, that it had just been one of her mad impulses, and that the whole thing had been as cool and scientific as could be, and that Francis had only agreed to go along with it *because* he was detached, because she, Caro, meant nothing to him whatsoever, and wasn't his type, wasn't the kind of woman who would sweep him off his feet with desire.

Was Marian? she wondered doubtfully. She tried to picture Marian in Francis Albany's arms. The thought made her uncomfortable, and crossly she turned and unplugged the iron. The dress looked perfectly all right. She would take it back to Jennifer now. She couldn't stand hanging about in the house any longer, and the walk to the Amhursts' might clear her head.

She folded the dress carefully in a carrier bag, pulled on an old mac and some wellingtons, and set off down the drive at a smart pace, wincing only slightly as the boots rubbed the blisters on her feet. At the bottom of the drive she turned into the road, and marched along, head bent against the wind. She

would think about Will, she told herself, and almost immediately forgot him.

A mile from the Amhursts', where the road forked to
Bodinnick and Fowey, she crossed to a stile between the high
hedges. From here she could walk across the fields at the edge
of the cliff; it was her favourite walk. She paused for a moment
on the stile, lifted the carrier bag over, and pulled her scarf
tighter around her head; it was quite cold, and she still felt a bit
snuffly and achey. A butterfly was poised on the gorse flowers
beside her; Caro froze, watching it, it was a tortoiseshell, quite
beautiful, its tawny back speckled with motes of gold. It
reminded her of something, though, just then, she could not
place it. The butterfly's wings trembled; the cold would kill it
within a day, she knew. It folded its wings, flicked them, and
flew off. Caro's eyes followed it until it disappeared from sight;
she felt sad.

Just as she was about to turn and clamber down from the stile
she heard the car; she paused, then stared. Coming to the
crossroads, from Fowey, was the great grey Bentley. It pulled
up at the turning, began to take the corner. Caro lifted her arm
to wave, suddenly excited. It must be Francis!

Then she stopped. It was Francis, and he was not alone.
Sitting beside him, looking flushed and animated, was Marian.
The two were clearly deep in conversation. Neither looked to
right or left as the car went past; neither saw her. The Bentley
accelerated into the distance, and Caro stared after it. Then
slowly, thoughtfully, she climbed down from the stile, picked
up the carrier bag and set off to the Amhursts'.

'The dress is all *right*, Caro, stop fussing! Honestly, there's no
need to get in such a state. Are you feeling okay?'

'Fine—I'm fine. I think I'm getting a cold, that's all.'

'Well, if you will go for midnight rambles in the rain, what
do you expect? What on earth were you doing, you and this
mystery man of yours? Walking in the moonlight?' Jennifer
looked at her closely and Caro sniffed.

'There wasn't a moon.'

'Well, thanks for bringing it back anyway.' Jennifer grinned.
'Peter rang this morning. The Brussels thing is a wash-out; he's

flying back and coming down here. He's decided to charm Mother, I think. So—I might get to wear it. Oh . . .' she paused, 'did you forget the shoes – the underwear?'

'Er—no.' Caro hesitated. 'I don't have them.'

'You don't have them?' Jennifer turned round very slowly.

'No. I—er—left them behind. But I can get them back, Jennifer, today. Honestly, I'm terribly sorry. I was in such a panic about the dress I totally forgot.'

A slow smile appeared on Jennifer's face.

'How long have you known this man, Caro?'

'Know him? I don't know him, not very well. About a week.'

Jennifer's eyebrows rose. 'A *week*?'

She sat down on the bed and there was a long silence. Caro shifted her feet on the carpet. She was still wearing the wellingtons, and they were making a little damp patch.

'You do know what you're doing, don't you, Caro?' Jennifer's voice was suddenly concerned. 'I mean, you're a terrible innocent, you know. Always were, and I'd hate for you . . .'

'I'm all right!' Caro snapped irritably. Jennifer was beginning to get on her nerves. 'I know what I'm doing, and I wasn't doing anything anyway, so stop looking like that.' She paused. 'I'll ring him up and get them back, today, I promise.'

'Ring him up? You mean you think he might hang on to them? What is this man, a fetishist?'

'No, of course not. He's just probably forgotten, that's all.'

'Forgotten? What kind of man forgets a pair of silk stockings, some Charles Jourdan shoes and a black lace suspender belt?'

'His type,' Caro said bitterly.

Jennifer laughed. 'Well, I can't wait to meet him,' she said. 'Tell you what, why don't you bring him over for dinner tomorrow? Peter will be here, and I'd love you to meet him anyway. Mother will be out, which is a pity. She's never met a fetishist before, I'll bet and . . .'

'Jennifer, will you shut up? I'm going home.' Caro turned grumpily to the door. 'I'll get the rest of the stuff today, I promise.'

'Well, bring him to dinner, then I can get a look at him, and see if I think he's good enough for you.' Jennifer uncoiled herself from the bed. 'You'd better, Caro. Otherwise I might start making some enquiries locally. I can be very embarrassing when I set my mind to it.'

'I know you can,' said Caro, remembering Jennifer's inquisitions from the past. She hesitated. 'I might. I don't know if I can. He mightn't be here . . .'

'Stop prevaricating. Fix it.' Jennifer put an arm around her. 'And now I think I'll give you a lift back. Tell me,' she said persuasively, teasingly, as they went downstairs together, 'is he tall, dark and handsome, Caro?'

'Yes,' said Caro, before she had time to think.

Caro put her hand over the mouthpiece of the phone. The door was firmly shut, her mother was in the kitchen making tea, and Marian was upstairs singing happily as she took a bath, but she had an irrational terror that someone might come into the room.

'Mr Albany,' she croaked into the telephone. The line crackled. Mrs Trelawney's breathing wheezed in her ear.

'Who, dear?'

'Francis. Francis Albany,' Caro croaked.

'Oh, Mr Francis! Hang on a minute, my dear.'

Caro hung on in agony. Damn, damn, double damn, she thought, what would she do if he were out?

'Yes?' Quite suddenly the phone at the other end had been picked up and a crisp cold voice sounded right in her ear. She nearly dropped the receiver.

'Francis?'

'Who is this?'

'It's me, Caro.'

'Oh, hello.' He sounded maddeningly unconcerned.

'I need my coat!' she hissed.

'Your coat?'

'I left it in your car, last night.'

'Did you?' There was a pause. 'Yes, of course you did. It's in my room. I brought it in to dry. I'd quite forgotten.'

'I need it, Francis.'

'Oh, fine, will it be all right if I bring it over tonight?'

Caro thought quickly; tonight both her mother and Marian

would be in. There might be questions; one of the goddamned shoes might fall out of the pockets, or the suspender belt. The possibilities for embarrassment were endless.

'No!' she hissed. 'Not tonight—I'm not alone. Tomorrow.'

There was a brief silence on the other end of the line.

'You're not alone? Does that matter?'

'Yes, it *does*. It might be embarrassing. I . . .'

'Embarrassing? To return a coat?'

'It's not the coat,' she moaned. How could he be so stupid? 'It's what's in the pockets. I don't even need the coat. I just need—that.'

'Oh, you mean the shoes and stockings and suspender belt?' His voice was not even lowered. Caro thought with horror of the tiny hallway at the guesthouse, with Mrs Trelawney no doubt listening to the whole conversation.

'Very pretty, the suspender belt. I like the lace. It's hanging in front of the fire in my room. It must be dry now.'

'Oh, for God's sake! I need it.'

'Then I'll be delighted and honoured to return it. And if you need any help putting it on—I seem to remember you found it rather difficult to take it off—I'd be delighted to oblige.'

If he'd been in the room with her now she would have hit him, Caro thought. Clearly he was enjoying the situation immensely. She attempted a haughty tone, and her voice came out in a tortured squeak.

'Francis, *please* . . .'

'Have you something wrong with your throat? You sound most peculiar.'

'It's a cold,' Caro moaned hoarsely. 'I have a cold. Francis, *listen*. Can you bring it back tomorrow morning? Marian and my mother will be out then, I know, and . . .'

'Just the suspender belt?'

'No, everything, dammit!' Caro's temper snapped. 'Stop teasing me, you're doing this deliberately!'

'Teasing you? Nothing could be further from my intentions, I assure you.'

'About eleven, please, Francis.' She paused, a dreadful idea suddenly coming to her. 'And Francis, you didn't say anything to Marian about this, did you? Over lunch? She said you'd had lunch.'

'Marian?' He sounded astonished. 'Goodness, no. We had much more important things to discuss.'

'Did you?' Caro said sharply. She wiped her hand across her forehead. Really, she might be ill, she felt most peculiar.

'Much more important. So.' There was a pause. 'Tomorrow at eleven. A clandestine assignation—what fun! Goodbye.'

He had hung up. Caro stared at the receiver stupidly. The dial tone buzzed in her ear.

She would go to bed, she decided. Now, with a hot water bottle, and she would take some more aspirin. And she'd read—yes, a book; something to take her mind off things.

In the library she searched around for a bit, and finally found the one she was looking for. The book on post-modernist architecture; someone had put it back in the wrong place.

It was only when she was upstairs and in bed, flicking dully through the pages of the book, which was not as up-to-date as she had hoped, that a thought suddenly came to her. What a state she was in! She had spoken to Francis, she had had the opportunity; and she had totally forgotten to ask about Will.

CHAPTER SEVEN

'I CAN'T think why I said I'd go to this thing. Maybe I should ring up and say I've changed my mind? That I can't get away?'

Marian and Caro were sitting across from each other at the breakfast table. Caro sat slumped in the old dressing gown, her elbows on the table, and Marian sat upright, eating a grapefruit without sugar. Caro looked at her cousin; she was looking extremely pretty. She was wearing a suit Caro had never seen before, made of some soft silky material in a torquoise green colour that intensified the colour of her eyes. She was delicately, carefully made-up; she had washed and set her hair, in a softer style; now it curled becomingly around her cheeks. Marian's face was heart-shaped, Caro thought; how odd she should never have noticed that before.

'You can't do that.' She watched her cousin carefully. 'It's not at all like you to break appointments. Besides, they're counting on you. You're a guest speaker.'

'I suppose you're right.' Marian sighed. She was going, as she did every year, to their school's old girls' association annual meeting. Caro had never been, and imagined it would be dire, but Marian liked that sort of thing; she kept in touch with people Caro was only too delighted never to see again.

'You've prepared your speech. It's a good speech.'

'I know—but I've never made one before. Maybe that's why I don't want to go.'

Caro looked at her cousin narrowly. She thought there were quite other reasons for Marian's reluctance to leave Trevelyans—she would be away all day, and staying overnight in London with one of her cronies—and they had nothing to do with making a speech. She looked at her watch.

'You're cutting it a bit fine anyway,' she said, 'if you're catching the eight-fifteen. How are you getting to the station?'

'Oh, Francis said he'd take me,' said Marian, in a casual tone of voice. She smiled, and a little dimple appeared in her cheek.

'I'd better hurry if I'm going. He said seven-fifteen and I should think he'd be punctual, wouldn't you?'

'I should think he lives his life by a stop-watch,' Caro said maliciously. So he was driving Marian to the station, was he? He hadn't mentioned that to *her*!

Marian looked at her cousin with a hurt expression.

'Oh, Caro,' she said, 'don't be like that. I know you two don't exactly hit it off, but . . .'

'What do you mean, don't hit it off?' Caro said sharply. 'You mean he doesn't like me?'

'No, of course not,' Marian said soothingly. 'But you're very different, aren't you? And I just thought . . .' She suddenly froze, and to Caro's fascination colour swept up in a wing from her neck to her cheeks. 'I think I heard a car,' she said. 'It must be Francis.'

Caro leapt to her feet and made for the back stairs, running her fingers through the tangle of her hair. God, she looked a mess, she thought, catching sight of herself in a glass as she passed. She'd go and wash her hair, have a bath.

Marian was flustered, fiddling around with her bag and gloves, and suddenly Caro felt contrite. She went back and quickly hugged her cousin.

'Have a lovely day,' she said more warmly. She paused. 'And a lovely drive to the station. You look terrific, Marian, really terrific!'

Marian gave her hand a grateful squeeze. The doorbell clanged.

'Oh, Caro,' Marian said, then she was gone.

Caro lurked out of sight in the kitchen regions. She listened to the car door slam, the engine fire. She curled her hair around her fingers. Something was wrong; why had it been so difficult to pay Marian a compliment? Why should she resent Marian's having a lift to the station, unless . . . But no, that was too stupid.

The next hour was agony. She thought of returning to bed, but knew she would not sleep. She went through all the books on modern architecture in the library, not one of which mentioned anyone called Albany, and she fell to imagining what might happen at the station. Was Francis, for instance, the sort of man who simply dropped you outside? Or did he go into the station and buy books and magazines, and get a platform ticket, and wait until the train came? Did he kiss people goodbye? More particularly, would he kiss Marian goodbye, and if so, how? A peck on the cheek? On each cheek, in the French manner? No, that would be Will's style, she knew it instinctively. Perhaps more than that.

An exceedingly sharp and detailed picture came into her mind of her cousin, held tight in Francis Albany's arms, with his lips pressed lingeringly against hers. The image made her feel guilty—after all, it was none of her business to think of such things—and it also made her feel sick. Quite suddenly a horrible griping pain started somewhere in the pit of her stomach, an ache below the heart which was as physical as the reaction to a blow. She put down the books and stared into space; the pain ebbed; a hideous blank depression followed it.

At nine-thirty Will telephoned. By the time the conversation was over, Caro had no more doubts. The sound of his voice came as a disappointment. He was in a jocular, teasing mood, and that irritated her. His excuses for his absence seemed unnecessarily protracted, and in any case did not interest her. She tried to conjure up his face as he spoke, and could remember it only imprecisely. Her colourless replies eventually seemed to irritate him.

'Missing me, I hope—just a bit?' he said.

'I was,' Caro replied; she always found it hard to be untruthful. He did not even notice the past tense.

'Well, I might be back tomorrow,' he said, clearly seeing this as consolation. 'Or the day after at the latest. There's a few loose ends still to tie up.'

'Good,' Caro said dully, thinking he sounded smug.

When she put down the receiver her hand shook a little. I haven't fallen in love with him, and I'm not going to, said a small voice in her mind. She knew it was true; she didn't even attempt to argue with herself. Her mind, in a snaking, insidious way, immediately began to suggest certain other possibilities, but those she turned away from, forcing herself angrily not to think. She would get washed and dressed; she would be practical. After all, Francis would be arriving at eleven.

To her horror, her heart instantly lifted, her spirits sang.
With perfect cosmic timing, the sun then came out, shining into
the room with great radiance. Caro, who knew herself to be
suggestible enough, without the assistance of the weather,
glowered at it, then hastened upstairs. The seconds ticked
nearer to eleven. Her feet felt winged.

She lay for a long time in a bath which she scented with some
of Marian's bath salts, then she washed her hair, and spent
what seemed like hours with Marian's dryer, trying to make it
smooth and shiny. Maybe her technique was wrong: her hair
looked more like a mane than ever. In her underclothes she
padded into Marian's bedroom and rummaged around on her
dressing table. From the other side of the wide galleried
landing she could hear her mother getting ready to go out; she
was seeing the agents this time, and Caro felt a momentary
wave of guilt. Her mother was having to do all this, she herself
was being no help at all. Perhaps she should have gone with
her?

She looked at her watch. It was past ten, she realised, and
she'd expected her mother to leave by ten. Heavens, why was
she delaying? If she took much longer she might run into
Francis, and that would be embarrassing, because she hadn't
mentioned his visit to anyone. Hurriedly she peered at the
bottles and lotions on Marian's dressing table; there was some
tinted foundation—she'd just borrow a bit of that. Marian
wouldn't mind, and really her nose still looked red.

Satisfied with the new pallor of her nose, she padded back
into her bedroom at the back of the house and began to dress.
She was just pulling on her most presentable pair of trousers
and shaking out the creases from an old silk shirt of her father's
that she had adopted years ago, when she thought she heard
voices in the hall. She listened; a door shut. She must have
imagined it. Probably her mother was just leaving; in a moment
she'd call out goodbye.

Hastily Caro fastened the trousers, which were cream cor-
duroy and tight, and did up the cuffs of the shirt. It was a
deeper colour than the trousers, very close to the colour of the
hair which now fanned out over her shoulders. She pulled on a

pair of old leather boots, rubbed the scuffed toes ineffectively on the rug, and surveyed herself in the glass. Not too bad, she thought grudgingly. She wasn't warm enough, but she'd suffer it. She wasn't going to put on one of those awful bald old cardigans. She still had her mother's scent, and hastily dabbed it at her wrists and temples, and then—as an afterthought—in the cleft between her breasts. She'd read somewhere that you should always apply scent where you expected to be kissed, and the memory of this bizarre piece of information made her blush suddenly.

Suddenly decisive, determined to waste no more time, she hurried from the room, along the corridor and out onto the landing. Then she stopped dead.

Below her, in the hall, were her mother and Francis Albany. They were standing side by side, their heads bent over a huge map which was spread out on a table. Francis' hands were moving rapidly over the map, pointing, emphasising, and her mother's head nodded.

'You see—here,' she heard. 'It's a sizeable amount of land. How much exactly, do you know?'

'I'm not sure, I . . . It's only grazing, you see, Philip never thought that . . .'

'Yes, but don't you see?' Francis's finger jabbed at the map. 'It's *good* grazing; I had a look at it yesterday. I'd have said some of it had potential as arable land. The soil's very rich here, and . . .' he paused, 'and that land is on lease, you say? You're quite sure about that?'

'Well, yes.' Her mother sounded dazed. 'I wouldn't be, normally, because I find all these agreements so confusing, and it was Philip who entered into them originally. But I know that's on lease, because that's the land Mr Wells wants to discuss with me. In fact, I was going to sign the papers today. Mr Wells says it will make no difference to the sale of the estate, and it will help with the—what is it? Cash flow problems—if that is sold separately. And really it seemed only fair. Jack Trelawney's been farming it now for over ten years and . . .'

'Mr Wells is quite wrong.' Francis spoke sharply, and Caro saw her mother jump. 'I'm sorry to be so direct, Mrs Trevelyan, but I assure you I'm right. Don't you see? Here, look at the map.' Patiently he directed her gaze back to the table. 'You see? That farm is the one sizeable farming unit on the estate. If Trevelyans remained in private hands it could make all the difference. If you could extend and develop that farmland, the estate's a viable financial proposition. It would still require a huge outlay of capital, of course, but eventually . . .' He paused. 'And, even more important, if what you say is true, that land is clearly key to anyone considering investing in the property for an hotel. Don't you see?' His finger traced a line on the map. 'With that land included in the sale you have an historic house, a potentially glorious garden, space for increased leisure facilities—tennis courts, pools and so on. And—' he paused, 'you have direct access, from the estate, to one of the finest beaches left on this coast. The value of that is—well, it's very high. If you sell to Jack Trelawney at—what's the going price for farm land here, and to a sitting tenant?'

'Mr Wells mentioned five hundred an acre . . .'

Francis's face became grim. 'That's ridiculous in any case,' he said angrily. 'Way under market value.'

'It would bring in about fifty thousand pounds.' Caro's mother sounded defensive. Francis sighed.

'Mrs Trevelyan, forgive me, but that's chicken feed. What would fifty thousand do? Pay off your bank loans? Is that why Wells is so keen on it? Look. Lease back that land—you have the option to do that, if I understand you correctly—and then sell it *with* the house and estate. You'll increase the value of the property to any developer by far more than fifty thousand, I assure you. I would estimate three times that amount. At least.'

'A hundred and fifty thousand?' Meg Trevelyan stared at him. 'On top of the price of the house?'

'That's right.' Francis paused. 'Look, Mrs Trevelyan, I think you should ask yourself something. Jack Trelawney is a small-time farmer. He uses out-of-date farming methods, there's been no plant investment on that farm for years—I took a look at his machinery the other day. Where is someone like Jack Trelawney going to raise fifty thousand to buy this land?'

'Mr Wells mentioned something about a loan . . .'

Francis sighed. 'On what security? Frankly, Mrs Trevelyan, I find it highly unlikely. Has he ever shown any interest in purchasing the land before?'

'Well, no, he hasn't, but . . .'

'You see?' Francis sounded triumphant. 'You realise it would be perfectly possible for a third party—someone with an interest in the outcome of this sale, a potential developer, for instance—to use Trelawney as a front man, acquire that land below value, transferring it almost immediately from Trelawney to himself and then purchasing the rest of the estate?' He smiled grimly. 'Someone doing that would save in the range of one hundred thousand on the purchase. Do you understand?'

Meg Trevelyan turned to him slowly. 'You can't mean that? Surely not? I've known Jack Trelawney all my life. He worked for Philip. He wouldn't be party to something like that.'

'People are, every day. This is business, Mrs Trevelyan, and the first thing that goes out of the window is personal loyalties. Trelawney may need the money—has that occurred to you?'

'Well, no, I hadn't thought . . .'

'Mrs Trevelyan, listen to me, please.' Francis leaned forward urgently. 'Do not sign that option for sale to Trelawney today. I beg of you not to. Stall if you like. Say you may renew the lease, and consider an option for sale at a later date—anything. But don't sign any sale agreement. Look.' He reached in his pockets and pulled out a small card. 'This is the firm of a friend of mine, in London. They specialise in estate management, in advice on questions of this kind. They're professionals. I've worked with them myself on several occasions. I can contact them for you today; they can send someone down within the week. Then, if you find I'm wrong—well, it will have made no difference. But I don't think you will. Please.' He reached across and took Meg Trevelyan's hand, and Caro saw her mother lift her face to him doubtfully.

'Ask yourself,' he said. 'Why the hurry? Why are you being suddenly pressurised on this? Please!'

Meg Trevelyan hesitated. Then, as if she drew strength from something she saw in Francis' face, she bowed her head, and nodded.

'Very well,' she said softly. 'Very well, I'll do as you say.'
She paused. 'I don't know why you should go to this trouble
. . . it's so kind of you, and . . .'

'I don't like double-dealing. And I've seen so much of it in
the work I do that I recognise the signs, that's all.' He took her
arm. 'Would you like me to ring Wells for you? I don't want
you to feel pressurised when you see him, and I think I can sort
him out fairly easily.'

'Oh, Mr Albany, would you?' Meg looked up at him with an
expression which Caro could see was now openly one of
hero-worship. She felt her blood go cold. It was the way her
mother had always looked at her father.

'Of course, I'll do it now.'

They disappeared into the morning room, and Caro heard
the sound of the telephone being lifted, then Francis Albany's
voice barking out a few crisp, curt sentences. It didn't take
long. A few minutes later, and they came out, her mother was
leaning on Francis' arm.

'Just give Caro a shout,' she was saying. 'She must be about
somewhere. And tell her I've gone, will you? I'm so glad she's
going to show you the house. I think you'll find it interesting.
How silly that I never realised you'd worked on the Blakeneys'
place. I hear that's quite magnificent now. Of course, I've
rather lost touch with them. It must be years since we met. But
such a lovely house . . .'

'Very lovely. Not as beautiful as Trevelyans, though . . .'

Their voices faded; the front door swung to. Caro clutched
the banisters, staring after them. Fierce anger mixed with
contrition fought in her heart. If only she understood that sort
of thing better! On the one hand it looked as if Francis Albany
were actively encouraging the sale of Trevelyans for development, and that made her hate him with a violence that shook
her. On the other, he did seem to be helping her mother, to be
guiding her away from what had obviously been a disastrous
course of action. If he was to be trusted, of course, and Caro
wasn't sure, suddenly, if she did trust him.

'Caro.' He had come back through the door, alone, and he
saw her instantly. They stared at one another in silence.

'I heard,' Caro said at last. 'I heard, Francis.'

He said nothing, but just looked at her, and on a sudden impulse Caro raced down the stairs, across the width of the hall, pulling up short just before she would have cannoned into his arms. He put out a hand to steady her.

She raised her face to him pleadingly.

'Francis, was that all true? Was it? Please don't lie to me.'

'Yes, it was true,' he said evenly.

'But why should you . . .'

He looked away. 'I like your mother. I came early so I could talk to her. It occurred to me I might be able to help.' He shrugged. 'I like the house. If it has to be sold, I don't want to see your mother cheated on the deal on top of everything else. That's all.'

Impulsively Caro flung her arms around him and hugged him. He drew back a little, as if embarrassed, and slowly, embarrassed herself, Caro let her arms fall.

'You're *good*,' she said simply. 'Thank you, Francis.'

Francis' brows drew together in a frown.

'It's not a great deal of help,' he said drily. 'It won't save Trevelyans from being sold. Nothing will.' He paused, and she saw the ghost of a smile lift the corners of his lips. 'Unless you take my advice, that is.'

She looked away. 'Don't talk about that,' she said sharply. 'That was stupid—a pipe-dream. I see that now.' She lifted her face to him bravely. 'Trevelyans will have to be sold. I just hope they don't spoil it, that's all. And anyway, before they get the chance—may I show it to you? It can be my last tour. A sort of farewell. I'd like to do that.' She paused shyly. 'I'd like to do it now, with you.'

There was a little silence between them. Francis regarded her carefully. Caro feared that he might ask her to explain, but he did not.

'Then lead on,' he said at last, offering her his arm. 'Where shall we begin?'

She saw the house with new eyes. Partly it was what he said, and what he left unsaid, for he was very clever and also very informed. But it was not just that. It is possible to know a great deal about buildings, and yet to have no love for them. Francis was not like that; his scholarship, which she had judged dry, was nothing of the kind; now she saw that. And seeing that he was capable of love for a building, she also saw his capacity for other kinds of love. She had, stupidly, judged him cold, and closed. Now she saw he was no such thing. The realisation set up in her heart a terrible ache; it was as if someone had opened a door and given her a glimpse of the most beautiful place—and then had banged the door shut. So, gradually, as they passed from room to room, she ceased to be aware of her surroundings. She saw only the man, his concentration, which seemed to exclude her. She became preternaturally aware of him, of the tiniest gesture he made, of every nuance of expression in his eyes and in his voice. It was as if some invisible thread connected his body to hers—so much so that she feared he might sense what was in her mind, and selfconsciousness took possession of her. Her remarks became duller and flatter; she could hear her own voice falter unaccountably. He touched some panelling; she looked at his hands. It took every ounce of her will power not to reach across and touch them.

She became brusque, as businesslike as she was capable of being. Francis sensed it, and it seemed to puzzle him, but he said nothing. She went on with her account of the house; a terrible constraint, a tension, grew up between them, and still they talked.

They looked at the old account books. Caro showed him the various plans that had been drawn up, at different times, for the gardens.

'But these are exact!' he exclaimed. He bent over the faded drawings, his narrow face intent, his beautiful, capable hands smoothing the folds from the paper. 'They even detail all the plantings. You could restore it, to the way it looked in the twenties, Jekyll's garden. It must have been exquisite.'

'Yes, you could.' Caro could not meet his eyes. 'Her designs were very beautiful. There was a white garden, with lilies and roses. And a water garden . . .'

Her voice trailed away; her lips felt dry. Francis rolled up the plans. 'Where shall we go now?'

Caro hesitated. 'You haven't seen the attics . . .' She braced herself, and deliberately lightened her voice. 'I love them, but they're in a terrible mess. The dry rot!'

'Show me.'

Together they climbed the main staircase, then up the smaller winding stairs that led to the rooms under the great pitched roof. The air there was warm and slightly dank.

Caro opened the door to the largest attic; there was a scuttle as a mouse fled into the wainscot. Through the grimy cobwebbed windows, the sun shone on the wide oak boards of the floor, striping the wood with gold. There was a flutter from the rafters where pigeons now nested, taking advantage of the gaps in the roofing. The attic was filled with things, the detritus of the past: old trunks and boxes, rolls of carpet, china that needed mending, gramophone records, stacks of books and photograph albums, boxes of toys, a harmonium, the rocking horse that had once stood in the nursery. Francis gave an exclamation of pleasure, and Caro watched him sadly.

'It is lovely, isn't it?' she said. 'So still. I used to come up here and play for hours when I was little. When I wanted to be alone. Look . . .'

She crossed, and picked up one of the old leather photograph albums, blew the dust from its covers, and opened it carefully.

Faded sepia pictures filled its pages. Women in long Edwardian dresses, their faces shadowy beneath wide hats. Men in heavy formal suits, with watch chains. In groups they walked, or sat, or picnicked on the lawns of Trevelyans; the house lay behind them, the wistaria, which now reached the roof, climbed then to the lower windows.

'The golden years.' Caro smiled sadly. 'Before the first war. Before the money began to run out. I suppose everything seemed very certain then.' She pointed to a tall figure of a man. 'My great-grandfather, I think. Though they're so faded, it's difficult to be sure. The others . . .' Her voice died. Then tears came, unstoppably, welling up from deep inside her, falling softly on to the book.

'Caro.' Francis took her in his arms. Very gently he drew her to him, encircling her body, holding her firmly against the rise and fall of his chest. Caro bowed her head against him, making no noise, crying silently. The tears wet his shirt.

'Caro,' he said again, rocking her very tenderly in his arms, stroking her long thick hair. She shuddered, unable to speak. It was the first and the last time she would cry—and she cried for Trevelyans, she thought.

Francis took out a white handkerchief at last, and tilting her face to his, gently dried her eyes. Caro, looking up at him, saw his face very close, its expression intent, concerned. Her eyes widened as she met his gaze; it held her absolutely, with a deep compulsion, the seriousness, the sobriety of that regard.

'Francis?'

'Yes,' was all he said; then, as she had known he would, known he must, he kissed her.

Then all thought stopped. Nothing existed except the touch of his lips, against hers. The room was quite still.

When they drew apart a little at last, she stared at him.

'Francis . . .'

'Don't speak.'

Then he drew her to him again, more fiercely this time, opening her lips under his, his arms tightening around her, his hands caressing her back, her thighs, her breasts, and the violence of his embrace shook her to the roots of her being. She trembled against the hardness, the undisguised arousal of his body, straining against him, conscious of nothing except that somehow out of her grief, out of his closeness, had come—this, and it overwhelmed her.

Her mind had gone; all that was left was touch, the questing of hands, an urgency. When his fingers reached, trembling a little, for the fastening of her shirt, she caught his hands and helped him, almost tearing the old material in her impatience. Then with a sigh that was close to a groan, he lifted her breasts in his palms, held them, lowered his mouth to her nipples, and took them hard with the stirring in her blood between the softness of his lips. She cried out, and caught him to her, wanting to touch him as he touched her, wanting to feel the warmth of his bare skin against her own. Impatiently, a little fearfully, she slipped her fingers beneath his shirt, touching the taut muscles of his chest, curling them in the dark hair which grew there, drawing his head up once more so their mouths could meet.

Her breath came short and shallow; against her breasts she could feel the beating of his heart. Neither spoke. Pausing a little taking her hand, he held it against his body, against his heart, and then down.

Caro gasped, a little short intake of breath, and urgently Francis again sought her mouth. She clung to him, her breasts pale and full, straining against his chest; stomach to stomach, thigh against thigh. It was as if the sharpness, the suddenness of this need, fused their bodies. She felt herself liquid, warm, infinitely pliant in his arms, her mind stilled against debate or questioning.

His kisses softened, grew more gentle. As she reached for him impulsively, he stilled her hands, touched her breasts once more, held her, and then drawing back a very little, so she cried out in dismay, gently began to button her shirt.

'Francis . . .'

'No,' he said. 'No, Caro.'

She obeyed him, quietening herself, until at last he simply held her close in the silence. He kissed her once more, one last lingering slow kiss, then he drew back and looked down into her eyes. Caro, looking up at him, felt a joy more intense than she had ever known catch at her heart.

'How did that happen?' Her eyes danced. 'How, Francis?'

'I thought it might.'

'How clever you are!' She sighed and leaned against him. 'You must think me such a fool.'

'No, I don't think that. You know I don't. I think . . .' He paused. 'Well, it has happened, that's all.'

Caro flung her arms around his neck; she felt suddenly so happy she wanted to sing, to dance, to shout. She looked into his eyes.

'You are quite wonderful, Francis,' she said. 'You are the most wonderful man I've ever met, and . . .'

Francis laughed softly.

'Caro,' he said, 'you're so sudden.' He took her hand. 'Think a little. Yesterday you . . .'

'Yesterday was a century ago! Yesterday I was a *child* still: I didn't know, I didn't see . . . believe me, Francis.'

He took her hand gently and raised it to his lips. 'No one grows up that fast, Caro.'

'They do! I have. Francis, I know what I'm doing. I . . .' She broke off in confusion, afraid suddenly to say what she wanted to say.

He put his finger to her lips very softly.

'Wait a little,' he said. 'Wait, and think.' He gave her a wry smile, tilting her face up to him as she tried to turn it away a little sulkily. 'You think it's easy for me to do that? To stop—now? It's not—not at all.'

'Did you . . .' she hesitated. 'Did you want me then, Francis? I wanted you—terribly much.' She looked at him wide-eyed. 'So much it hurt almost. Here, and here.'

'Yes, I wanted you, Caro,' he said, quite seriously. His grip on her hands tightened, then relaxed. 'But we shan't talk of that now. You shall . . . behave yourself. With decorum. Keep your distance, you hear me?'

'Yes, Francis,' she said meekly, backing away. He laughed. 'Not that far, idiot! Just like this.' He drew her back to his side, and put his arm around her shoulders. 'There,' he said. 'A suitable, decorous distance, enough to keep a man's passions in check—for the time being. Now—' he gestured across the room, 'we shall complete our tour, I think.'

'Just as you say, Francis.'

'And don't overdo the meekness, either,' he said sternly. 'It's entirely unconvincing.'

Caro grinned. She would agree to anything. Anything. She cared only that he should stay. The thought of his absence, of an hour without him, made her whole body rebel.

She took his hand. 'I'll show you the East Wing,' she said. 'It's the only part we haven't seen. Mostly it's shut up now.' She paused wickedly. 'There are some wonderful four-poster beds there . . .'

'No bedrooms,' he said. 'We'll skip those. I wouldn't be responsible for the consequences.'

CHAPTER EIGHT

FRANCIS stayed for lunch, they sat for hours in the kitchen, eating baked ham and a not very successful salad, drinking half a bottle of wine that Caro found at the back of the cupboard. To Caro the indifferent meal was like a feast; she could not take her eyes from Francis' face. His very existence, his closeness, filled her with delight. They talked: she could not have said, after, of what they spoke. She simply felt that after an hour she had known him all her life, or—more—that the discovery of him had begun her life anew.

He was still the same Francis, she thought happily, watching him as he talked: cool, clever, watchful, reticent even now, taciturn, preferring to avoid all her personal questions. He was the same, and yet he was translated. He was infinitely precious to her, someone it now seemed inconceivable she should be without. How could she have been so *blind*? she thought impatiently; it was as if a bandage had been ripped from her eyes. He was kind, good, truthful, funny, and when she met his eyes, the force of the current between them was so strong it hit her like a wave. He was a man, she thought, why—beside him, Will was a mere boy and . . .

'And so,' he was saying, 'since we spoke I'd been trying to think of ways in which I might be able to help with your problems. I'd come up with very little, I'm afraid, but I could see how important Trelawney's land was from the point of view of the estate . . .' He hesitated slightly. 'Then this morning, in the car, Marian mentioned something about sale documents— suggested that perhaps I ought to advise your mother. I hesitated because . . .'

Caro did not hear the rest of the sentence. She stared at him: Marian! An image of Marian's face as it had looked that morning when Francis Albany's car drew up sprang into her brain. Marian, her dearest friend, who was twenty-seven, who should be married, who would make a man a perfect wife,

117

Marian, who was clearly falling in love for the first time in her life . . .

'Is something wrong, Caro?'

'No,' she lied quickly. 'Nothing, nothing at all.'

He was watching her closely and Caro turned her face away. Concentratedly she looked at the table in front of her, the pattern of plate, knife and fork. Shame and self-disgust surged within her. She stood up abruptly.

'Francis,' she said, 'would you mind very much? But I feel awfully tired suddenly. I didn't sleep very well last night, and . . .'

He rose and crossed to her side, his face full of concern.

'Do you feel unwell? Would you like to lie down? Why didn't you say something sooner? I should have realised—that walking in the rain . . .'

'No, I'll be all right. I'm fine.' She moved a little away from him. 'I think if you don't mind I might just go and try to sleep a little.'

'Do you want me to stay—until your mother gets back?'

'No—really. I should prefer to be on my own.'

'I see. Of course.' He drew back at once. 'I've stayed far too long in any case, and . . .' He paused. 'I still haven't returned the coat. And the other things—I'll go and fetch them now from the car.' He gave her a teasing glance as he said this, and Caro managed a smile in return. She sagged despondently into a chair, listening to the sound of his footsteps cross the hall, the bang of the car door. The thought of his leaving caused her such pain it frightened her. She stared fixedly at the table, trying to make her mind work, to sort out her feelings, but it blurred, refused to function with any clarity. She looked up sadly as Francis came back into the room, and laid her coat and a small carrier bag on a chair.

'Well,' he hesitated, looking awkward, 'I'll leave you, then. You're sure you're all right, Caro?'

'Oh yes, yes,' she said quickly. Their eyes met. There was a long silence.

It seemed to Caro thronged with questions which neither of them then had the courage to ask. She clung to her resolution—let him think her capricious if he liked—as far as the hall, as far as the door of his car. Then it left her, and she asked him to take her to the dinner at the Amhursts'. Out came the words, before she could stop them, and immediately they were followed by a thousand rationalisations. After all, Marian was away that night, it could do no harm, just once—to be with him just that once.

He asked if Lady Amhurst would be there. When she said no, he agreed, a little curtly, and made some reference to Will's absence.

'I don't want to go with Will, I want to go with you,' she said, before she could stop herself, and she felt treacherous to Marian and glad she had said it.

'I must talk to you, in any case . . .' Francis hesitated. 'Properly. I . . .' She must have flinched; anyway, he took her hand, grasped it a little wildly, and then turned abruptly to the car.

When he had gone, Caro went back into the kitchen and paced back and forth, then she sat down and immediately stood up, and at last cried for the second time that day.

She knew, before she stopped crying, that she loved him.

'Have one of these cheese straws, Marian darling. Or what about one of those—divine filling, mushrooms and parmesan, I think, *too* more-ish. You've hardly eaten a thing.'

Marian hesitated, but she felt hungry, and the gin and slimline tonic had weakened her resistance.

'Well, perhaps just one . . .'

Charlotte Anstruther-Lamont had her pinned in a corner. The speechmaking part was over, thank goodness, and now familiar faces from her past moved in and out of her vision; much the same as they had looked at school really, but made-up, enamelled with the confidence befitting their new roles as wives and mothers and adornments of the West London marital scene. For the first time at such an occasion, Marian felt depressed; she was acutely aware that Charlotte was staring at her ringless hands as she reached for the canapés.

'How *are* you, Marian?' Charlotte was looking at her keenly. Marian raised her eyes reluctantly to Charlotte's flushed, somewhat horsey face. 'Do tell! Such a good speech, but then you were always so frightfully clever.' There was a pause. 'Still—teaching, wasn't it?'

'Yes, I'm still teaching.'

'A career woman—too impressive! I can see you now—headmistress at Cheltenham or somewhere, and all us boring mothers coming down and cringing while you assess our daughters' chances. Too funny!'

Marian took a large swallow of her gin; such a picture of her future was one she too had had. In the past it had seemed to her desirable; now the prospect dismayed her.

'And how's darling Caro? Still as harum-scarum as ever? She hasn't married, I hear. Odd, isn't it? I mean, most people always thought her *so* pretty, though I never could see it myself. Too eccentric, always striving after effect.' Charlotte leaned forward. 'She was most terribly rude to my brother once, you know: walked out on him at dinner—just left, not a *word* of explanation. He was still on the soup, I think. However . . .' she gave Marian a wide smile, 'I mustn't be bitchy. I know you two are as close as can be and . . . tell me, darling, is it true Trevelyans is going to be sold?'

'Where did you hear that?' Marian turned back to her sharply, her attention suddenly focussed.

Charlotte assumed a vague expression. 'Oh, I don't know, darling. I thought it was common knowledge. Did I see it in *Country Life* last month?'

'You can't have done. The advertisement is in the current issue. It's just out.'

'That's cutting it a bit fine, isn't it? The auction's this month, I heard, and . . .' She broke off, then smiled engagingly as Marian looked at her suspiciously. 'Of course, I remember now. Jamie was intrigued, of course . . .' Marian frowned, then remembered; Jamie was Charlotte's husband. 'Yes, that's it. Jamie was interested—you know he's left Sotheby's now, don't you, darling?—because of all that Chinese stuff. One of Caro's uncles—great-uncles?—was rather famous, he said. Went to China and Nepal and collected botanical specimens, something like that?'

'Her great-grandfather.'

'That must be it. Well, Jamie says he brought all *kinds* of things back with him, as well as plants. Was quite a famous collector, he said, and it must be ceramics, because that's Jamie's field, so when he heard Trevelyans was going to be sold he was positively *sparkling* with enthusiasm . . .'

Marian smiled coldly; she had met Charlotte's husband once, and could not imagine his sparkling about anything, even ceramics. Still, Charlotte had her attention now.

'I imagine they're going to sell the contents, aren't they? Such a huge draughty place, filled with stuff—I can't imagine they'd keep it—in fact Jamie was going to get in touch, but he hadn't realised the sale was so soon, and you know how stuffy they all are about ethics and so on . . .'

'Oh, I'm sure,' Marian said drily.

'And I knew I'd be seeing you here and so I said if I had a chance I'd mention it . . . Jamie has his own company now, you know. Just ceramics. Doing frightfully well . . .'

Marian smiled. So that was why Charlotte had sought her out so deliberately; on previous occasions they had hardly exchanged a word.

'How did your husband hear of the sale?' She looked Charlotte directly in the eyes. She had the grace to blush a little.

'Darling, I really don't know . . .' She hesitated, and when Marian did not lower her gaze, rested her hand confidingly on her arm. 'Oh, you know how it is. One of those City lunches, I expect . . . you know what men are. Such gossips! Someone was biting because there might be a chance of turning Trevelyans into an hotel . . . could that be it?'

'It might be.' Marian still held her gaze stolidly.

'That's it, of *course*!' Charlotte gave a passably good imitation of someone who has just remembered a vital fact. 'How silly of me! It was Athertons'—you know, darling, the development people. William Atherton is a friend of my brother's—Simon, you remember? He was looking for more funding and wanted Simon in on the deal. Anyway, they and Jamie were having lunch last week. That's it. Athertons' are *huge* now. A positive empire, expanding here, there and everywhere. All over Europe. Paris, Brussels,

Rome—Milan. Frightfully clever—William Atherton; started off with asset stripping, then into property and now hotels. He bought the Davignons' place up in Cumbria, and it's too wonderful now. As soon as he heard rumours about Trevelyans . . .'

Marian stared at her; slowly she put her glass down on the table beside her. 'William Atherton?' she said.

'But you must know him, darling. You must! Frightfully thick with Mark Amhurst at one time—not any more, I hear, but then William drops people like hot coals if they can't be useful to him. Frightfully ruthless and madly attractive . . . one can't help liking him.'

Marian forced her voice to sound natural. 'I'm not sure . . .' She paused. 'I think I might have met his cousin . . .'

'What, Francis?' Charlotte laughed. 'Well, if you haven't, darling, you probably will. I mean, you're on the fund-raising committee for the new building, aren't you—you mentioned it in your speech. Well, Francis Atherton is designing the building. Don't you read your brochures?'

'I . . . I must have seen it. I'm not very up in architecture and . . .'

'Oh, but darling, he's the best—bar none. Frightfully hot at the moment. Everyone wants him, so it was rather a coup for the school. Doesn't do that many new buildings, frightfully snobbish and selective, not to say madly dictatorial, but brilliant. And *the* best, Jamie says, when it comes to restoration of old houses.' She paused. 'You wouldn't forget him if you had met him, I think. Beastly man, no manners at all. *So* conceited! He was frightfully rude to me. I can't think he gets on very well with William, but of course they make an unbeatable combination—William's business acumen, and Francis's contacts, not to mention his famous ability to take a wreck and turn it into a palace . . .'

'Yes, I see. As you say—an unbeatable combination.' Marian looked at her watch; if she hurried she could just catch the seven o'clock train. Suddenly she felt very cold; her mind was working slowly, but with an ugly unhurried precision. Her hands shook a little.

'You're not going?' Charlotte grabbed her arm. 'Just when

we were beginning to have fun. Why, there's masses of things I . . .'

'I'm sorry, I must go.'

'Marian *darling*!' Charlotte bent forward and kissed her cheek. 'Not back to Cornwall at this hour, surely? Go tomorrow.' She paused. 'Come and have dinner with us—I've been meaning to ask you for ages. Stay the night. Jamie's dying to meet you and—'

Marian turned back slowly.

'You're forgetting, Charlotte,' she said coldly, 'Trevelyans isn't my house. I can't help you, or your husband. If he's interested in the ceramics, tell him to contact Caro. I'll tell her we met.' She disengaged herself firmly; Charlotte's high colour had deepened.

'Darling, *honestly*—'

'I know you've never called before. But you'll get the number from enquiries.'

She turned, leaving Charlotte expostulating to the air. A quick explanation to her friend that she had changed her plans, would not be staying on in London after all, and in under five minutes she was out of the room.

The reunions were held in a small, old-fashioned and charming hotel in Knightsbridge, much favoured by women who came up to London to shop. A group of such women sat now in the lobby; exactly like the women upstairs at the party, but older. They were discussing the best place to buy cashmere sweaters. Marian looked through them as if they were invisible. In a moment of acuity, sharp and without pain in its clarity, she saw her own future. *I shall not marry, after all*, she thought. *Everyone was quite right*.

An image came to her then, of her small book-lined room at school; of the exercise books piled for marking; music playing softly in the background. Charlotte might be right; she might well end up a respected and admired headmistress, but in just such another room, distinct only in that it was larger, more impressive. Marian turned away quickly; the doorman was entreated to find her a cab, urgently. He raised his eyes to the heavens; outside it was raining; traffic was at a standstill.

Marian moved aside and ducked quickly into the telephone

kiosk. Her hands still trembling slightly, she leafed through the directory.

She found it quickly enough.

Francis Atherton. No mention of his profession. The address was brief: Albany, W.1.

'You've just been in Europe, I believe?' Francis turned to Peter Dalton with an air of polite enquiry.

Peter laid down his knife and fork; there was a little pause. He took off his horn-rimmed spectacles, and polished them on his napkin, put them back on, and looked at Francis across the Amhursts' wide mahogany dining table.

'Yes, that's right,' he said. 'Brussels, as a matter of fact.'

'Brussels? You work for the Commission?'

Again a little pause. 'No,' Peter said at last. 'Caro didn't tell you? I'm a journalist. I work for *The Economist*.'

'Really? A fine journal.' Francis too put down his knife and fork rather slowly, then took some time lining them up precisely on his plate. His eyes were lowered. There was a little silence, and Jennifer leaned forward.

'I hope you don't share my mother's antipathy to journalists, Francis. I can't tell you what it's been like today—sticky in the extreme, Lady Bracknell isn't in it! Peter's been trying frightfully hard, poor soul, but . . .'

'What story took you to Brussels? Something interesting?' Francis cut across Jennifer.

Again her husband paused. Really, Caro thought, he was quite nice, obviously very gentle and kind, but not exactly the most witty man she'd ever met. He had such an odd hesitant manner, particularly marked when he spoke to Francis.

She caught Jennifer's eye, and then, rising, began to help her remove the dishes from the table. The two moved to the end of the room, and Jennifer rang the bell for the housekeeper.

'Pudding, Caro? Or shall we skip it and leave them to jaw on a bit and just have coffee? I'd rather—don't want to undo the effects of the diet!'

Caro grinned. 'Yes, let's. They're going to get on to something frightfully masculine and boring any minute, I can tell. Let's go and gossip by the fire.'

Caro glanced back over her shoulder; Francis was sitting quite still, listening attentively. Peter Dalton had leaned forward slightly, and seemed to be hitting his stride. Goodness, she would never have expected Francis to be so polite, Caro thought. He had more social graces than she had anticipated. She turned back to Jennifer with a grimace, and Jennifer smiled conspiratorially.

'I don't expect you two will notice,' she called to the two men, 'but Caro and I are going to have some coffee in the drawing room. The port's over there, darling. You won't be too long, will you?'

The two men rose to their feet, Peter turned briefly with some remark, but it was apparent that his mind was elsewhere. Before the doors had closed both men were again seated, and had picked up their conversation.

In the drawing room Caro moved to the fire, paused, then turned to face Jennifer who was watching her sardonically.

'Well?' she said.

Jennifer laughed. 'You know what I think. You must be able to sense it. Come on, Caro.'

'Tell me.'

'Well, I think he's quite disgracefully good-looking. Unfairly so. Just a suggestion of haughtiness, and then something about the mouth which implies that in the right circumstances he wouldn't be haughty at all—far from it. Witty. Obviously extremely clever. Astute—doesn't miss a thing. *Not* very tolerant of bores, I should guess. And, beneath that impeccable suit, behind those impeccable manners, a hint of something else.' She paused, wrinkling her brow. 'Difficult to say quite what. Ruthlessness, perhaps. No, not that exactly, something rougher, more physical. Not an easy man to know, I would think. Puts lots of barriers around himself . . .' She grinned. 'Not at all what I would expect a fetishist to be like!'

'Do you think—' Caro paused. 'I mean, would you say he liked me?'

Jennifer turned, eyebrows raised.

'You mean you don't know?' She shrugged, and pushed a coffee cup into Caro's hand. 'Well, I observed he had extreme difficulty in turning his face away from contemplation of yours.

And there was—just very slightly—a dazed look about the eyes which I think I recognised. It generally indicates a man who has recently been poleaxed and is still reeling from the first blow. But perhaps he always looks like that.'

'Oh Jennifer, did you?'

Despite all her resolutions earlier, Caro felt her heart lift. Instantly her thoughts began to wing. Francis looked very fine, she thought; so tall, so straight; so admirable in every way. A pattern of a man, she thought idiotically, the phrase coming to her from nowhere from some set text at school. And, in the car that evening he had said, yes, that he had something important which he wished to tell her, but that it must wait until they returned to Trevelyans after dinner.

Her hand shook; coffee splashed from the tiny delicate cup on to her wrist, burning her, and she set it down. What could he want to say? There seemed to Caro, in her heightened state, fed by an afternoon of depression and painful self-examination, that it must be something of great significance. Perhaps it was something to do with Trevelyans, but she felt instinctively that it was not. So what could it be?

Her mind whirled; a thousand alternatives seemed to spin in it at once. Maybe he cared for her—could that be it? But no, she felt Francis was too cautious, too careful a man to make any such declaration so soon, and in any case, he probably felt nothing of the kind. Her own feelings were of such intensity they seemed to sense reciprocity where perhaps there was none. Perhaps, on the contrary, he cared for Marian, was going to explain that what had happened that morning had been a mistake, a passing temptation, which must not be repeated. Perhaps he cared for neither of them.

The pace of her mind accelerated. Perhaps he was going away, miles away, the other side of the world, for months. Years. An image of Francis standing in the middle of the desert came to her, and of herself, sitting in front of sheets of blue airmail paper, writing letters he never answered. She groaned aloud, and Jennifer gave her a startled glance.

'Caro? Whatever's the matter?'

Caro stared at her bleakly. 'I love him,' she said, in dolorous tones.

Jennifer's lips twitched. 'Well, you don't have to look so miserable about it. And I knew you did anyway.'

'But what if he doesn't love me?'

'Ah well.' Jennifer contrived to sound sage and smug.

'That's not much help—sounding like a sybil!'

'In your state nothing's much help. But I'll put you through a catechism, if you like.'

'All right.' Caro sat down. Jennifer curled in the chair opposite.

'When did you realise?'

'The second—no, the third time I met him.'

'Bad. Much too precipitate. And why do you love him?'

'Because . . . I just do. I feel it.'

Jennifer pulled a face. 'Inarticulate,' she said. 'Honest, but inarticulate. Do you like him? Any little flaws? Things you hardly notice now, but which might seem much worse later?'

Caro thought. 'I think he could be obstinate,' she said at last. 'And he has a temper, but I don't think he'd sulk. He's reserved—I don't know very much about him. He can be sarcastic. But those aren't such bad faults, are they?' She looked at Jennifer pleadingly. 'I have much worse ones, and there's nothing mean about him. He's not petty, or pompous, or devious, or vain. He might be proud. He's very truthful . . .'

'Mmm—promising. Truthful is good, of course, if you're sure he is. I thought husband Jack was a fountain of truth, and look how wrong I was. And reserved—well, I don't think that matters. It's probably why he likes you. Because you're not. I expect you just went crashing right through all the barriers he'd erected around himself, and suddenly he found he had no defences left. How splendid!'

Caro looked away. 'Oh, I don't think I did,' she said sadly. 'I didn't mean to do anything. I was thinking of someone—something—else. Then, quite suddenly . . .' She spread her hands; the memory of the night in Francis' car came back to her, and at once it became urgent and imperative that she should be with Francis again. She could not bear his absence, not now, when so much seemed to be beginning.

'Oh, Jennifer! Do you think you can know—almost at once—quite quickly?'

'Yes, I think you can—sometimes.' Jennifer's face grew serious. 'Though whether that will last . . .'

'How can I know that?'

'You can't,' said Jennifer.

After that, as if by common but unspoken consent, both changed the subject. Words and analysis would not help her now, Caro felt it instinctively, and too much talk felt like desecration. So she sat quietly, and listened to Jennifer, who told her about her husband, and his work, which had taken him to Brussels, and now, it seemed, brought him here to Cornwall.

'He never tells me much until it's over, but there's someone he has his eye on, and I think that's what brought him down here. You remember that big construction company scandal story he broke last year? It's something like that, I think. Even Mother's nervous. That would liven things up, don't you think, Caro? I have my suspicions, of course. Major Penniston in some nefarious deal with the churchwarden! Maybe the WI is indulging in land speculation . . .'

'Land speculation?' Caro had hardly been listening. The two men seemed to have been an age over the port. Now she heard their footsteps, and her heart leapt.

As Jennifer rose, offering brandy and coffee, she looked at Francis. He appeared oddly constrained, slightly pale, with a tightness around the lips that made her think the two of them might have quarrelled. She turned to Peter Dalton; his gaze slid away from her, and he blushed a slow crimson.

'Forgive me,' Francis refused a drink. 'I'm afraid I must take Caro home. She wasn't feeling frightfully well earlier today, and I promised her mother I would take her back early.'

Caro stared at him open-mouthed. The untruth had been spoken totally easily, perfectly convincingly, and in a tone of voice which excluded the possibility of argument.

'Of course.' Jennifer gave her a look heavy with understanding and mockery. 'I'll ring for your coats. Francis, so glad to meet you! I hope we shall have the chance to see you again soon. Peter, come and see Francis and Caro off . . .'

It all took less than five minutes, from the time the men returned, to the time Francis and Caro were safe in the Bentley and accelerating down the drive. The two men had shaken hands, rather formally, Jennifer had placed a kiss on Francis' cheek before he could draw back.

'Look after Caro,' were her last words as he closed the car door.

'We must talk,' said Francis, and he turned out of the drive and on to the main road.

'Will you come in for a drink when we get back? We'll be alone . . .'

'Fine.'

His manner was odd, abstracted, tense, and for a second, unable to suppress it, Caro felt optimism surge through her body like blood. Could her hopes have been justified? She glanced at his profile, then back to the narrow road ahead. Happiness began to flood her heart; she fought to suppress it.

By the time they reached Trevelyans her mind was in a ferment; curiosity, excitement, nervousness, fought for dominance within her. She tried to order her thoughts, to consider Marian, her own feelings, dispassionately, but she could not do so. Not knowing what he meant to say to her shaded all her thoughts with such tense anticipation that she could force no clarity into her mind. Francis glanced at her once, but he said nothing, and his silence sharpened her emotions until, by the time they reached the house, they had narrowed and refined to just one simplicity: she ached, physically, for him to touch her.

In the shadowy hall, as he reached his hands up to take her coat, she turned to him impulsively, knowing suddenly that he must read her heart in her face. Their eyes met for a second; she saw him falter, as if unprepared for the entreaty he saw in hers. In an instant exhilaration soared inside her; it was as if she stood on the clifftops, looking out to sea; she saw clearly, joyfully, and without conscience.

'Francis,' she said.

His hands caught her tight, gripping her arms. He bent his head to her uplifted face; she reached for him. The door into the hall behind them opened and a man laughed; not pleasantly.

As she and Francis drew back, sharply, and he swung round, Caro saw beyond him.

Standing in the doorway of the drawing room, lolling against the jamb, as if posed selfconsciously for just such an entrance, was Will. Behind him, very pale, her hands clasped in front of her, was Marian.

'So, you're back,' said Will. 'Your mother's gone to bed, Caro, and so Marian and I have been waiting up for you both. Why don't you come and have a drink by the fire?' He looked from Francis to Caro, then back to Francis. He smiled. 'Do . . .' He held back the door. 'Marian is about to make her second speech of the day—aren't you, Marian? It looks as if it's going to be quite an evening of revelations!'

CHAPTER NINE

'You lied—both of you. You lied!'

Caro's eyes blazed with anger; Marian bowed her head. Neither of the two men answered. Will was standing by the fire, leaning against the mantel, holding his whisky glass in his hand, his attitude one of concerned concentration. Francis was seated, alone on the sofa, his legs stretched out in front of him. He had refused a drink, and was smoking a cigarette. He did not look up when Caro spoke. Marian's hands moved restlessly in her lap; Caro had never seen her look more miserable. Her own gaze moved contemptuously between the two men and rested, finally, on Francis.

'*You* lied,' she said. 'It was you who said your name was Albany—I remember now. You lied, and Will went along with it.'

Still Francis did not look up. Will made an impatient movement, and crossed the room. He sat down beside Caro, and turned to her.

'It wasn't quite like that, Caro. Do try and see it from our point of view. Francis isn't to blame—not entirely. It was my idea not to use Atherton here. After all, you may not have heard of it, but it is quite well known . . .'

'Of course I've heard of it!' Caro rounded on him angrily. 'I'm not such an idiot or an ignoramus as you seem to think. I know quite a lot about architecture, as it happens . . .' She broke off. Francis had looked up, a gleam of amusement in his eyes. She set her mouth. 'I've heard of your cousin,' she went on coldly. 'I've even seen some of his work. I hadn't heard of you, or your company, but then . . .'

'Caro,' Will leant across and laid his hand over hers, 'don't you see? All this had nothing to do with you personally. I was coming down here to look at a house—a house I was interested in professionally, that's all. If word got out that I was here, that I was interested in Trevelyans, well . . .' He shrugged.

131

'Then you mightn't be able to buy the place so cheaply? You might have a bit too much competition? Is that it?'

Will smiled reproachfully. 'Caro, I'm a businessman. I won't attempt to deny that entered into it. It did. But that wasn't my only reason. I care about this house—I care about all the properties I work on. If Trevelyans is going to have to be sold, if it's going to become an hotel—no, let me finish—then better Francis and I should work on it than any of my so-called rivals. If I buy Trevelyans, if I convert it—well . . .' he paused, modestly, 'it will look splendid, Caro—almost the way it did in the old days. It will be saved, preserved. I know it won't remain your family home, but you must be practical. This kind of house is impossible to keep up privately now. What would you prefer? Some rich Arab absentee landlord, who would sell it again the moment the market rose? Some kind of institution? Or just to let it gradually decay, until it was too late to save it? It happens, Caro, to thousands of houses as fine as Trevelyans, every year. Don't you see that my way . . .'

'Your way!' Caro stood up angrily. 'Your way—which is so underhand you don't even use your own name! You lie and cheat . . . you deliberately deceive Marian and me. Both of you! I despise you both!'

Will looked down at his hands. He sighed. He glanced at Francis, then back at Caro.

'Look, Caro, once I realised who you were—well, of course things seemed different then. Francis and I discussed it, that first night.' He shrugged. 'I'm an impulsive kind of person— Francis is more cautious. I was all for coming out with the truth then, trying to explain. Trying to make you see the advantages of what we wanted to do . . .'

Caro hesitated. 'Then why didn't you? You had the chance.'

There was a little silence. Will looked at Francis. Francis said nothing. He put out his cigarette and looked at Caro imperturbably, as if his sole interest was her next reaction.

'I see.' She drew in her breath sharply. 'You don't need to be loyal, Will. You were dissuaded—I can imagine by whom.' Her eyes met those of Francis, and in the pause that followed she thought she saw something flare briefly in his eyes, a dart of anger. Almost at once it was gone. Still he said nothing.

'Look, Caro . . .' Will stood up and crossed to her side. 'Please try to understand. The last thing I wanted was for you to find out this way. That's why I came back tonight, to tell you . . .' He took her arm. 'It was difficult for me, Caro. My personal feelings were involved—you must have realised that. After I met you . . . after that day on the beach, well—' he glanced at Francis as if defiantly, and then back to Caro, forcing her to meet his gaze, 'I went to London, Caro, because I wanted to see if some kind of backing or loan could be arranged. I saw some friends in the City—I hoped. I might point out that it wasn't in my own interests to do that, but by then . . .'

He broke off. Francis gave a low laugh. Will glared at him.

'It's *true*, Caro. Ask Marian. I was in the City. That's how her friend Charlotte heard about it. Her brother . . .'

'*Charlotte's* brother?' Caro swung round to Marian, who shrugged miserably. 'I don't believe it. Of all people!' She moved angrily away. 'I wouldn't accept his help if I were destitute! I'd rather see Trevelyans pulled down brick by brick than save it with a penny from him . . .'

'Caro, please!' Will sounded irritated for the first time. 'Try and keep to the point. That's all irrelevant. It was obviously hopeless in any case. There's a recession on—you know what that means? A few years ago there might have been some hope, but not now. Believe me, if you want to see Trevelyans saved . . .'

'Stop patronising me! I don't believe anything you say. You lied once, why shouldn't you lie again? We're easy enough to deceive, Marian and I, aren't we? I expect you both find it rather amusing, how gullible two women can be!' She paused. 'What about the farm land, for instance—Jack Trelawney's land? The land you were so interested in when we walked back from the beach that day? Francis says . . .'

'Francis?' Will frowned.

'Yes, Francis. Your precious cousin!' Caro swung round furiously. 'Why he should take it into his head to help, I can't imagine!' She broke off, for Will had paled very slightly. Caro stared at him. 'It was *true*, wasn't it?' she said at last. '*You* were trying to buy Trelawney's land, weren't you? You were using

Jack as a front man, so you could get it cheaper. God, it's disgusting!'

'Caro, that's not true . . .' Will gave Francis a venomous look. 'I suggested to Trelawney that he should buy that land, I don't mind admitting it. I was setting up the loan for him. But not for the reason you think. I was trying to help, goddammit! I thought it would at least raise some money for you, in the interim. It would help with immediate debts. Then, if I could have raised some finance in London . . . Francis knew that. Why the hell Francis should go behind my back . . .' He broke off suddenly, and looked down at the floor. 'Oh hell, what does it matter now?' he added.

Caro stared at him in confusion. There was a silence, and then Marian stood up.

'Are you saying . . .' she said, her voice sounding oddly small and tight. 'Are you saying Francis misled Caro about Trelawney's land? Misled me?' She turned to Francis. 'When I spoke of it's being sold, you gave no indication that you knew about it already. You said quite clearly it was undesirable. That was why I suggested you talk to Caro's mother. You said . . .'

Her voice had taken on a sharp accusing note. Francis stood up, but before he could speak, Will stepped forward with a placatory gesture.

'Marian, Caro . . . please, don't let's make this any worse than it already is. If Francis said anything of the kind then I'm sure he had his reasons. I admit I don't understand them, but . . .' He gave an odd smile. 'Though perhaps, after tonight, I do understand them a little.' He looked directly at Caro. 'I think, perhaps,' he began in an insinuating tone of voice, 'I think perhaps Francis had some personal motivation, Caro. I was away in London, and obviously while I was away . . .' He shrugged. 'If Francis saw some way of recommending himself to you, Caro, of apparently helping you, he might have wanted to take it. That's understandable. Any man might do the same—you're a very beautiful woman.'

He glanced at Francis. 'I wouldn't say it was a very honourable thing to do, the moment I was out of the way. I wouldn't even say, frankly, that it was the right advice, but in the circumstances . . .' He broke off, looking meaningfully from Caro to Francis. There was a silence.

Across the room. Caro saw Marian's face take on a pinched, crumpled look. She sat down slowly. Two tears welled, veiled her eyes, then fell down her cheeks. She lifted her hand slowly and wiped them away, then turned her face to the fire. Looking at her, Caro felt guilt and pain knot in her chest; anger and indignation so intense swelled in her heart that she could hardly speak, and when she did so her own voice sounded strange to her ears.

'Go away,' she said. 'Both of you. Now. I never want to see or speak to either of you again.'

'Caro, my dear—please!' Will took a step towards her, then stopped. 'You're being very childish, Caro. You can't go on like this, you know, ignoring realities. Francis and I may be at fault in some ways, I grant you, but at least now it's all out in the open, surely we can talk sensibly about this? I should tell you that my intentions remain unaltered. I'm a business-man—I'm being straight with you now. And as a business project I can see the possibilities for Trevelyans . . .' Will paused, and when Caro did not answer, seemed to gain confidence. He gave her his quick warm smile, and Caro saw it now for the cold thing it was, a movement of the lips only, that never lit the eyes, that sickened her.

'I can envisage it only too well,' Caro turned on him fiercely. 'I can envisage it so well I feel sick. I don't want to hear any more. Go—both of you!' She hesitated, and her eyes met those of Francis for the first time. He was watching her, still silent, his face betraying nothing, his eyes dark. For a moment she faltered, then gave a quick angry gesture with her hand. 'And you?' she said. 'You haven't said a word, not one word. And yet you can be so eloquent when you try. Aren't you going to try and persuade me, Francis? I'm sure you'd do it more subtly than your cousin. Is that why you were so interested in the house, in the garden? Because you could envisage just the way it would be—Will's money and your talent—creating the per-fect playground for rich weekenders? And to think I was once foolish enough to admire your work . . .' Her words choked her, and she turned bitterly away.

Francis stood up slowly. There was an angry silence, during which Will made a move towards his cousin, and was brushed contemptuously aside. Francis looked straight across the room at Caro, as if they were alone.

'Just a few things,' he said, his voice cold and low. 'First: Trelawney's land. I believe I gave your mother the correct advice. I telephoned Will and told him what I'd done this afternoon. I would imagine that's why he's here. Second: I regret the business over the names. Third. Now is hardly the time and place to discuss the ethics of your house or of luxury hotels, but you might just ask yourself why "rich weekenders", as you call them, have less right to stay in this house than you have. Do you find it more justifiable that a house this size should be occupied by two women, and fall into disrepair because they're both lamentably incapable of managing it? Fourth,' his mouth tightened, 'don't make cheap, disparaging remarks about my work, or . . .'

Caro's eyes blazed with anger. 'Or what?' she taunted furiously. 'It's all right for you to make them about us, it seems. How dare you say that about Trevelyans, about my mother and me? My family built this house, they've lived here for four hundred years and . . .'

'And mismanaged it for at least the last three decades!'

To her fury Caro felt tears start to her eyes. 'You mean my father!' she cried. 'That's what you mean—why not say so? You think he mismanaged Trevelyans. I hate you for that! He cared about this house. He loved it. At least he didn't simply think of how he could use it, make money from it. I thought that you . . .'

She broke off. Across the room their eyes met, his as angry as hers. Caro faltered. For a moment, through the anger, she felt the instinct to trust him. Some of what he said was true, she knew it in her heart, however much it hurt. She stood still for an instant, and felt herself poised. If she could not make the leap of trust now, she knew it was finished between them. Francis seemed to know it too, for the anger died from his eyes.

He lifted his hand. 'Caro . . .' he began.

His voice had softened, there was a tenderness and a plea in it now. Marian heard it as clearly as Caro, and bowed her head.

Caro turned abruptly away, and moved to her side.

There was a pause, then Francis, without another word, walked out of the room.

In the silence that followed, Will for the first time appeared awkward, even angry. He hesitated for a moment, picked up his whisky glass, seemed to toy with the idea of saying more, then put it down with a bang on the table—which tilted. Caro, seeing the gesture, began to laugh softly, a little hysterically.

'Goddammit!' With an irritable gesture he righted the table before the glass crashed to the ground. 'I have to say, Caro, formally as it were, that this doesn't alter anything as far as I'm concerned. I came down here with a purpose. I've tried to explain that to you. I'm willing to explain it again if need be. As many times as you like. Or need.' The patronage in his voice was now unmistakable. 'But nothing is changed. The auction is next week. I intend to buy Trevelyans, and it will make no difference whatever attitude you take. Obviously I'd much prefer it if we could be reasonable about it. There's no reason why we shouldn't have an amicable . . .'

'Will, go away. Please, now!'

Still he lingered, fiddling with his tie, and then suddenly, as if aware that his staying was undignified, that he had somehow been robbed of an effective exit, he walked out, and banged the door unnecessarily loudly.

In the sudden quiet of the room, Caro bent down and knelt beside Marian, encircling her in her arms. The two looked at each other.

'What an awful pompous man Will is,' Caro said at last. 'How was it I never noticed?'

Marian shrugged and gave her a weak smile. 'He's very handsome. And he's not pompous all the time. Only when he's crossed perhaps. By a woman.'

Their eyes met and they laughed softly, together.

'Well,' said Caro, 'what fools we've been, you and I. Dupes, the pair of us.'

Marian took her hand. 'I was the dupe,' she said slowly. 'I, most of all. I thought Francis . . . I hoped . . .' She sighed. 'I should have known. He talked about you all the time, and

I thought . . .' Her voice caught, and Caro pressed her hand sadly.

'He wasn't thinking of me, either, Marian. Just the house, that's all. Maybe he had a twinge of conscience about the farm, maybe Will went a bit too far then, but that's all.' She lowered her eyes and thought one last time of the morning in the attic, and then, quite deliberately, she put the memory from her. She would never allow herself to think of it again.

'So—what do we do now?' Marian looked down at her sadly.

'Do? We stop them. You and I, Marian. That's what we do.'

Caro rose to her feet as she spoke, and pulled her cousin up beside her. Her face, to Marian's surprise, was lit with a new, fierce determination; the firelight caught it strangely, throwing its planes into relief, giving it strength, tingeing it with gold. Marian, looking at her, thought she had never seen her more beautiful, with an air of desperation that made her beauty all the more touching. Her own face softened, and their eyes met.

'This evening, in the hall, when you came back with Francis . . .' she said, 'I saw you both then, Caro, and I thought—' She broke off. 'Tell me what you felt. I would prefer to know.'

Caro met her gaze. 'I thought—that I loved him. I did think that. And it made me feel guilty.'

'Because of me?'

'Yes.'

'And now?'

Caro hesitated, then bowed her head. 'Now,' she said at last. 'Now I realise—our friendship matters to me more. It will outlast—all that.'

'Will it?' Marian smiled gently. 'Maybe.'

She looked at her cousin: privately she thought that when love weighed against friendship love would win, because it was the more ruthless emotion. But she did not say that, not then, not to Caro. Instead she smiled.

'Listen,' she said. 'I talked to Charlotte tonight. Her husband is a Chinese ceramics expert. He is also, as I remember, one of the coldest fish I ever met, but we'll let that pass. Listen, Caro. There might just be a way . . .'

*

Two days and one telephone call later, James Anstruther-Lamont drove down to Cornwall in his new Lamborghini, and arrived in an irritable mood, the car's bodywork spattered with mud from Cornish roads. He was taken on a tour of the house. At some point on the tour, quite when she could not exactly have said, but fairly soon, Caro suddenly realised the extent to which, in the past, she had traded on vague feminine charm. She realised only because, transparently, it was not working.

Anstruther-Lamont had eyes as nimble as a cash register, but not for her. Indeed, he appeared hardly to see her. He set his weak chin; his gaze revolved and revolved. Occasionally, his long thin hands twitched at the pockets of his long, slender grey suit, as if a calculator lurked in their regions. He showed no sign of animation until Caro took him to the east wing, where the possessions her great-grand-father had brought back from China were displayed. Then the faintest of pink flushes coloured his sallow cheeks, the hands twitched a little more frequently. He did not speak. Caro watched as he moved from object to object, lifting a dish here, a vase, an urn, and setting each down with an air of reverence tempered by caution: they had not yet, after all, discussed anything so vulgar as price.

At last, when he had seen all there was to see, he paused, and looked at Caro speculatively. She saw wheels, cogs, click behind his pale blue eyes, and she gave him a charming smile, slumping down in a chair.

'How much?'

He winced. 'Well, really, Miss Trevelyan . . .' The faint colour in his cheeks deepened instantly, and he appeared to register her presence—and with distaste—for the first time.

'How much?' Caro stretched her legs out. She was beginning to enjoy herself.

'I really cannot make snap judgments of that kind—I thought I made it clear on the telephone.'

'OK, fine—I'll get someone who can. Thank you for coming.' Caro stood up.

'No, no, please. You mustn't misunderstand me . . .' He hesitated. 'There are some fine pieces here, of course. I'd need more time to evaluate quite how fine, naturally. And the whole market is depressed at the moment and so . . .' He paused, eyeing her. 'I realise that there may be reasons why you would appreciate a swift sale, and if that were the case I could perhaps put you in touch with various private individuals who are interested in this field . . .'

Caro tilted her chin. 'I want the pieces to go to auction, Mr Lamont, so I can be certain of realising their value, and I want you to give me a reliable estimate of what that value should be. My mother and I are not so desperate for money that we're prepared to undersell.' Caro paused; it was a new role, and she thought she was doing awfully well. Dislike for the man before her, who now visibly squirmed, made it easier. 'So—if we could start again. I'll be interested to hear what you think, and of course I have a friend who can give me a second opinion.'

'A friend?' He looked at her suspiciously.

'Carl Rubinger,' Caro said airily: she had never laid eyes on the man, but the book she had consulted the previous day on Chinese ceramics had named him as Europe's leading authority on the subject.

'Professor Rubinger?'

'An old family friend. So,' Caro tapped her foot idly on the carpet, 'which items, and how much?'

'Well . . .' Caro saw anger and cupidity fight for dominance briefly in his face; she knew it was a foregone conclusion which would win. His fingers twitched a little.

'This.' He picked up a small insignificant vase, of plain shape, its pinkish glaze unornamented and covering a thousand tiny hairline cracks. 'And that.' He pointed to a shallow blue and white dish. 'And possibly that.' A tiny figurine, of a horse, unevenly glazed green over dull yellow clay, one hoof lifted, a saddle on its beautifully arched back. 'Of that I'm not certain. It could be T'ang, but there are so many very fine early copies I should need a second opinion. The other two—the other two I am certain of.' He gestured to the pink vase: 'Famille Rose—the best period, Ch'ien Lung. And the dish, slightly earlier, late seventeenth century. K'ang Hsi. Not unique, but excellent. There should be museum interest.'

'Just those three?' Caro concealed her disappointment with difficulty.

His eyebrows quivered in outrage. '*Just* three, in one house? My dear Miss Trevelyan!'

'It's a pity about the horse—I've always loved that. But still . . . ' Caro turned and faced him. 'How much?'

His thin lips almost gibbered with rage. But he knew when he had lost and he named a figure. Caro knew her eyes rounded, but—she hoped—she managed to betray no more than that.

'You're certain?'

He shrugged. 'I should like a little time—to do some checking. Perhaps consult. But I would say yes, a conservative estimate which could be outstripped at auction. Or not,' he added maliciously. 'I am suggesting a reserve figure, of course.'

'And your house could arrange for them to be included in one of your sales—how soon?'

'Six weeks. No sooner—we have to print our catalogues, and where serious collectors are involved, one needs time to alert them, and so on.' He paused. 'There would be no problems over provenance, presumably?'

Silently Caro blessed the books she had consulted. 'Provenance? Absolutely not. The details of my great-grandfather's purchases are all fully documented in the estate account books: dates, figures, information as to where bought and from whom . . . I should imagine they're rather more fully documented than many of the pieces you handle.'

The thin hands twitched once more. Caro pressed on:

'I should of course need confirmation from you in writing. Your opinion as to the pieces' authenticity, with further expert opinion if necessary. And the stated reserve price you would expect us to realise at auction . . .'

'Certainly, certainly.' He was moving reluctantly to the door, his eyes still on the china. 'As long as you realise that this is no guarantee, of course . . .'

'Of course. I stopped believing in guarantees quite recently in any case.' Caro gave him a brilliant smile. 'Nothing's certain in this life, is it, Mr Lamont?'

He looked at her blankly. 'I don't quite follow you, Miss Trevelyan. If you're referring to ceramics, I would point out that they represent one of the more certain hedges against inflation. Better than silver, for instance. Why, the percentage increase in value over the last ten years has . . .'

Caro opened the door. 'I wasn't referring to ceramics,' she said.

The day James Anstruther-Lamont came down to Trevelyans, Marian telephoned Trelawney's guesthouse, giving in at last to an impulse which had been with her for days. It came as no surprise to learn that Mr Will and Mr Francis, as old Mrs Trelawney called them, had checked out separately two days before, leaving no forwarding address. After that, screwing up her courage, but secure in the knowledge that Caro was occupied and unlikely even to find out what she had done, she went to see Jack Trelawney. She walked to the farm at a time she knew he would almost certainly be at home, knocked and opened the door at once, to find him sitting before the fire, just as she had hoped. He rose to his feet when she came in, his wide handsome face blushing as pink as a girl's, and with his wife's help it did not take her long to get the truth from him.

'We wasn't certain, all along, Miss Marian,' he said at last, when his story was over.

'*I* wasn't that certain. You was quite took in by him, Jack,' his wife Doris interjected.

'Well, he were that reasonable, like,' he said, looking at Marian pleadingly. 'I was never a one for figures—I didn't understand the half of it. And it sounded so simple. I buy, then he buys from me. There's a tidy little sum over, and Doris and me, we've bin talkin' a while now of leavin' here, makin' a new start. There's her brother now, out in New Zealand, says you can do well at the farmin' out there. If I'd knowed then as how it might be hurtful to Mrs Trevelyan, as always been so good to Doris and me, and her husband afore her—well, I'd have told him no, straight out. But it weren't until the other one comes along, his cousin, that I began to see the lie of the land. I didn't take to him at first . . .'

'I did,' said Doris.

'Dark as the devil,' Jack went on. 'And cold—seemed cold. Not like Mr William, all smiles he was, now I sees why, of course. But after a bit, I took on him. He explained it, very clear and proper, to Doris and me, as how it'd be damagin' to Mrs Trevelyan, how it wasn't all honest and above board the way his cousin made out. He had a head on his shoulders. A gentleman, of course, only need to look at his hands to see that, but knowed about the farming, understood the land— and him not a Cornishman, neither. He had ideas, he had. How this farm could be built up, things I'd never thought on before. If it weren't all sold and turned into one of them fancy hotels like they have on the Rivieera . . .'

Marian leaned forward. 'This was Francis? Francis Atherton?'

Doris nodded. 'That was him. And a kinder man than that, straight as a die, I haven't met in a twelvemonth.' She paused, and smiled. 'Sweet on Miss Caro, too—I'd have said so.'

Jack gave his wife a reproving look. 'So—after I talked with him—well, then it were clear as glass, weren't it? And Mrs Trevelyan she wouldn't sell, anyhow, but even if she'd bin willin', I wouldn't have gone along of it, not after I talked with him. But I've bin worryin' and worryin' since, so I was glad to see you, Miss Marian, so's I could put the record straight.'

'You'd have gone up the Hall, wouldn't you, Jack?' his wife put in, turning to Marian. 'He would have gone up, but he's shy, my Jack is, and his best suit bin in the cleaners, so he held off.' She paused. 'Will it be all right now, then, do you think?'

Marian stood up. 'I'm sure it will be all right,' she said. 'Please, you mustn't worry.'

She stayed a little longer, drank some hot sweet tea, ate some of Doris Trelawney's scones, and then when she judged that she had allayed all their worries, and repeated several times her promise to explain exactly to Caro's mother, she left, and walked home across the fields. As she walked, she thought of Caro, who had been so odd these past two days, so odd Marian felt she scarcely knew her. Since the evening when they had discovered the true identity of the two cousins, Caro had been filled with a kind of desperate energy which Marian found it impossible to pierce. It was as if she had shuttered something of herself away, Caro, who was normally as open as the day. It reminded Marian suddenly of a Caro she had almost forgotten, the little girl who had once said to her: 'I was going to have a brother, but he was born dead, Mummy says. Daddy says we won't talk of him ever again, so I shan't. But how can you be born and dead both at once, Marian?'

Marian paused a little; she was standing just by the bank of flowers where, the last time she had walked this way, she had met Francis Atherton. She thought, though, not of him, but of Caro, who talked now so fast, so excitedly, and who had violet shadows under her eyes, and who, when she met Marian's gaze, looked curiously deadened and hopeless, even as she talked of her plans.

She looked around her at the wild scene: cliffs, gorse, sea, sky. And, almost without pain, a resolution came to her.

CHAPTER TEN

'HE's rich, Caro. I mean really rich—ridiculously so. You know, the way only Arabs and Americans are rich these days. I just don't understand how you can't have realised . . .'

Jennifer had arrived five minutes after James Anstruther-Lamont's Lamborghini had accelerated down the rutted drive in a spattering of angry gravel. Now she and Caro sat in the kitchen, Jennifer leaning across the wide deal table, Caro leaning back in her chair, absently stroking one of the cats.

'I don't care how rich he is,' she said dully. 'It's irrelevant.'

'But Caro—he's so *famous*! And you've always been interested in architecture, how can you not have *known*? Peter recognised him instantly of course—even I knew a bell was ringing somewhere, I just couldn't place it till you'd gone and Peter told me. I mean, you do *know* who he is, don't you?'

Caro turned her head slowly. 'No,' she said at last, 'I don't know who he is. You tell me.'

'He's the only son of Jeremy Atherton and Frances Vanderglas Atherton, that's all!'

'So? I've never heard of either of them.'

Jennifer sighed. 'OK. We'll begin at the beginning. It's quite simple. First of all there's his grandfather, Thomas Atherton. Late Edwardian property developer, built the parts of Chelsea Cubitt didn't reach, plus large areas of Westminster and Kensington. Not a pleasant man, by all accounts—obviously his great nephew William takes after him. Dies, at a suitably ripe old age, one of the richest men in England.' She paused, holding up one finger, and then lifted a second. 'Two. His son, Jeremy, Francis' father. *Not* a chip off the old block. A dilettante. Cashiered from one of the best regiments. A gambler. Bred racehorses—successfully—very successfully. He took my mother to Ascot once, and even she's never forgotten the experience. Marries late, said Frances Vanderglas, whose

Daddy started out in the sticks and ended up one of the richest oilmen in Texas. Marriage not a success from the first: Jeremy dies early and conveniently, leaving a lot of London society ladies with happy memories, and his widow with a taste for chemin-de-fer and young—what shall one call them?—escorts.

'Widow, contrary to all expectations, does not make a disastrous marriage with a man twenty years her junior, but spends the declining years of her life touring the gambling casinos of Europe, and usually winning. Not the motherly sort. Francis, so the story goes, is farmed out from the age of two and scarcely knew Daddy or Mummy. Eton of course, and holidays in a tiny cottage in Cumbria with a Calvinist nanny from the Outer Hebrides of unimpeachable credentials. When he's fifteen—this is from Mark, he knew him quite well at school, as well as anyone ever knew him—Mummy dies. Spectacularly. Halfway along the Baie des Anges, clutching some more unbelievable winnings from the Casino, with two Italian twins aged twenty-four, from Trastevere, one on either arm. A heart attack. Poom! She's gone. Little Francis inherits the lot. Granddaddy's property empire; Daddy's celebrated racing stud; Mummy's winnings and the Vanderglas oil millions. Quite disgusting, really. The minute he comes of age he sells the property, sells the stud, cashes in the Vanderglas holdings, and enrols at the Architectural Association. Buys rooms in Albany—next door to where Byron lived—and all the gossip columnists in London sharpen their pencils. He disappoints them. He does not live it up. Lives alone, never marries.' Jennifer paused. 'Has affairs—but very discreetly. Turns out, to everyone's amazement, to be the best bloody architect this country had produced in a long, long while. Gets involved—two years ago, Peter says—with cousin Will, who's always been hovering in the background, who had to make it from scratch. Apparently takes him under his wing—Will, who wouldn't know a good building from a bad, and couldn't care either way so long as it raked in the cash. Mysterious that. They couldn't be more unalike. Works with Will on—to date—one project. The Davignons' place in Cumbria. Now it's a dream palace, and you have to be bankrolled by an Onassis to stay there. End of story. Caro, he could buy and sell Trevelyans without noticing—do you realise that? He could buy three Trevelyans in the morning and hardly change the noughts in his stockbrokers' account. Can't you understand what I'm saying?'

'I don't care.'

'I thought you said you loved him.' Jennifer's lips tightened. 'If you loved him when you didn't know he was first cousin to Croesus, why can't you love him now? Presumably you can see he could solve a few of your problems?'

'He lied, that's all.' Caro shrugged. 'He lied to me and he misled Marian, and I'm not interested. Neither, I might point out, is he. When it all came out he didn't apologise, didn't even explain. He just took off—and good riddance.'

'But he was going to tell you the truth. He told Peter that.' Jennifer reached across the table, but Caro ignored her hand. 'Caro, he and Peter had it out—to some extent anyway. It was Will Atherton's little empire Peter was interested in: Francis was incidental. When they talked that night after dinner, when Peter said he knew who he was, they talked about Will. Peter said it was quite obvious Francis hadn't realised half the things Will was up to.

'Will's clever,' she went on. 'He sails close to the wind, but even Peter thinks it's impossible to nail him. Francis had an inkling, perhaps, because of the Trelawney business, but he wasn't that involved with Will.' She paused. 'Peter said Will had clearly been using him, and that if Francis had suspected that—and Peter thought he had—he'd deliberately turned a blind eye. He seemed to feel guilty about Will, protective towards him—maybe because Will was his cousin and he had to make it the hard way—god knows. Obviously he didn't even begin to realise what Will was really like until he came back and came down here. Honestly, Caro, you mustn't be rash. I liked him. Peter liked him. He admires him enormously. Even the other night, when it can't have been easy, when the simplest way out for him would have been to blame the whole thing on his creep of a cousin—even then he wouldn't. Oh, Caro, can't you see . . .'

'No, I can't.' Caro stood up. She turned away for a moment,

and when she turned back Jennifer was startled by the pain that
suddenly disfigured her face.

'Listen,' she said fiercely. 'I'll just say this and then I never
want to talk about it again.' She hesitated. 'He lied—that's the
first thing.'

'But, Caro . . .'

'Wait. And he misled us. He misled me.' Caro paused. 'And
more important, because I probably deserved it, he misled
Marian. He hurt her, Jennifer, and I just intend to make sure
he never gets the chance to do it again. That's all. So . . .' she
spread her hands, 'everything you've told me is beside the
point, irrelevant. I shall never speak to him again.'

There was a little silence.

'He misled Marian?' Jennifer looked at her curiously.

'Yes, he did.'

'Intentionally?'

Caro stared at her, then dropped her gaze. 'I don't know.'

'Well, it does make a difference, you know,' Jennifer said
gently.

When Caro did not answer, and was clearly unprepared to
say more, she stood up.

'So,' she said, 'what are you going to do now?'

Caro laughed sadly. 'Now? Now I'm going to save Trevelyans. If I can.'

'And then?' Jennifer looked at her friend with compassion.

'Then? I haven't the least idea. No more than I ever had.
Grow old in it, I expect. Develop into an eccentric old Cornish
spinster. Be godmother to your tribe. Who knows? I shall be
perfectly happy.'

'Will you, Caro?'

Caro looked at her for a long while before she answered;
then, for a second, Jennifer glimpsed the Caro she had always
known, yet changed somehow, grown older. Her eyes cleared,
her beautiful mouth lifted in the old wry grin.

'Perhaps not,' she said. 'Perhaps not too happy. But I expect
I'll get used to it.'

'Don't dramatise,' said Jennifer, uneasily, for something in
Caro's eyes frightened her.

'How right you are. I mustn't,' was all Caro said. Then she

laughed and stood up. 'Come on, let's change the subject,' she
said. 'Let's not be morbid and dull. Let's walk in the garden,
shall we? And I'll tell you about Mr Anstruther-Lamont who
came to see me today, and who is going to solve all my
problems. A nasty man, but useful, Jennifer. Useful.'

Marian sat on a pearl-grey sofa, her feet neatly crossed on a
pearl grey carpet, in James Anstruther-Lamont's outer office.
She was exhausted; tiredly her eyes ranged over the white
shelves on the opposite wall on which, carefully arranged,
carefully lit, stood some of Lamont's own collection of Chinese
ceramics. In the pale, selfconsciously tasteful room the colours
of their glazes glowed like jewels. She looked at her watch;
Lamont seemed to be taking an age.

It had been easy enough to persuade Caro to let her come to
London: at Trevelyans the preparations for the auction had
speeded up. The house seemed constantly filled with agents
and the packers who were assembling the furniture to be sold.
Caro's mother was growing increasingly distraite; all Marian
had had to do was point this out to Caro, with the wry addition
that if Caro took the three Chinese pieces on the train to
London she was quite likely to drop them or lose them en
route. So Caro had agreed, and Marian had risen at dawn and
solemnly taken the small wooden packing case on to the train,
then off it again at Paddington. Then, unknown to Lamont,
she had taken a taxi straight to the Victoria and Albert
Museum, where the custodian of the Chinese ceramics department had confirmed Lamont's identification and tentative
evaluation.

Now it was nearly one, she felt as if she hadn't slept for a
week, and Lamont was escorting the pieces to his firm's safe,
and having the receipt documents and the confirmation of
the sale drawn up, together with his formal estimate of their
worth.

'And then, when you have that, when you come home, we'll
tell Mother,' Caro had said, her eyes glittering with that
frightening excitement which now seemed to drive her. 'When
it's certain. I daren't tell her until then, Oh, Marian, thank
you! Aren't you excited?'

Marian closed her eyes. What she felt now was not excitement, but a sick terrified dread that, try as she would, she couldn't force down. When all this was over, before she took the train home, she had one more thing she had to do: of that, Caro knew nothing.

In the inner office the last details took very little time.

'Might I just briefly use your phone?' she asked, when it was all over.

'Please . . .' Anstruther-Lamont waved languidly at the bank of ivory phones on his desk, and then left her alone. She lifted the receiver and dialled. As soon as a voice answered at the other end—he was in, it was all she needed to know—she replaced the receiver.

A moment later she was out in Bond Street; the sun was shining, there was a hint of autumn, a slight chill in the air. She turned left. It was less than five minutes' walk to Albany.

For a moment, seeing the inner courtyard, the pillared doorway, the marble halls, Marian had almost given up; it was so grand, so discreet, so overwhelming that her nerve momentarily failed her. Now, as she stood in the corridor outside Francis Atherton's door, she lifted her hand to the brass bell pull and hesitated again. It was one thing to confront the Francis she had known in Cornwall, it was quite another to come here, where so many famous people had lived in the past, and confront someone she now knew to be one of Europe's leading architects, and—if what Jennifer had told Caro was true—one of the richest men in the country. Francis was formidable when she had thought him just an ordinary anonymous architect; now the prospect of seeing him terrified her. After all, he had made no attempt, by telephone or letter, to contact anyone at Trevelyans: perhaps to him that whole episode seemed remote, unimportant, trivial. Her hand wavered at the bell; it would be so easy to go home now; to do nothing. Then she thought of Caro again; she pressed the bell.

Francis himself opened it; they stared at each other, and Marian caught her breath. In a week he was so much changed. He looked thinner, and tired, as if he had not slept. He needed a shave. He was in shirt-sleeves, the neck of the shirt open, the sleeves rolled up.

He looked at her in silence for a moment, Marian fearing he might suddenly slam the door in her face; then, with a wry grimace, he stood back and held it open.

'You'd better come in,' he said, not very graciously.

He led her quickly through a hall, then flung back a wide pair of doors into an enormous pillared drawing room which he obviously used also as a working studio. The room was beautiful, but at the moment a mess. Everywhere Marian looked there were books and papers, empty coffee cups and glasses, huge sheets of paper marked with what appeared to be half attempted and abandoned designs. Francis gave a grimace.

'I'm sorry, I've been working.' With a swift gesture he pulled the design sheets roughly together and turned them face down. He tossed a pile of books from a chair, and Marian, since he seemed to expect it, sat down.

'I'm interrupting you,' she began nervously.

He shrugged. 'You are, but I shouldn't let it worry you.' He paused. 'Was that you who telephoned just now—and hung up?'

Marian nodded. He didn't seem interested to ask why, but the information clearly disappointed him. With an impatient gesture he pushed his black hair back from his face, and Marian, seeing him in full light for the first time, realised he looked more than tired.

'Have you been ill?' She leaned forward. 'I'm sorry, but you look—'

'I haven't been sleeping.' He slumped down in a chair opposite and stared at her moodily. 'I often don't when I'm working on a project, that's all.'

Then there was a silence; it hung between them like a cloud, embarrassing Marian. She clasped her hands together, nervously fiddling with her gloves, and moved forward a little so she sat on the edge of her seat. Sentences revolved insanely in her mind, sentences she had rehearsed in the train, but which now seemed absurd, impossible to utter. Francis was looking at her, yet she had the impression that he hardly saw her. He picked up a book, put it down again. His hand clenched, then relaxed, and in that instant it occurred to Marian that he might in many ways be almost as shy, as reticent, as she was.

'Did Caro send you?'

His words jolted her. 'No,' she said quickly. 'No. I decided to come. Caro doesn't know I'm here.'

He said nothing, but she saw something which had lit in his eyes die. He looked at her now with an expression that reminded her of Caro, as if he were dulled by pain.

'I came because—' her voice shook a little and she nearly gave up, but she forced herself to go on. 'Because I wanted you to know various things.' She looked down at her lap. She could go through with it now, she thought, provided she kept it as cool and impersonal as possible, and as long as she did not meet his eyes.

'First, I think I understand the part you played in the whole Trevelyans thing. Not all of it, perhaps, but enough. I talked to Jack Trelawney, and I learned . . . that Will was lying that evening. So—I realise we shouldn't have attacked you as we did that night—that in fact we owe you a good deal. I wanted to apologise.'

He shrugged. 'It's of no account.'

'Secondly.' Still she did not raise her eyes. 'I wanted you to know about Caro.'

'Yes?'

'It's possible—not certain, but there's a very good chance— that she may have found a way of saving the house. There are some ceramics—it turns out they're really quite valuable. They won't raise as much as the sale of the house would do, of course. But enough, if her mother agrees, to keep the house on, make the major repairs. They're being put up for auction— it's all arranged.'

'How fortuitous!'

'More important than that . . .' Marian twisted one of the gloves tight round her finger, 'I thought you should know that Caro is desperately unhappy.'

'Even though the house may be saved?'

'Oh yes.'

'You surprise me. I thought that was her sole concern.'

'It was—once. Before she met you.'

Francis looked at her for a while in silence, and then abruptly rose, with an odd agitated gesture of the hand.

'I don't know what you're talking about,' he said sharply. 'I'd prefer not to discuss your cousin. I have work to do and . . .'

'Do you always take refuge in work?' asked Marian, without thinking, and because she saw her words stung him, she suddenly felt an extraordinary calm take possession of her. She stood up.

'Caro cares for you,' she said simply, meeting his eyes at last. 'That's really what I came to tell you.'

'Did she tell you that?' He swung round sharply.

'Not exactly, no—not quite. But I know I'm right.' She regarded him calmly.

'Then why couldn't she tell me so herself?' His voice was angry and bitter now. 'She showed very little trust in me on the last occasion I saw her. She seemed only too ready to listen to Will's fabrications. No doubt she's listening to them still?'

'She made Will leave almost immediately after you—I thought you would have known that. And she hasn't seen or spoken to him since. Nor will she.'

'I wouldn't know, I drove back to London that night. I've severed all connections with my cousin. I've spent the last week working. Really . . .' his voice became cold, 'this can be nothing to me now—you should understand that. It's not my concern.'

'I can't speak for you,' Marian said gently, 'but I can speak for Caro.'

'I think you should tell your cousin to speak up for herself—she's old enough.'

'That's not fair!' Marian rounded on him fiercely. 'You know Caro, you know how direct, how straightforward she is. She speaks from her heart, she's not a person for subterfuge, and . . .'

'The last time she spoke to me from her heart it was to tell me she was in love with Will, on the basis of a few days' acquaintance,' he said savagely.

'Is that true?' Marian looked at him curiously, and he did not answer.

There was a silence. Marian turned her eyes away to the floor, where the richly coloured rugs were striped with light from the windows. There was just one more thing which she had resolved to say, and if she could summon up the courage to do it, she could then leave, the whole ordeal would be over; she would have done as much as she could. Slowly she wound the thin leather of her glove tighter around her finger, until it almost stopped the flow of blood; she saw the skin whiten. If Francis had spoken then, she thought afterwards, she could not have gone on, but he said nothing, and so, at last, she began to speak, precisely, dropping the words one by one into the pool of silence between them.

'Caro won't contact you herself,' she said, 'and I came here to tell you why, because I thought you should know.' She paused. Francis' back was tense; he had not moved. 'As you know, Caro is very impetuous. She leaps to conclusions, and is very often wrong. She thought—she thinks—that my feelings were involved. She thinks that I'm in love with you.'

There! It had been said. Her heart beat wildly. As she said the words, in her small, flat precise voice, she realised in a second of despair that, even now, she had a little hope left. It might just conceivably be possible that this man would turn on his heel and say, 'But I love *you*, Marian.' He turned.

'You?' he echoed, in a tone of such astonishment it was clear he could have no idea how her whole being seemed to shrivel as he spoke.

'I'm afraid so.' She laced the glove a little tighter. 'I've tried to disillusion her, but it's not always easy to make Caro see reason. Of course, she's completely wrong.' She managed a tight headmistressy little smile. 'I am not in love, I have never been in love, and frankly I don't expect to be in the future. I'm not a romantic, I . . .'

Francis gave an odd convulsive gesture. 'Don't say that—you can't. These things happen. They take one unaware, when you least expect . . .'

'Not to me.' Marian's voice dropped. 'I'm not particularly attracted to men, which is fortunate, of course, because they are unlikely to be attracted to me . . .'

The lie brought him up short; he reddened slightly, and

Marian gave a wry smile. She had been right. He was easy to embarrass; he was as reticent, as shy as she.

'So—I thought you should know this. Caro would like to see you again, I feel sure of it. When she knows the full truth about your cousin, she'll want at least to apologise to you herself. But she can be very obstinate. She won't see you again because she thinks I would be hurt. I can't convince her—I thought I must tell you. Then . . .'

At the last her voice failed her; it shook slightly. She saw his eyes darken, grow intent.

'Marian?' He had guessed she was lying, she could see it in his face. It grew suddenly gentler, with an expression of embarrassed concern. He paused awkwardly, then held out his hand. 'Marian, I like you very much. I assumed . . .'

'But of course.' She pressed his hand lightly, then at once turned away. 'I like you too—it's why I came. And now I must go, I'm afraid, or I shall miss my train.'

They looked at each other for a moment, and the second of intimacy, of understanding between them, passed and was gone. They were strangers again, and the faint trace of admiration she saw in his eyes hurt her more than anything else which had happened. It was admiration, but not of the kind she craved. She moved to the door.

'The auction is the day after tomorrow,' she said. 'But once Caro explains to her mother about the ceramics, I expect it to be cancelled. In any case, term begins this week. I go back to school immediately after, so I don't know if we shall meet again . . .' She paused and turned, on a quick irrepressible impulse. 'Oh, Francis, what shall you do?'

His eyes glittered a little feverishly in his drawn face.

'I don't know,' he said. 'I don't know.'

Marian smiled. She thought she knew. She hoped she knew. In the meantime, she resolved to say nothing more—to him or to Caro. It was safer, in case she was wrong.

'Goodbye, Francis,' she said. 'No, please don't see me out.'

And she closed the heavy door firmly between them.

She arrived back at Trevelyans in the early evening, to find Caro in a state of tense elation.

'Marian—Marian, we've done it! I knew we could. Oh, thank you!' There were tears in her eyes as she clasped Marian to her. Marian tried to turn the subject to Will, and then to Francis, but Caro's mouth set.

'Don't let's speak of them, please, Marian. It's so much better not. All that's over now.'

Marian looked at her uncertainly, for she spoke with great finality, and yet dully, flatly. The animation died from her face. Her eyes, usually so candid, slid away from her cousin's gaze.

'Over?' Marian reached for her hand. 'Caro, why pretend? You may feel that now, but later, when we've told your mother, settled all this . . .'

'Then I shall feel exactly the same.' Caro turned back to her, her eyes full of pain and bewilderment. She hesitated, then pressed her hand to her chest. 'It's an odd sort of feeling— empty, dead, as if I didn't have a heart any more. Have you ever felt that, Marian?'

Now Marian avoided her eyes. 'Once or twice.'

'And does it go away, do you think?'

Marian paused. 'Of course.'

'I don't think so,' Caro said seriously. 'I expect it eases—it would do that, wouldn't it? So you imagine that everything is quite all right again. I'm sure I shall laugh again, and dance, and go to parties, all those things . . .' She broke off, and shook her head, as if she could shake away her sadness. 'Anyway, we're going to forget all that, aren't we? No more melancholy!'

She turned briskly away to the door, then came back and drew Marian after her.

'We'd better hurry,' she said. 'I mustn't waste time. We'll have to notify the auction house, the agents, the bank . . . How cross they'll be!' A dart of the old humour and spirit flashed for a second in her eyes. 'Trevelyans is safe, and that's all that ever mattered, isn't it? Let's find Mother, and tell her . . .'

She picked up the papers from Lamont, and, Marian following, walked slowly across the hall to the door of her mother's office. It was evening, the light was fading, and the air was cold. As she passed the looking-glass she touched her own watery reflection with the tips of her fingers, and shivered.

CHAPTER ELEVEN

THE auction was to be held in the long drawing-room. It had been cleared of furniture for the occasion, and now the bare boards echoed to the feet of the auctioneer's men as they placed the last of the small wooden chairs for the bidders, and made the final adjustments to the dais where the auctioneer would stand.

Marian could see him now, in a far corner; a tall, distinguished-looking man with silvery hair. He had come down from London that morning. He was talking to Meg Trevelyan, obviously going over the final arrangements. Even from where she stood, at the very back of the hall, Marian could see the strain on Meg's face. Behind her, to one side, taking no part in the discussions, was Caro. Her head was bowed; she twisted her hands nervously. Marian's heart went out to her. Meg's refusal to stop the auction had been so unexpected, so entirely unforeseen that Caro still seemed numb with shock. She looked as if she had not slept for nights; her features were waxen.

Even as the men stationed the last of the chairs, the room began to fill up. There were a hundred hired chairs; now it looked as if there would be too few of them. As the people began to file in, Marian watched them carefully. Many of them she knew: friends who had come to commiserate but who also took a gossipy interest in the outcome of the sale. The Major was there, and Lucy Amhurst, wearing a voluminous tweed suit and a battered felt hat set at a combative angle. Jennifer was beside her mother, trying to attract Caro's attention, but Caro did not look up. There were some reporters, all the local papers had sent someone, so had *The Times* and the *Daily Telegraph*. Many of those present were obviously dealers, there for the sale of the furniture rather than the house, clutching catalogues already dog-eared and scribbled upon.

Lucy Amhurst's voice boomed, but everyone else seemed

157

curiously inclined to lower their voices; the room buzzed with whispers. As Marian watched, the crowd before her swelled, moved, with a life, a suppressed excitement of its own. Fragments of conversation reached her; faces turned palely in her direction, then away again. There were nudges, nods, scraps of accents, an American voice, a French one. A couple of German dealers were in a huddle in a corner, arguing with a Dutchman about rugs. Mingling discreetly with the dealers were the security men, recognisable by their noticeable plainness of dress, the way their eyes moved constantly over the ebb and flow of people. Their main contingent was in the library, where the most valuable articles remaining in the house, and the silver, would be sold that afternoon.

Seeing them, Marian felt a sudden fierce dart of anger against her aunt. None of this was necessary; the money raised from the sale of the Chinese ceramics would have paid off all the debts, have left enough to make many of the major repairs the house needed. If that wasn't enough, there were other things, some of the silver for instance, which could have been sold at a later date as other repair work became necessary. Meg was so timid, so cautious. Nothing Marian herself or Caro could say had swayed her, Marian had never seen her so adamant. 'It isn't *enough*,' she had repeated, again and again, as they argued with her. 'Can't you see that? It's enough for now. But it will run out. There will be another crisis, four years from now, five, maybe sooner. We can't go on. It's destroying me, Caro, and it will destroy you. I don't want to see that happen. My mind is made up.'

Glancing at her now, Marian felt compassion. She was wrong to be angry, she thought. Meg looked haggard with exhaustion; she and Caro had underestimated the strain, the toll of the past few weeks. Perhaps it was simply that Meg felt she couldn't go on any longer; maybe that was it. 'But I can work,' Caro had cried pleadingly, kneeling by her mother, her face white, two brilliant patches of hectic colour on her cheeks. 'Please—can't you see? If we can pay off these debts, get the major repair work done, then I can take a job—a well-paid job. I could go back to that modelling firm. They'd take me, I know they would . . .'

'No,' Meg had answered. 'No.' Flatly, resolutely, appearing hardly to listen to their arguments.

Marian sighed; there was very little time left; the auction was due to start at eleven. One of the security men, tall and beefy, moved in front of her, blocking her view. Marian moved slightly to one side, craning her neck to look over the heads in front of her. There was still no sign of William Atherton. Perhaps he didn't do his own bidding, she thought; perhaps, after all, he had changed his mind. Some seats in the front row seemed to be being kept vacant: a large American in a plaid check suit had just stationed himself there, but there were still five empty seats, and the crowd near the door searching for places to sit were clearly growing restless and resentful.

'This is preposterous—why shouldn't I sit there?' The speaker was a woman of about fifty, tanned, expensively dressed, her throat weighted with rows of heavy gold chain necklaces. One of the auctioneer's men said something to her in a low voice, and she pushed him aside.

'Well, I'm afraid that's just too bad. I intend to sit, not stand at the back . . .'

So saying, she brushed past the man and seated herself in the centre of the front row. Now there were just four empty seats left, two on either side of her. The security man, following Marian's gaze and obviously not knowing who she was, gave her a wink.

'Got all the big boys in today, I see, out in force. That'll mean fireworks.'

'Really?'

'Sure.' He nodded in the direction of the tall American. 'Know *him* for a start. Conrad Hartnet—Hartnet Leisure Developments. Big in America, two or three places in France. Moving over here now, and looking for opportunities, so they say. At the Dunsforth Castle sale—you must have read about that?'

Marian shook her head.

'Lost out there. Weren't prepared to go high enough. On the lookout for places they can pick up cheap. That's why they're here.'

'And that woman?' Marian nodded to the one who had

manoeuvred herself into the front row. The man grinned.

'Her? Madame Boulardier, she calls herself, though she's as English as you or me. Married to some Swiss—loaded. Health farms. Facelifts on the quiet—monkey serum, you know the kind of thing. Eternal youth.' He chuckled. 'Big money in eternal youth. A place in Switzerland, one in Paris, opened up in London last year.'

Marian frowned. 'But why would she be interested in Trevelyans?'

The man shrugged. 'It's got class, this place. Run down, of course, but that's no problem to someone like her, the fees she'll charge. And it's remote. Has its advantages, that does, in her line . . .'

From behind Marian someone swore, a curse of moderate obscenity. The security man glanced over Marian's shoulder, reddened, and disappeared quickly. Behind her were Caro and her mother. It was clear they had overheard the last of his remarks.

'You see?' Caro turned to Meg with a gesture of passionate pleading. 'You see what will happen? Those people—they're hateful! Is that what you want for Trevelyans? Please, Mother, please! It's not too late, even now. You can change your mind. Don't you see . . .'

Meg Trevelyan looked dazed with tiredness. She turned her eyes from Caro to Marian.

'Please,' she said, in a low voice, 'don't start this up again, Caro. Marian, make her see sense! I've made up my mind. I've had enough. As long as I can remember there's been worry about money—borrowing, selling, pinching and scraping. It's no way to live, Caro . . .'

'You can't do this! Mother, please . . .' Caro kept her voice low, but she was visibly shaking. 'Not now you see them, the kind of people who want the house . . . you can't!' Her voice broke. 'If Father was alive . . .'

'Caro,' Meg put her hand on her arm, 'not even Philip would have gone on as long as I have. He'd practically decided to sell just before he died. Even he had realised . . .'

'That's not true! He can't have done! You never said . . .' Although she was trying to control her voice, it had risen in pitch. Heads turned curiously in their direction, and Meg flushed.

'Caro, it is true,' she said quietly. 'Even Philip, who was an optimist and a romantic, just as you are, darling. He knew it was becoming impossible.' She hesitated, looking hopelessly from Caro to Marian. 'If we'd had a son it might have been different, but Philip thought that . . .'

'If you'd had a son?' Caro's voice shook; she was chalk white.

'Darling, don't misunderstand me . . . He was just being realistic. You might marry. You might move away from here— your father was always aware of that. Whereas a son . . . Well, maybe a man could have made a go of the place. Developed the farm land—I don't know, darling, it's different for a man.'

'It's not! It isn't! I could make a go of it—I know I could. If we sold the ceramics, cleared the debts—Mother, please . . .'

Meg Trevelyan looked at her for a moment; there was a little silence. Then she looked down at her watch. Across the room the auctioneer was signalling to her. Her eyes met Caro's and her face crumpled; tears came to her shortsighted eyes.

'Caro, please, try to understand,' she begged. 'It's too late. I can't . . .' She turned away, and the storm of protest from Caro which Marian expected never came. She looked at her mother, her eyes blazing dark in her pale face, then very slowly she reached out her hand and caught at her mother's sleeve. Then, abruptly, awkwardly, not speaking, she hugged her tightly. They held each other for a moment, then gently Caro released her.

'Go on,' she said softly, as if she were speaking to a child. 'The auctioneer wants you. You're right . . . I'm sorry. It's my fault. I left it too late . . .'

For a moment Meg seemed to hesitate, and Caro gave her a little encouraging push.

'Go on,' she said again. 'Don't give them the satisfaction of seeing we care. I'll come and join you in a minute.'

Her mother looked into her face a moment. Surreptitiously Caro passed her a handkerchief. Meg turned away, dabbed at her eyes, and when she turned back had composed herself.

'OK, Mother?'

'Fine.' Meg grasped her daughter's hand briefly, then dis
appeared into the throng.

The effort that gesture had cost her now showed on Caro'
face. She met Marian's eyes, and reached for her hand.

Silently they turned together to look back across the room.

'What time is it?'

'Five to.'

Caro nodded.

Across the room the auctioneer had left her mother's side
and was moving towards the dais. A slight hush of expectation
fell over the crowd. Marian scanned the seats in the front row
Four were still empty; there was still no sign of William
Atherton. Caro must have realised that too, for she was now
staring round the room, her eyes raking the rows of heads, the
knot of people still gathered by the door. Suddenly her hand
tightened painfully in Marian's, and Marian, following her
gaze, froze.

There was some kind of altercation going on in the hall
outside; voices were raised, men's voices. The knot of people
by the entrance ebbed, joined; heads turned curiously. One of
the auctioneer's men was attempting to close the doors, but
before he could do so they were thrown back sharply. The little
crowd parted; Marian caught a glimpse of a tall figure, heard
the tail-end of some angry-sounding remonstrance, though she
could not make out the words. A whisper went through the
room—'Atherton'—and the crowd finally parted.

She saw Will Atherton in the same moment Caro saw him
He entered quickly, as if breaking away from someone who
had sought to detain him, and there was the briefest moment
before he recovered his composure, when his handsome face
was distorted with an ugly scowl. Then he paused; stopped. He
glanced around the throng at the door, over the heads of the
people seated, with an expression of arrogant dismissal. Then
unimpeded and without hesitation, he moved to one of the
empty seats in the front row. He nodded at Madame Boular
dier, and received a cool nod in return. He sat down on her
right, leaving one chair between them ostentatiously empty.

Again there was the sound of voices from the hall: again the
little group by the door shifted, moved, and finally parted.

'Marian. Oh, Marian!' Caro muttered, and her nails dug into the skin of Marian's arm.

Francis Atherton had come in. A head taller than any other man in the room, distinct in his conservative black suit, as if attired for a funeral, he too paused in the doorway. His eyes moved over the heads before him, to the back of the room, rested for a second, then moved away. It was only as he moved to a seat in the front row, on the other side of Madame Boulardier, that Marian realised he was not alone. In his wake, looking distinctly embarrassed, was Jennifer's husband, Peter Dalton. He clearly sensed the attention this late arrival had caused. He looked flustered and embarrassed, and was wiping his spectacles with a large handkerchief as he moved to sit beside Francis. Caro and Marian stared at the front row. If Will saw his cousin he gave no indication. Both men sat straight, staring ahead of them at the dais where the auctioneer had now taken his stand. To the side of the room, Meg Trevelyan moved quietly to a seat on an aisle. The auctioneer cleared his throat; silence fell.

'Ladies and gentlemen . . .'

There was very little preamble. Once he called for quiet as another late arrival caused more pushing and shoving by the door. Then he moved quickly on to enumerate the details of the house and the land to be sold with it.

'So, ladies and gentlemen,' he looked quickly at his watch, 'if we could open the bidding now. As I have said, an historic house, encompassing four thousand acres of gardens and farming lands, the exact specifications being in your catalogue. The house listed Grade One by the Department of the Environment, with permission for statutory change of usage having been granted in outline.' He raised his gavel, an actor manqué, Marian thought sourly, disliking his mellifluous tones.

'Ladies and gentlemen, shall we open the bidding at—' he paused, 'two hundred thousand pounds?'

'*Two hundred thousand?* To *open* the bidding?' Caro turned to Marian, her face pale. 'But Mr Wells said we'd be lucky if . . .'

'Sssh!' Marian grasped her arm.

No one appeared to have moved, but the auctioneer nodded.

'Two hundred thousand I am bid. Any advance on two hundred thousand?'

The American in the front row gave the slightest inclination of the head, scarcely perceptible.

'Two hundred and twenty-five thousand . . .'

Madame Boulardier lifted her catalogue half an inch.

'Two hundred and fifty . . .'

The American nodded again.

'Two hundred and seventy-five . . .'

The auctioneer turned his head. Someone standing by the door must have moved.

'Three hundred I am bid . . .'

Marian stared at the crowd by the door, then stiffened.

'It's Simon,' she whispered to Caro. 'Charlotte's brother. Look, isn't that him?'

Caro stared. Her lips tightened, colour flamed in her pale cheeks.

'What's he doing here?'

Marian looked at him grimly. 'I know what he's doing,' she said tersely. 'He's bidding for Will. He's in on that deal—I *thought* so! They're splitting the bids between them to discourage the others. You wait!'

'Three twenty-five . . .'

The American leaned back in his seat. It had been his bid, and Marian sensed it had been his last. He glanced at Will Atherton beside him, but he still had not moved a muscle.

Madame Boulardier bent her wrist.

'Three-fifty . . .'

Caro gave a stifled gasp. 'What are they doing, Marian? They must be mad—so much money! I can't believe that . . .'

'Three-seventy-five.'

This time Marian saw Simon lift his hand, and nod. He had not quite mastered the understatement of the other bidders; his cheeks were flushed with excitement. Even as he made the bid she saw him glance at Will, and receive in return a tight little smile.

There was a pause. The auctioneer glanced at the tall

American and he gave a scarcely perceptible shake of the head.

'Three-seventy-five. The bidding stands at three hundred and seventy-five thousand pounds . . .'

Madame Boulardier glanced across at the American, let her gaze rest with a second of puzzlement on Will Atherton, then lifted her catalogue once more.

'Four hundred thousand . . .'

Marian's eyes were riveted on the door. So that *was* Will's ploy, she thought angrily. He was going to stay out of the bidding as long as he could; perhaps he would have no need to enter it at all. She saw Francis turn his head to the door, just as Simon's hand fell once more.

'Four hundred and ten thousand I am bid . . .'

Francis remained staring at Simon; Madame Boulardier glanced over her shoulder, but it was obvious that the bidding had gone too high too fast; there were no bids coming from behind her. She shot Will Atherton a glance of pure dislike; obviously she had tumbled to his ploy. Her mouth set. She fingered her gold chains, then abruptly made a small irritable gesture of the hand.

'Four hundred and twenty thousand . . .'

The rate was slowing down. It couldn't be long now, and it was a foregone conclusion, Marian thought, who was going to win. Yet the bidding had gone so high. Surely there must be a cut-off figure, even for Will, beyond which the whole project became uneconomic. It was obvious, though, that Madame Boulardier was already stretched; she might drop out at any second, and there seemed to be no other contenders. Will made a tiny gesture and Simon inclined his head.

'Four hundred and fifty thousand . . .'

Caro gasped and Marian bit her lip. He had made a big jump, thirty thousand on one bid. Even at the moment she most disliked Will, she had to admire his psychology; Madame Boulardier was already wavering. Such an increase was designed to stop her in her tracks, to show her Atherton meant business.

'Four hundred and fifty thousand I am bid. Any advance on four hundred and fifty thousand?' There was a brief silence.

Will continued to stare straight ahead of him; Madame Boulardier appeared to hesitate, then she too gave the minutest shake of the head.

'Going for the first time, at four hundred and fifty thousand pounds . . .' The room was silent as a church. Caro, her eyes wide, was staring at the auctioneer.

'Going for the second time . . .'

'Five hundred.'

The curt crisp voice made Marian and Caro jump. Even the auctioneer was palpably thrown. He looked around the faces before him in a second's confusion.

'Sir?'

Francis Atherton leaned forward slightly. 'I said, five hundred thousand.'

There was immediate pandemonium. Voices broke out on all sides; heads craned, a couple of people stood up in their seats. Will Atherton did not move, and Simon stared across the room aghast, clearly waiting for a signal. None came. The auctioneer gathered his wits.

'Five hundred thousand,' he said in a satisfied croon. 'Half a million pounds I am bid . . . Any advance on five hundred thousand?'

Caro turned to Marian. 'It was Francis—Francis made that bid! Marian, what's going on? He can't be bidding for Will, surely? If you're right, Will had it already, with the other bid. I don't understand . . .'

'Going for the first time at five hundred thousand pounds . . .'

Will Atherton moved at last. Very slightly he lifted one hand from his lap.

'Five hundred and twenty-five thousand pounds . . .'

A man in front of Caro and Marian turned to the woman beside him.

'Who's that bidding against Will Atherton, for God's sake?' he muttered. 'He must be mad! They're way over the odds, surely? The place is a wreck!'

'Six hundred thousand,' said Francis.

There was an audible intake of breath. The auctioneer, clearly intent on betraying no more emotions as inappropriate as surprise, did not raise an eyebrow. He glanced quickly towards Simon at the door, then back to Will. Will lifted his hand.

'Six hundred and fifty thousand I am bid. Any advance on . . .'

'Seven hundred.' Again Francis' voice cut through the hubbub of whispers and enquiries and stifled excitement around him. Madame Boulardier turned to him with an expression compounded of sudden interest and amazement.

'Seven hundred thousand I am bid . . .'

The man in front gave a sigh of disbelief. 'They're potty,' he said roundly. 'They must be. What on earth does Atherton think he's doing?'

'Going for the first time, to the gentleman here,' the auctioneer indicated Francis, 'for seven hundred thousand pounds.'

'Oh, my God!' Caro looked as if she were about to faint. 'What is he doing, Marian? It's hateful—it's obscene! So much money! I don't understand . . .'

Marian looked grimly before her. She didn't understand either. Clearly no one in the room did. All they knew was that a gladiatorial combat was taking place, with money for weapons, and they scented blood. Everyone in the room was on the edge of his seat now; silence had fallen; all eyes were focussed on the two tall men in the front row, the fair and the dark, neither looking in the other's direction.

'Going for the second time at seven hundred thousand pounds . . .'

Will leaned forward: 'Eight hundred thousand,' he said.

Caro jumped. The auctioneer's gavel hovered in mid-air.

Francis leaned back and crossed his arms over her chest. A little smile played around his lips.

'Nine hundred,' he said.

'Now I know they're both mad,' said the man in front. 'Certifiable! Who the heck is he—that dark one?'

'Ssh, darling!' The woman beside him placed a restraining hand on his arm. She leaned forward avidly, passed her tongue over her painted lips. Suddenly the room seemed very close, very hot, and Marian realised she felt sick. The atmosphere in the place had become thick; with envy, with a kind of restless excitement akin to a sexual arousal. All eyes were focussed on Francis now.

Will seemed to hesitate. He glanced towards Simon at the door. He looked up at the auctioneer. Marian stared, her nerves strained as taut as wires. He was rich, of course, but not as rich as Francis. Will's money was presumably tied up, in investments in his other hotels. There must be a limit as to how high he could go—especially as he wasn't bidding just with his own money, but with that of co-investors like Simon. Whereas Francis . . . She looked at him, and felt fear. His money was his own; according to Jennifer, it was well nigh limitless. He could, if he wished, presumably outbid anyone in the room, including his cousin, and he seemed to intend to do just that. His ruthlessness then repelled her, and in a shaft of understanding she saw the reason for this confrontation. They weren't bidding for a house at all, they were bidding for a woman, for Caro. This was not financial rivalry, it was sexual. A sexual power game was taking place in front of her eyes, with Caro as a prize, or as a pawn—it could be either. A pawn, she thought; in spite of her visit two days before, Francis had made no attempt to contact Caro. What seemed to be involved now was simply pride, a stupid male pride, pointless except to the victor.

She could not be sure, but Caro seemed to have realised the same thing in the same moment, for she had gone quite white. Her hand fluttered against Marian's sleeve.

'I hate them!' she whispered passionately in Marian's ear. 'I hate them for this. What are they doing? They don't care about the house at all. It's something else . . . oh Marian, it's hateful!'

'Nine hundred and fifty thousand,' Will said clearly. He might have been speaking the time, for all the inflection in his voice.

Before the auctioneer could even pick up the bid Francis had leaned forward again, his face now grim.

'One million,' he said.

Caro gave a muffled cry, midway between a gasp and protest. Her eyes blazed in her face. She gripped Marian's arm once more.

'I'm going,' she said sharply. 'I can't bear it. I don't understand it and I don't care. They're doing it out of hate, that's all, hate for each other—I don't know. It's vile! All that money . . .'

Before Marian could restrain her, she was gone, pushing through the ranked chairs, shoving people aside blindly, as she made for the door. There Simon put out a hand to restrain her, and she brushed him off angrily; a buzz of whispered comment passed through the room. Both Francis and Will must have seen her leave, though neither moved. There was a silence. The crowd parted, Caro disappeared, the doors opened and swung shut.

'Going for the second time at one million pounds . . .'

Marian felt pain choke in her throat. She wanted to cry out: two million, three million, as many millions as you like—but no words came.

The auctioneer gripped his gavel; he was looking at Will, who had not spoken. In the stillness that had succeeded Caro's abrupt exit, Marian saw from the corner of her eye that someone had moved. At the far side, Meg Trevelyan had risen to her feet, consternation on her face.

'One million pounds I am bid. Going, for the third time . . .'

The auctioneer raised his gavel.

Caro ran. Out of the house, down the drive, along the road. It was a beautiful autumn day; the air was clear, the sun shone, there was a scent of raked leaves, of burning wood tinged with the salt of the sea. But the air was also a little cold; it seared her lungs. She did not pause.

It was a shock to be outside, to smell the air, to see cars progress along the road, cows graze on the fields above the cliff. She stopped for a second, dry-eyed, panting, staring ahead of her at the path that led across the fields to the cliff and to the beach. Everything was as it always was. Out to sea the gulls circled, freewheeling on the up-currents. The path was rutted, muddy still from the previous week's rain, and deserted as it usually was. The world went on.

And yet, back in that room, everything outside had seemed suspended, as if nothing existed outside its four walls, outside the contest which had so suddenly sprung up between two men. She did not know why they had challenged one another so, nor even which of them succeeded. Both had money, both were prepared to use it as a weapon against each other in some challenge in essence so masculine, so foreign to her, that she could feel nothing but bewilderment and repulsion.

She paused for a second, wondering if her ancestors, the men who had built Trevelyans, acquired the money to put up its walls, to expand its boundaries, maintain its grace, had been men such as Francis and Will, and she felt, for the first time (the thought had never come to her before) that they probably were. She gave a little strangled half sob; the realisation sullied the house for her. She saw it for a moment not as the house she had always unquestioningly loved, but as a possession merely, an instrument in a war of subservience and mastery between men.

The clarity of that thought was no sooner with her than it was gone; she was left with nothing then but pain and confusion, and an aching sense of loss. She began to run again, stumbling a little on the path, towards the cliff edge, and the track that led down to the beach.

When she reached the summit at last, she stopped, and looked down, then out to sea.

On either hand the headland curved away from her, sloping around the bay with such a perfection of symmetry it was as if some god had cut away the land, had sculpted it, in a moment of idleness with a lazy yet exactly sure touch. Green grass curved to the horizon on either side. And below, a drop so sheer to the pale sand that it was invisible even at low tide, unless you stood at the very edge, which was dangerous.

Caro looked down at her feet. Close to the grass was not green at all, but compounded of hundreds of different tiny plants, yellow, amber, bronze, vermilion, violet and blue.

As she had known it would, the prospect calmed her. Her breath came less fiercely in her chest; she stood still. A view was no kind of surety, and yet, even now, it had this power over her as it had always done. She stepped forward a pace, looking out over the water. It was tranquil, lapping against the rocks. Her father had loved it here.

She was not at the very edge when she felt the ground give. She was perhaps a foot further back; the movement of the earth beneath her feet seemed at first very slow. She reeled back, clutching at air, certain for a moment even as she lost her balance, that she could step back from the brink. Then she felt herself fall; not painfully in the least, but with a slow, inevitable slide, out and down, dry earth scattering around her, rocks tumbling out of the earth and over into space. Grass slipped through her fingers; she slipped, and then was still.

For a second the sky tilted, then steadied. The frozen calm deserted her, and panic leaped in her chest. She had fallen only a few feet, ten at the most. Above her, where the cliff edge had given way, she could see an ugly jagged raw edge, like a bite out of the earth. Below her were the rocks; a long way down—eighty feet at least, perhaps more. She held her breath, scarcely daring to turn her head. She had fallen into a position where she was half crouching, half lying on a tiny narrow ledge. She was not hurt; there was one long scratch—that was all—on her leg. But she could not move. The ledge was not rock; tentatively she moved a foot, and instantly heard the earth crumble away and fall; she withdrew it gently, feeling the ledge stealthily with her fingers. It was gritty, sharp, made up of small sharp stones and turf and dry earth; all that seemed to be holding her weight was a thick clump of gorse below, and a small out-jutting of rock. One move and she would be over.

She lay there a long while, how long she was uncertain, perhaps half an hour. The breeze had got up; it was starting to whip the waves into peaks; she grew very cold, and her legs felt desperately cramped. She must not panic, she thought. When they realised she was missing, they would send out a search party; they would think of looking here first—Marian would know she would come here. Then, if she kept still, if they found a rope . . . She must just keep calm. She must think of something else, occupy her mind, so she forgot her fears, the terrible aching cramp that was starting in her legs.

Deliberately she set her mind: she thought of the auction room, of the sequence of bids, all of which had happened so fast that at the time she had been unable to follow them coherently. Francis had bought Trevelyans, she thought; that was almost a certainty, if not with his bid for one million, then with a higher one. Just before she had left she had seen on his face an expression of grimness and singlemindedness that left her with no doubts. As to why he had done it, she could not decide, though she struggled with a score of alternatives as they surged into her mind.

Revenge of some kind against Will, that seemed the most likely, because Will had angered him, perhaps because there had been some rivalry between them—over herself, she felt instinctively, and yet that made no sense, for she had been mistaken over Francis, just as Marian had been, she saw that now. If he had cared for her, he would at least have tried to see her, to speak to her, in the awful endless sleepless week that had passed.

And then, before she could fight it down, there crept into her mind the memory of his touch, of his embrace, of his face close to hers and the truth she had seen in his eyes. She cried out aloud, a soft moan of pain, for the instant that memory came to her she knew her longing for him was as intense and as fierce, as demanding as it had ever been. She had been at fault: she had disbelieved him, listened to his cousin, and then—then she had done nothing. Now it would be impossible. If she sought him out now, even if she tried to apologise to him, he would think it was because he had bought Trevelyans. She moved her face a fraction, turning her head, feeling gravel bite against her skin.

I love him, she thought. Then, seeking to be rational, telling herself she was a fool and an impulsive fool at that, she put herself through a catechism. Was she sure? Why was she sure? *How do I love thee? Let me count the ways* . . . That this, an old tag, should come into her mind then struck her as ridiculous, but even so it had no power to alter the state of her emotions. She felt something grow within her, strengthened by admission; a force as intense and as powerful, as necessary, as breath in her lungs. She knew; that was all.

The emotion was so strong it revived her; suddenly she felt determination return. No one had come: surely there was something she could do? If only she could rescue herself, return to Trevelyans, why then she could see Francis. She had no notion what she would say to him; it no longer seemed to matter in the least how he might regard what she said, there was only urgency. She had to see him.

Very cautiously, she lifted her head and turned it, scanning the cliff behind her. Even that slight movement sent a scattering of dry earth, but she did not care. Her situation seemed to her so ridiculous, so absurd, that she could no longer believe in her own peril. She must escape.

She narrowed her eyes, looking at the cliff. Once, years ago, she had climbed it, looking for gulls' nests. It was not so sheer, so unscaleable as it looked from a distance. To the right of her now she could just see the cliff path snaking down to the beach. That was unreachable: at least thirty feet of sheer rock separated it from the ledge where she lay. But to the left: she hesitated.

The cliffs were granite and quartz; there were seams of rock, although it was difficult to trace them under the skin of red earth and shallow-rooted plants that clung to them. If she could only move a fraction to the left she thought she could inch her way along the cliff face to a narrow chimney of rock that plunged straight down; under it the water boiled against sharp rock; but it was narrow. She might wedge herself there; descend gradually; it was possible, perhaps to get a purchase . . .

Very slowly and delicately, often pausing, she levered herself into a crouching position, facing in towards the rock. Then, scarcely daring to breathe, she began to inch her feet around until she felt the solidity of the rock beneath them. As she did so she saw the earth crumble and heave; half the ledge that had supported her before now fell away to the sea. She made one swift quick move, standing, swaying against the cliff face, her breath catching in her throat, but she had managed it, she was upright. There! An inch at a time, painstakingly, her face pressed close against the rock, she began to move. One hand, one foot, then the others. The rock bit into her skin, she dared not look down, but it was possible, surely it was. There were tiny ledges, minute handholds invisible from far away, but like landmarks close to: she inched forward again; now she was two feet from the ledge where she had lain, and perhaps three from the chimney of rock. Another six inches; another two. She paused. With a sudden whisper the ledge where she had lain fell away in a crumble of red dust; she stopped, suddenly afraid. Now there was no going back; she had to move on. Her hands and feet were not strong enough to cling to the rockface indefinitely. She set her mouth. Another inch.

Her world had contracted now: she could hear the sea, the cry of the gulls; she could see nothing but the face of the rock in front of her, the slow testing passage of her own hands as they sought and found a tenuous purchase. Dear God, she thought wildly, did I really climb this once? I must have been insane! Another foot. Now she could see the outline of the rock chimney ahead of her quite clearly. She paused, panting, strain in every muscle. She must go on. Another inch. Another.

'Caro.' The voice came from just below her. It was pitched quietly and low, but even so it alarmed and startled her. Her foot missed a tiny ledge, scrabbled against the rock. A shower of earth fell.

'Caro, listen to me very carefully and do exactly what I say.'

Her foot found its grip; she froze, huddled against the rock. It was Francis. She couldn't see him, but she could hear him quite clearly and for a wild moment she thought she must be hallucinating, that she had gone quite mad. Then he spoke again.

'I didn't see you until you moved from the ledge; but I can see you now. Don't look down. Can you stay where you are, just for a moment?'

'Yes—yes, I think so . . .'

'Very well, now, listen carefully. I'm nearly level with you and I'm going to bring you down, but you'll have to do exactly what I say, all right?'

'All right.' She bit her lips between her teeth. The pain in her arms was excruciating. Now the foot or so to the chimney looked like a mile.

Above the sound of the sea and the wind she heard a vague movement; breathing, the crumbling and falling of earth, an expellation of breath as he heaved his weight higher.

'Francis!' she cried in sudden terror. 'Leave me. It's dangerous, you could fall—if I can just get to the chimney . . .'

'We're both perfectly safe.' His voice was soothing, perfectly calm, and though she knew it was a professional tone, she was reassured by it. 'I'm a couple of feet under you now. In a moment or two I can help you directly. Now . . .'

There was a silence; Caro froze. Her arms felt as if she were stretched on a rack. Then he spoke again, very gently.

'Now. Just to your right, about three inches from your hand, there's a ledge. And another, two inches from your right foot. Move your hand first, slowly—that's right, then the foot. Very good. Now transfer your weight, and move your left foot. Look at the rock face, keep your head tight against it. Don't look down. Pitch your weight forward against the rock, it will hold you, I promise—that's right . . .'

She moved. It was slow, painfully slow, but she moved. It was as if she read Braille, she thought wildly, as if someone guided her fingers across the bumps and indentations and made them sense. The chimney was closer now: a foot, six inches, three.

'Fine. You're doing very well, exceptionally well. Now, this is the hard part, after that it's plain sailing. Listen carefully. You'll have to stretch a little, and lean back a fraction to get round the corner of the rock and into the chimney. Now.' There was a second's pause. 'You must swing your body, out and round, in one movement. You can't see it from where you are, but there's a perfect hold just inside the chimney, about an inch higher than your right hand, and about six inches from the grip you have now. Don't move your feet. Feel for it with your hand—that's it. Now, when I tell you, move your right foot round and swing your body. There's not much purchase for the feet, you'll have to move so you get your back against the rock on the other side and then wedge yourself with your feet flat against the rock, do you understand?'

'Yes . . .' She turned her head. 'Oh God, Francis, I can't!'

'Don't be damn ridiculous—of course you can. I thought you had guts. Now, when I tell you, move.' There was a moment's pause. '*Move!*'

Caro's body swung out into space; for a second she believed she must fall. Then, with a gasp of pain, she felt the rock bruise every bone in her spine as she made contact with it.

'Your feet. Push them hard against the rock—that's it! Push outwards with your back and your feet . . .' His voice caught, then grew calm again.

'Well done. Now, if you've muscles in your legs we'll be all right.'

He was close now, she could sense it, though she still could not see him. Her whole body screamed with pain, and only his voice, like a drug, kept her from the easy way out. Let go, a part of her mind cried. Just let go.

'Now. I'm about three feet below you, and in a second I'll be able to take some of your weight. Keep pressing with your feet, then very slowly let yourself slide down the rock. Not more than a few inches at a time, then move your feet so they're parallel. Imagine you're a cork in a bottle. That's it! A bit more . . .'

The rock cut her; she gave a little cry of pain. Then she felt his arms, his hands, as they roughly came round her.

'Keep absolutely still now. I've no rope, so this will have to do.' His movements were so quick and deft she hardly knew what was happening. She felt the leather of his belt cut into her skin as he slipped it under her arms and across her breasts and tightened it. His arm came around her waist with an iron strength. Suddenly she felt the hardness and warmth of his body cradling hers from below, his thighs pressing hard up under hers, his chest supporting the weight of her back. His breath was coming fast.

'Now,' he spoke through gritted teeth, 'if either of us goes we both go, so concentrate. I'm going to start going down. Keep your feet and your back wedged, but not so tightly you can't move. Let yourself rest against me, but not your full weight. Move with me, let yourself slide when you feel me move, but not too fast. Brake yourself with your back and your feet. Don't talk. Ready?'

'Francis . . .'

'I said don't talk. Just do exactly what I say.'

He moved. For a horrible lurching second she felt the pressure and warmth of his skin gone. Then the leather of the belt cut painfully into her breasts and she let herself slide a little. A pause, then again. And again.

The effort of pressing with her feet and her back was becoming intolerable. She cried out at the pain of it:

'I can't, Francis. Let me go—I can't!'

'You'll damn well have to. If you don't, we'll both be killed. Now, again, when you feel me move. Just go with it, don't think . . .'

She was trembling now, her whole body shook from the strain. Each time she felt his closeness then his loss. Air and vacancy against her body, then the heat, the power of his, the scent of his sweat close to her nostrils, acrid and sharp, the pained catch of his breath.

'Another few feet. Can you make it?' He had paused. The chimney was narrowing, the strain was less. Caro looked up to the clear wide sky above her face, and through the pain in her body she felt something else, sharp and clear, incongruous in this moment but there; a sharp, physical desire for him so intense she had to close her eyes and wrench her consciousness to blot it out. They had paused and she was pressed tight down on him with her full weight; against her body she felt him stir, for a second his grip on her tightened.

'Dear God,' he cried sharply, 'concentrate! We're nearly there.'

'Francis . . .'

'Shut up. Move when I move, goddammit!'

He moved; she lurched after him, her muscles so weakened now she had hardly any control over her own movements. Desire sharpened by fear surged in her body, even then. It blinded her; she felt as if her senses had all been destroyed except this one; sweat trickled from her brow into her eyes.

'Again, Caro. You must push. Try—again!'

He was down. She had no strength left. As her legs gave, and she fell, the belt caught her fall, then his arms. Her feet were plunged into water; it sucked and pulled against her thighs. Blindly she reached for him, and he caught her, held her upright. She swayed against his body, felt him hold her tight. Then she lost her footing, slipped. For a moment of cold shock she felt icy water soak her clothes, splash her skin as she sank up to her shoulders. Francis had bent with her, then he was lifting her, dragging her, and she managed to stumble as he pulled them across the rocks to the sand.

'Hold me—tight. That's it. I've got you!'

CHAPTER TWELVE

CARO felt firm ground beneath her feet. Francis' arms around her tightened, and she slumped against his chest, her legs shaking, pain from her raw hands shooting up her arms. She sagged, unable to support herself, resting her head against his firm shoulder, feeling the harsh rise and fall of his chest.

She opened her eyes. They stood in a circle of wet sand. The tide had just turned, and only this tiny island of the beach was uncovered. As the water receded so it sucked and drew the pebbles and granite gravel after it, leaving the sand in a pattern of rivulets, as delicate as lace. All around them was sea, and before them, gaunt and threatening, the cliffs they must have come down.

She could only cling to him; she could not speak. He must have discarded his jacket before starting his climb to her, for he wore only trousers and a shirt torn and soaked with salt. His feet were bare and bleeding. His belt still bound them to one another, and now, with a soft exclamation, he loosed it.

As it fell away, their eyes met, in a second of inquiry, pain, indecision—want. She could never have said what exactly, for it was all those things. Then, for she knew it was inevitable and thought he must also, Francis bent his head angrily, and their mouths met in a second of impatience, of searching. She opened her mouth under his, strained her body against the hardness of him and did not think—could not have thought.

When at last he released her, she sank to the ground, and moving quickly away, he came back with his jacket and wrapped it around her, then knelt beside her and clasped her tight in his arms, rocking her back and forth gently in a strange ecstasy of happiness and pain.

Neither spoke. He took her hand and pressed it against his lips. He held her, then looked into her face, then held her again, and she felt his body tremble against her own.

At last she said, 'Francis, I love you.'

178

And he said, 'Do you, Caro? Do you?'

And a little hysterically she began to laugh, could not stop, until he drew her down beside him on the damp sand, and held her close so his body warmed her, and they were both silent, not daring to look at each other, just staring sightlessly before them at the sand and the sea. After a long while he turned to her, and lifted her face to his. She looked into his eyes, and she saw into their depths, saw that he laughed at her a little, but that the shock of everything that had happened had not quite gone away.

'You realise you shouldn't have moved?' he said. 'I was here below. I came down to the beach—I was looking for you. Until you moved, I didn't even . . . You would have been safe, you realise, on the ledge?'

Caro stared into his eyes: she felt as if she could never turn her gaze away.

'Maybe,' she said. 'I didn't care, really. It wasn't very safe and I could have been there for hours, and—I wanted to see you.'

'Did you now?' He gave an ironic smile. 'Well, fate contrives these things very oddly. Once you'd moved and I saw you . . .' He paused. 'We were lucky, that's all.'

'Not at all.' Caro smiled. 'You'd have saved me. That's nothing to you . . . You climb, you told me . . .'

'Yes. Well, maybe I'll take you to the Cuillins some day and we'll see . . .'

He paused, and left Caro a second in which to savour the joy of that casual suggestion, of the promise of a time in the future when they might be together.

'However, before we do that, you'd need to do a lot of work. You may boast that you climb like a man but . . . ouch!' He gave a mock cry of pain as she pushed him. 'But,' he went on, catching her wrist hard, 'but you'll have to learn not to do foolhardy things like that. Do you realise . . .' his face sobered for a second, 'do you realise how close a thing it was?'

'You saved my life, you mean?'

'No.' He was looking at her seriously. 'I helped. You might not have got down without me. However, I have to admit, you were a good pupil. You were sensible. You did what you were told, when you were told, and . . .'

'So I did once before. Don't you remember?' Caro laughed, suddenly feeling so acutely a sense of relief, of disaster averted, that she cared no longer what she said, that caution, all caution could go. She stopped, and looked at him.

'I do love you,' she said. 'Very much. Isn't that odd? I thought I'd never be able to tell you. And now . . .'

'Now you're in shock,' he said, a little sharply, his arm tightening around her. 'I might have to ask you to say that again in less stressful circumstances. After all, heroines generally love their rescuers, don't they? And—'

'Don't you dare mock!' Caro turned on him fiercely. 'I do, and there's an end of it. I didn't want to, and I didn't expect to, but I do. I think you're quite wonderful. Now, what do you say to that?'.

Francis smiled a little. 'I say you don't know me very well. That I'm arrogant, and occasionally very hot-tempered. Far too cautious sometimes. Too cautious with you, perhaps . . .' He paused, and their eyes met. 'But in mitigation there are perhaps reasons for that. I can be suspicious, and jealous. I'm still too rich. I work too hard.' He paused. 'You might dislike me a good deal first thing in the morning . . .'

'You don't tell lies.' Caro paused.

'Not often. I told you some, when we first met, and I regret it.'

There was a little silence. Caro shivered.

'Did you buy Trevelyans?' she asked at last.

'No.' He reached for her hand. 'I didn't. And neither did Will. I would have stopped him that way, because he wouldn't listen to me, or Peter Dalton, and I couldn't stop him any other. But I didn't buy Trevelyans.' He paused. 'Your mother stopped the sale.'

'She did?' Caro looked at him wonderingly. Then she took his hand. 'I'm glad,' she said. 'It makes things simpler. Between us.'

'They don't feel in the least simple,' he said.

There was a little silence. Caro looked away, down at the sand and the receding sea. She hesitated. At the back of her

mind she could feel it all beginning to creep back, the uncer-
tainties, the complications, and she feared them, feared to lose
the perfect clarity she had known before. She bent her head.

'Why did she do that?'

'I don't know. I think she found the whole thing as obscene
as I did. Perhaps she sensed what was going on—the battle
between Will and me.' Francis paused. 'It was a kind of mad
battle, you know. He'd gone far above his limits, he was
hopelessly overstretched . . .'

'If Mother hadn't done that, if you had bought our house,
what would you have done then, Francis?'

'Found some way to give it back to you, I imagine. Presumably there are ways.' The corners of his mouth lifted a little.

'Give it back!' Caro stared at him. 'How could you give it
back? How could you think I could accept . . . a million
pounds?'

'Why not? I don't want it.' He paused. 'There would have
been provisos, naturally.'

'Provisos?' She looked at him suspiciously.

'But certainly. Your business acumen is improving. I hear
you handled Anstruther-Lamont like a dowager, and they're
generally tougher than the sharpest City operators. In fact, I
think you might develop along those lines. I can just imagine
you at sixty—a beautiful version of Lucy Amhurst, with a heart
of plated steel.' He paused teasingly. 'However . . .'

Caro stared at him. 'Did you say beautiful?'

'I said with a plated steel heart.'

'But you know that's not true!' She paused and met his eyes.
'I think you do, Francis. Don't you?'

'I'm reserving judgment.'

'I see.' The oddness of his tone, his mockery and his gentleness confused her. She buried her feet in the soft wet sand and
drew a small circle with her toes.

'So. What would have been the provisos?'

'That you accepted my advice. To begin with, at least, until
you yourself had more experience. That you listened to my
suggestions.'

'And they were?'

Francis looked away from her then, out across the sea. 'The

estate has to be developed, the farming side of it. I think that's possible. I also think parts of the house which are hardly used now could be developed. The stables, for instance. They're huge. They would make wonderful workshops. If you could find some small craft firm, a good one. There's a friend of mine who makes furniture, for instance. He has apprentices, he's looking for new premises. And the house itself. Whether you and your mother decided to involve the Trust or not, I think the house should be opened to the public at least part of the year; people should be able to see it. The library is very fine. It should be available to scholars . . .'

His voice tailed away and Caro felt herself suddenly cold.

'How clever you are,' she said slowly. 'I can see that, with some money, if we sell those ceramics—yes, all those things might work.' She paused. 'And you would help us?'

'But of course. That's also part of the provisos. I would suggest to your mother, and to you, that you might let me stay at Trevelyans for a while. I've already drawn up a lot of plans. But I should need to be here . . .'

Caro swung round, her eyes lighting up. She clasped his hand. 'You would stay here, Francis? Not go away? Not go back to London? Oh, I should be so happy if you would do that! I . . .' She broke off. 'I do love you, you see.'

'Even though I don't own your house?' His voice sharpened.

'How can you say that?' She took his hand and raised it to her lips. 'You know anyway, I'm certain you do. You can read it in my eyes. You must be able to . . .'

With an abrupt movement he stood up, then very gently helped her to her feet. Her legs trembled and almost gave way, and he caught her. He looked into her eyes intently.

'Caro,' he said, 'don't tell me that now, I beg you. Tell me again. In a little while. In six months, maybe. A year, however long it takes. If you still feel it, of course. And then . . .'

'You think I shall change. You doubt me.' She looked at him sadly.

His face softened as he looked down into hers. 'This isn't a good moment for such declarations,' he said with mock grimness. 'Not in the least. It's altogether too odd, and too . . . charged. And too sudden.' He gestured around them. 'We've just made a dangerous descent of a cliff. Your hands are bleeding. I still don't know how I shall get you back up the cliff . . .'

'I feel as if I could fly back up the cliff,' Caro smiled.

'Exactly. In six months, then. Now.' His arm moved around her waist, and the touch of his skin shot through her body. 'Start walking.'

. They walked a little way. Caro, to her chagrin, stumbled. A little way up the path, she paused, and clung to him.

'Mayn't I kiss you?' she said.

'Certainly not.'

'But my lessons . . .'

'Well, once a week then. But very primly. I want your mind to be quite clear and unclouded.'

'What about yours?' she cried indignantly.

'Mine even more. You know that quite well.'

Caro smiled. They walked on. Once she kissed his shoulder, and caressed his arm, and their feet came to a halt, their lips met, and then Francis—with difficulty—made them move on.

Almost at the top of the path, Caro paused.

'Marian,' she said.

'I know what you thought about Marian. She came to see me in London. She told me.'

'Marian did that?' She stared at him a moment, her eyes wide.

'She says she doesn't love me, Caro.'

'Did you believe her?'

He paused, then shook his head. 'No. It was my fault. I hadn't realised . . .' He turned to her with a look of pleading. 'Caro . . .'

She bent her head. 'It's no good,' she said quietly. 'I tried. But even so, I can't . . . I love you so much. If I didn't tell you I should feel dead. I'm not strong enough. I ought to be strong enough perhaps, but I'm not. There it is.' She turned to him passionately. 'I *can't* deny it, Francis, not even for Marian, I can't.'

'That is the way of things,' he said, as she leant on him again. 'Now, come home, Caro.'

*

Six months had passed to the day; Caro, turning the pages of her diary for the third time, counted them impatiently. It was almost Easter; the sun shone; a little ground mist still hung over the garden outside, for it was morning. The air was luminous, with a milky radiance; later—when the mist lifted—it would be hot. Her hand trembled a little, she lost count, began again, then sighed. She was right; six months.

She stood up—she was alone in her own room—and went to the window. Three men and one woman were crossing the courtyard towards the rear of the house, where the conversion of the stables was now complete; one was carrying a lathe, another a box of tools. The furniture workshop was already in operation; these must be the new apprentices. Her hand reached to the sill and to the small oblong wooden box which Francis' friend had made, and which Francis had given her. It was of rosewood, quite plain, the grain beautifully marked, the curvature of the lid so exquisitely worked it invited the touch. She lifted its lid; inside there were some shells from the beach, three letters from Francis, written on a visit to London, and the small card he had attached to her Christmas present.

At Christmas it had been three months. It had snowed, which was rare here, and she and Francis had walked to the woods to look for holly, and she had said then, clasping his hand, their breath coming white in the air, 'Is three months enough, Francis?' And he had kissed her, and laughed, and said, no, it was not. To be patient.

Patient. She could be patient no longer.

She turned away from the window, listening. The house was still. Her mother was away, visiting a cousin in Rome. Marian was here for the school holidays, but perhaps she still slept; it was quite early. From the distance, in the East Wing, came the sounds of hammering. The work on the main roof of the house was complete; now only that wing remained unfinished. Caro thought with a moment's affection of the three little Chinese pieces which had made all this possible, of the small T'ang horse, bought by a collector in Germany who had fallen in love with it despite the continuing doubts as to its complete authenticity. With Francis' help, those three objects had achieved so much—more than she would have believed possible: the new roof, repairs to the brickwork, doors and window frames; a heating system, which had banished the old clammy dampness that had always hung over the house in winter. Trevelyans was still shabby, there was still so much to do, but it was sound, for the first time in many years. The process of decay had been halted.

She thought of the hours she had worked, and the astonishing joy of them. Hours when, late into the night she and Francis had bent over plans and measurements. When they had argued with builders, with troops of experts, with the dry rot specialists and the glaziers, and the London brick company who were matching the old bricks exactly in shape and in colour. Of the hours of physical labour, helping with the less technical work, sanding wood and stripping old paint, clearing paths in the garden, digging, beginning the hard, back-breaking work of reclamation there, where weeds had had a hold for decades. She looked down at her hands ruefully, for they were roughened, the nails chipped and broken. She had never known that work, hard work, could be so pleasurable; for the first time in her life she had a sense of purpose.

And Francis, who had given her this? She loved him, with a steadiness of mind, a surety of heart so intense it sometimes frightened her. Only one thought was unbearable to her, that he might leave, that a future might exist without his company. She had not said that to him, though it had been difficult often. She knew he liked her; she prayed he loved her; if he left she felt as if the heart of her would die. But she was certain of so little, because surely, if he did love her, he must have said so.

Sometimes, of an evening, sitting by the fire, she would look up and catch him looking at her, and she would think then that she saw something in his eyes, in the tenderness of his mouth, but still she was not certain. And sometimes, more and more often of late, when he kissed her, when he held her in his arms, she sensed he held himself back with great difficulty. Some demon in her then made her lead him on, determined to break that damnable resistance of his, and sometimes she knew she had come near to succeeding. Then she saw he avoided being alone with her, and she suffered the withdrawal of his presence as she would have done the denial of food or light.

Well, no more, she thought. Six months, he had said, and six months it was, and now she would wait no longer. He slept in the West Wing of the house; there he had set up a studio next to his bedroom, and often, late at night, when she could not sleep, she would look out of her window towards his, and see the light burning there until three or four in the morning, and Francis' dark figure between the light and the glass, pacing backwards and forwards, backwards and forwards.

Caro ran to her window now; his curtains were still closed. She touched the little box like a talisman. She was still in her nightdress; it was eight-thirty. Opening her door, holding the folds of cotton against her skin, trembling a little, she tiptoed along the corridor, turned a corner, began to run. Portraits on the wall seemed to look on her disapprovingly, and she laughed softly. Down some stairs she ran, an odd apparition, she thought, were there anyone to see, and then along another corridor, his corridor, and then she stopped. She opened the door soundlessly, her eyes adjusting with difficulty to the shadows of the room. His clothes lay tossed across a chair; there was a tumbler of whisky, half drunk, on a table, a pile of books by the bed. She hesitated; he slept. She moved to the bedside, her feet silent on the rugs, and looked down on him.

His hair, black against the pillow, was tousled with sleep; in repose his face had a gentleness and a beauty that caught at her heart. One arm was thrown back across his pillow; she could see the pale veins in his wrist, the flicker of a pulse in his strong throat. He was naked.

She paused, then very gently lifted the covers at his side; he stirred but did not wake. Very gently, moving stealthily, she slipped under them, paused, and then moved against the warmth of his body. He was so warm, so still; it was wonderfully peaceful, in the silence of the room, with something else, the stir of desire in her, just a heartbeat away. She gave a little sigh, and rested her head against his arm, pushed back the sheet a fraction, and lowered her lips to kiss his arched throat. He opened his eyes; looked at her, his face at once alert, his expression unreadable. His arm moved, came around her shoulders, tightened, drawing her full against him, in one easy powerful movement.

'Francis,' she said firmly (she had rehearsed the sentence as she ran), 'it's six months, and I shan't wait any longer.'

'I quite agree,' he said lazily, turning with a swift movement that took her by surprise in its suddenness, so he lay half against her, half over her, so she felt the quick hardening of his body against her thighs.

'You weren't asleep at all!' she cried indignantly, as he bent his mouth to her parted lips.

'Certainly I was.'

'But . . .'

'Don't you start one of your damnable arguments now,' he muttered. 'Be quiet, Caro.'

His mouth silenced her protests. His kiss was so fierce she trembled in his arms, then moaned, as his strong hand, so easy, so assured, moved in one clear arc, from her thighs, up over her stomach, to her breasts. The pleasure made her exultant; she turned to him, slipping her arms around his neck, wrapping her thighs around his. His heart beat fast against hers; the skin of his face felt rough against her own. Their eyes met in a long teasing look of great happiness, then very gently he lifted her arms, and pulled her nightdress off over her head.

Later, considerably later, Caro lay back and stretched. They had slept a little; now in the same moment it seemed they both woke.

'Well?' she said.

'Well what?'

'My report.' She paused. 'My graduation report.'

The corners of Francis' mouth lifted. 'Remarkable facility,' he said. 'In fact, considering the circumstances, somewhat suspicious facility. However . . .'

'However what?' She turned to him indignantly.

'Well, they say, I believe, that the professor can always learn from his best pupil. I might need further—research.'

He moved his hand lazily, in such a way and in such a place that she moved at once in an arc of response. She clasped his hand and held his fingers tightly.

'Did you have cramp in your arm? Were you thinking of your newest designs, perhaps?'

He looked at her solemnly. 'No cramp, and not one thought of a design, not even in passing. Remarkable.'

'In that case,' Caro released his hand, 'you may continue the research.'

Later still, she lay back, her body shaking, and salt tears of happiness trickled from her face to his shoulder. They clasped each other tight.

'My darling,' Francis said brokenly. 'Oh, my darling!'

Then they slept. When she awoke at last, he was lying, propped up on one arm, looking down into her face.

Gently he lifted a hand, and pushed the thick strands of hair back from her forehead.

'I love you very much,' he said slowly. 'I fell in love with you on a Cornish beach, when we were there for a picnic, and you behaved like a lunatic. I particularly fell in love with you when you gave me an earnest lecture on how you should be treated like a man. And since then . . .'

Caro sat up abruptly, her hair in wild disarray.

'You loved me then?' Her voice came out in an exceedingly undignified squeak. 'You idiot! Why didn't you say so at once?'

'I really don't know.' He smiled at her lazily. 'It was hard not to then, and it's been harder ever since, and . . .'

'I know quite well why you didn't!' She stared at him accusingly. 'You thought I was frivolous, changeable—even when I told you how much I loved you, even then . . .' Her voice tailed away, and she lowered her eyes. 'Yes, well,' she said finally. 'I suppose you were quite right. But not now.' She lifted her eyes fiercely to his face. 'I love you, Francis, and I shall always love you. Nothing to do with Trevelyans, even, just you.'

'Then we'd better get married, don't you think?'

'Oh *yes*, I do! As soon as possible. And I'd like to have lots of children, your children—would you like that, Francis?'

He gave an amused shrug. 'There's twenty-five bedrooms to fill. How many had you in mind?'

Caro grinned. 'A tribe,' she said. 'Then you can build a new wing.'

Francis buried his head against her hair.

'You're a mad, impossible thing, do you know that?'

'No more than you. It just shows more in my case, that's all.' She flung her arms around him. 'Will you take me to Scotland, to Skye, for our honeymoon?'

'I might.'

'Can we do it all very quickly—no fuss, no parties, just a few people?'

'If you like.'

'If I buy a lacy, seductive, utterly disgraceful suspender belt as part of my trousseau, will you fasten it for me?'

'I might unfasten it.'

'And will you love me—a long time, Francis, do you think?'

He smiled. 'Oh, most certainly.'

'Then I agree.'

'You've already agreed. In fact . . .' he looked at her suspiciously, 'you seem to have given the matter considerable thought already.'

'Only in my madder moments.' She kissed him. 'You know what I'm like. And this is a bit different. I rather imagined you going down on one knee.'

'Then I shall!' He moved swiftly, pulling her upright. 'Come on. It's the most beautiful day. We'll go into the garden, to the old white garden, where you can see the house and the sea . . .'

'And there are tall hedges so no one can see you . . .'

'Of course. If I'm to make a fool of myself, I prefer to do so in private. And then . . .' he raised her hand to his lips, 'I'll propose all over again. On one knee if you like. And I shall proffer a suitable ring . . .'

'You have a ring?'

He gave her an injured look. 'Of course I have a ring! I'm an exceedingly practical man. And it is six months, to the day, isn't it?'

'To the hour almost.'

'Then we shall hurry.'

'And after I've accepted you. What then, Francis?'

'Why, then we shall come back here,' he said. 'What else, my darling?'

*

Marian had sent the letter. She had walked to the post office in the village, and was now walking back. It had taken all morning to write, not because the letter was long, or even complicated, but because indecision as to whether she should send it had clotted her style and clouded her mind, so the simplest sentence had been tortuous. Now she was glad it was done, glad she had not weakened, glad she had discussed it with no one, and had made the decision alone.

She turned into the driveway of Trevelyans, pausing to admire the restoration work on the gates; she nodded to the builder working on the roof of the lodge, and then, wanting to prolong her walk, for the air was warm and clear, turned down one of the side paths that meandered around the garden. It was bordered with daffodils and delicate scarlet tulips, branches of wild cherry arched over the path, and under the thick shrubs, where the ground was shady and moist, there were still prim-roses and cowslips in bloom; their slight delicate earthy frag-rance hung in the air.

She would go to France, then; it was decided. One more term, and then she would go. The college was in the Midi, near Arles; her duties there appeared unlikely to be too onerous; a class on the structure of English language; conversation clas-ses; an introduction to English culture, with special reference to *les romans les plus importants du dix-neuvième ciècle*. The professor suggested it might be particularly useful for the students to compare the works of Balzac and Flaubert, with which Mademoiselle Fox would discover they were well famil-iar, with those of such writers as George Eliot, Trollope and *l'incomparable Charles Dickens*.

Marian smiled to herself. If the students were as well familia-rised as all that she would have to work. She had been to Arles, once, years ago, when she was a child, with her parents. All she could remember was dry heat, a stuffy over-upholstered hotel that served six-course luncheons, and city squares. She had liked the squares: they had been bordered with pollarded limes, the trunks of the trees whitewashed neatly as far as the branches.

Caro would be upset, of course, when she heard. Marian would have to prepare the ground very carefully before she told her: otherwise, she could see it, she would undo all her own careful work of the past six months, in which, by argument and persuasion, and by use of an acting ability she had never suspected she possessed, she had convinced Caro that any feelings she might ever have had for Francis Atherton were now a thing of the past, that she welcomed the growing relationship between her cousin and the architect, that she rejoiced unconditionally in Caro's transparent happiness. Yes, she must be careful. Caro, guilty, reticent at first, had grown confident enough in the last few weeks to confide in her; she must make no connection now between that happiness and Marian's decision to go to France.

Marian turned off the main path on to a side path. Her own talent for duplicity amazed her; why, sometimes she almost convinced herself. And indeed, why not? She was a realist, she told herself firmly. In life, a woman such as herself did not spend the rest of her years grieving for a man who loved someone else. In novels, now, perhaps . . .

She climbed some narrow worn stone steps, damp with lichen and moss. She would stand on the terrace for a while; it was peaceful there and the view from the shelter of the garden to the bay was beautiful.

On her left were the high yew hedges that surrounded the old white garden; Francis and Caro were restoring it together, but the hedges were still overgrown and straggling; their branches now brushed her skin, and she pushed them aside irritably, as she came out on to the terrace. There she sat down on an old stone seat, looking out to the sea in the distance. She heard voices, laughter, from the garden; but they were muffled by the hedges and indistinct. Still, she had no wish to be an eavesdropper, and so reluctantly she rose to her feet.

As she stood, she saw Francis and Caro in the distance. They had come out of one of the lower gates and had begun to walk across the lawns to the house. Neither saw her.

She stood for a moment watching them. Caro's amazing hair glinted gold in the sun; she tilted her face up to Francis and said something, and Francis paused. They stopped, turned, took each other's hands, standing still in the sunlight. Caro bent her head to his chest, and he bent his face, and touched her hair with his lips. Then they turned again. Francis put an arm around Caro's shoulders; Caro put her arm around his waist. In step, they moved slowly back across the grass towards the house. A blackbird called; their shadows wavered on the grass.

Sharply Marian turned away, the pain of her own exclusion suddenly violent in her heart.

She looked out to sea again, and watched a small white yacht sail alone across the bay, and after a little while, glad for their happiness, she felt calmer.

They were waiting for her, they had seen her, she realised, turning back to the house. They stood, hand in hand, by the central doorway; as Marian looked, Caro raised her arm in greeting. Marian turned, hesitated; still they waited.

What a fine aunt I shall make, she thought. Slowly at first, then more swiftly, she walked back up the steep slope to join them.